"So you're an old pro at bringing girls here then," Callie teased.

"Of course," Luke played along. "But now I've stepped up my game. I offer mojitos instead of strawberry wine in paper cups."

"I used to drink strawberry wine too!" she giggled.

They walked down to where the waves were breaking and sat in the dry sand just close enough to get their feet wet when the tide came in. Callie slipped her sandals off and set them beside her.

"I haven't been to this beach in a long time," he admitted.

"Who was the last person you were here with?"

Luke pursed his lips as he sifted through the memories. Then that crooked grin spread across his face. "Sally Johansen. I was eighteen." He laughed and then turned to Callie. "Sally Johansen is married with six children—all a year apart."

"Wow." She let that sink in for a moment.

"It would be fun, though," he said, and she noticed that he'd moved his foot nearer to hers, only a small strip of sand between them.

"To be married to Sally Johansen?"

"No," he said, with a burst of laughter. "Having a bunch of kids. That would be enough children to start our own beach volleyball team."

They both laughed. Then his eyes met hers.

PRAISE FOR JENNY HALE

THE SUMMER HOUSE

"Hale's rich and slow-building romance is enhanced by the allure of the North Carolina coast...North Carolina's beautiful Outer Banks are the perfect setting for this sweet, poignant romance, and authentic characters and a riveting story make it a keeper worth savoring."
—*Publishers Weekly* (Starred Review)

"Like a paper and ink version of a chick-flick...gives you the butterflies and leaves you happy and hopeful."
—*Due South*

"*The Summer House* is the perfect beach read. Prepare yourself to meet your next book crush and to spend hours gushing about it."
—This Chick Reads

"A satisfying and heart-warming story. I can thoroughly recommend it as a perfect summery beach read!"
—Great Reads and Tea Leaves

"Jenny Hale has outdone herself once again by creating raw, emotional, and extremely thought-provoking situations, all of which were surrounded by the serenity of the beach house...completely blew me away."
—The Writing Garnet

IT STARTED WITH CHRISTMAS

"This sweet small-town romance will leave readers feeling warm all the way through."

—*Publishers Weekly*

CHRISTMAS WISHES AND MISTLETOE KISSES

"[A] tender treat that can be savored in any season."

—*Publishers Weekly* (Starred Review)

ALSO BY JENNY HALE

Christmas Wishes and Mistletoe Kisses
It Started with Christmas
Summer at Firefly Beach

the
summer
house

JENNY HALE

FOREVER
New York Boston

Copyright © 2017 by Jenny Hale
Excerpt from *Christmas Wishes and Mistletoe Kisses* © 2015 by Jenny Hale

Cover design by Emma Graves. Cover copyright © 2020 by Hachette Book Group, Inc.

Forever
Hachette Book Group
1290 Avenue of the Americas
New York, NY 10104
read-forever.com
twitter.com/readforeverpub

Originally published in 2017 by Bookouture, an imprint of StoryFire Ltd.
First Forever edition published in paperback in May 2019.

First Mass Market Edition: May 2020

Forever is an imprint of Grand Central Publishing. The Forever name and logo are trademarks of Hachette Book Group, Inc.

The publisher is not responsible for websites (or their content) that are not owned by the publisher.

The Hachette Speakers Bureau provides a wide range of authors for speaking events. To find out more, go to www.hachettespeakersbureau.com or call (866) 376-6591.

ISBN 978-1-5387-3439-1 (mass market)

Printed in the United States of America

OPM

10 9 8 7 6 5 4 3 2 1

the
summer
house

Chapter One

"The changes are coming along nicely!" Gladys said to Callie as she shuffled across the little road that sat quietly between their two beach cottages. She was in her sandals with the little wedge heels. Her familiar perfume overpowered even the briny air when she planted a kiss on Callie's cheek. While most new neighbors didn't greet Callie quite that affectionately, Gladys could, because she was like family.

Gladys tipped her head back to view the whole house. "I can tell you've been working hard today."

Having labored all morning on the yard, Callie's body was sandy and hot. She wiped her forehead with her arm and ran her hands through her long, dark tendrils, her fingers catching on tangles at the ends. Allowing herself to take in a tired breath, she stepped back to survey her work, shielding her eyes from the sun.

The cottage was something out of Callie's dreams— dark wood-shingled siding with white trim; the whole thing was on stilts to keep it safe from the rising tide in storms. It had a long porch across the front with a cascading staircase that Callie loved. She had been working on the walkway and the flowerbeds today, and she could just imagine the cottage as a bed and breakfast once it was finished, with weary travelers resting on rockers or on the upper deck, taking in the view of the island, the sound of the Atlantic lulling them from behind.

On the other side of the house, the rush of ocean waves beckoned, and the warm sea breeze whipped around Callie. The salty wind was always there for her, calming her and bringing her peace. She loved the quiet solitude it provided, the way the sound of it rushed in her ears, making her sleepy. It was hard to get her work done in such a paradise. But she'd managed to clear the plot today of all the overgrowth, leaving mostly sand in its place.

They stepped aside for a passing car, and Gladys watched it suspiciously as if it wasn't supposed to be on her road. Gladys had lived in the same little cottage across the street for most of her life. She'd weathered more coastal storms than she could count and seen the shift in other nearby villages from remote landscape to the towering cottages and hotels that were eating up the coastline. Despite the changes, she'd never regretted staying for a moment. "It's just heaven," she'd said.

"Hello, you two!" Gladys called to Olivia and her son, Wyatt, on the porch, raising the glass of iced tea she'd brought outside with her. The ice clinked as condensation fogged the surface, causing drips to slide down onto her fingers. There was a lemon wedge floating on the top. "You're gonna work yourselves to death!" Gladys said.

Wyatt's head popped up briefly, his red curls wet with perspiration, a grin on his face when he saw his great-grandmother. He was almost hidden except for his head and shoulders behind the large railings as he sat on the porch, pounding nails that had shimmied up from the floorboards, his lips pursed, a crease of concentration between his eyes. At eight, he looked exactly like his mother had at that age, with that brilliant red hair and freckles.

Olivia giggled and shook her head. "We're fine!" She was repainting the railings a bright white, making the original, peeled paint look gray in comparison. Her hair was pulled up into a bun held by a rubber band at the top of her head, showing her high cheekbones and bright green eyes. She waved to her grandmother.

"We're not even tired!" Wyatt said, his concentration waning for only a moment before resuming his task. Callie and Olivia had just bought the beachfront property, and there was a lot of work to be done if they wanted to open in time to catch the end of the summer season. With the landscaping and porch rebuild still looming it would be quite a stretch, but they were hoping to unveil The Beachcomber to the public at the end of the month. With the warm temperatures extending into October, it would be just enough time to get their feet wet, testing the market.

Their whole lives, Callie and Olivia had dreamed about having this cottage across from Gladys. They'd seen it on their visits, walked the small path that went beside it down to the beach, and fantasized about what it would be like to live there. When they were older, Olivia had inquired about the property with her grandmother, just out of curiosity, so when it went on the market, Gladys called her immediately. Olivia was on the phone to Callie within minutes to see if they could scrape up enough money together to realize their dream of opening the bed and breakfast. The opportunity was like some sort of amazing dream.

"I'm going to take a lunch break—run into town. Do you need anything?" Callie asked Gladys as she tied her hair back into a ponytail and secured it with the band she'd kept on her wrist.

"Oh, I'm just fine, dear. But I am glad to see you taking care of yourself. A thin girl like you needs to eat or you'll waste away."

She smiled with amusement. "Olivia," she called. "I'm going to stop for a little while and get lunch. Want me to pick something up for you?"

"Wyatt just had a sandwich when we went inside a minute ago, and I'd like to get the front steps painted before I rest," Olivia said, wiping her forehead, leaving a milky streak of paint and sweat. She and Callie had divvied up the "to do" list according to their talents and timeframe. Callie, who'd always loved the artistic side of things, took the landscaping and interior painting, while Olivia painted a lot of the exterior and handled the demolition.

Gladys fluttered her hand in the air. "I'm heading back in—all this heat. I'm painting some mason jars for flower arrangements. I'll get back to it. Just wanted to give my old fingers a rest."

Callie ushered dirt from the front walk back to its proper location with her foot. "Want to go with me anyway, Wyatt?" she asked, worried he might be getting bored.

"No, thanks," Wyatt said. He was still focused on the unruly nails, his little face pink under his freckles. The porch was completely empty with the exception of a watered-down glass of lemonade on the top step that Wyatt had brought out with him, which wobbled slightly every time he hammered.

He'd been so sweet and helpful since they'd arrived. He'd spent most of the last months of his summer repairing the house. They'd worked all evening one night, and they knew he was tired, but he hadn't said a thing; he'd just let them work. The moon and stars were so bright that night that it was as if someone had turned a giant light on outside.

Gladys had been working with them that night, and Callie remembered her pulling Wyatt aside, without telling Olivia or Callie what she'd done. "Psst. Wyatt. Look at this," she'd said. He'd followed her out onto the old walkway leading to the beach. It was shimmering in the moonlight. Wyatt bent down and ran his finger in the sparkles that looked very much like Gladys's silver glitter.

"What is this?" he'd asked.

Gladys offered a big smile. "Stardust," she said. "Whenever you've had a big day at the beach, you know it's time to rest when you've found the stardust. There's all kinds of magic here at the coast. You just have to know where to look…"

"Okay, then," Callie called up, returning from the memory.

"You know, it might be a good idea to get us a few sandwiches for dinner, though. I'm not sure if I'll be up for going out to get something, and we're low on groceries. We're down to orange sherbet popsicles and a bag of Cheetos," Olivia said.

"That's a good idea. I'll pick something up for later then." Callie wiped her hands on her shorts and headed to her car, where her wallet and keys still were from her trip to the nursery to get shrubs earlier that morning.

Leaving Olivia and Wyatt at the house, Callie waved goodbye to Gladys, who was walking back across the street, and drove toward the small strip of shops that lined the beach. Sandwiched between the towns of Rodanthe and Salvo, the village of Waves, North Carolina, was so small that if a person wasn't careful driving through it, they'd miss it. It was a quiet little town, but it was known for being the home of a group of watersports giants whose offerings attracted people from all over the country. Callie and Olivia planned to reopen the bed and breakfast in Waves, hoping to capitalize on the clientele its watersports brought every summer and hoping there were still people who wanted a small-town seaside escape. She was banking on it.

Callie found a parking spot and got out of her car, her feet still sandy in her flip-flops from pulling spiny weeds all day in the front yard. She grabbed her sunglasses from the center console that held a price quote from a local landscaping company and a receipt for the six pots of thimbleweed she'd planted herself along the stone front walk and by the front picket fence this morning.

She rounded the corner and headed for a place to get a bite to eat. The shops were crawling with people, the summer months in full swing. There was a surfing competition in town, and the tourists had filled the street with a buzzy excitement.

"Excuse me, sir." She heard a man's loud voice from up ahead, her attention shifting toward it like it had some sort of magnetic pull. "I'd just like a statement." A man with an iPad and a bag slung across his body—maybe a reporter of some sort—was parting the crowd hurriedly.

Callie watched for a second, wondering what he was up to. She hadn't seen that kind of eagerness in this small town before. She quickened her pace, curiosity getting the better of her. In only a few steps, she'd caught up with the man and realized he was nearly chasing someone. She followed him into the small crowd near the shops as she continued to look for somewhere to eat. When she caught sight of the person the reporter was after, Callie recognized him just as he zeroed in directly on her.

"Oh!" he said, linking arms with her. "There you are!"

"What? I—" Callie found herself being hurried along by Luke Sullivan, the multimillionaire heir to the Sullivan fortune. She'd read about him in the local paper. His family had made their money in early real estate development along the barrier islands and expanded nationwide. With Luke's return to the Outer Banks, heading up their latest project—Blue Water Sailing, one of those watersports giants—he'd brought with him quite a bit of press. Blue Water Sailing had taken off just like the yacht company they also owned, based in Florida. With rumors of his father's retirement, Luke stood to take over a goldmine, being the Sullivans' only son. Their daughter, Juliette Sullivan, was pursuing other interests, Callie had read.

Luke's hand was gently wrapped around her bicep as he led her forward, the face of his Rolex reflecting the sun into her eyes, despite her sunglasses, as the reporter gained speed behind them.

"I'm sorry," he said to the reporter over his shoulder. "I'm having a…lunch date. I can't speak to you right now."

The reporter was still behind them, but he was slowing just a bit. They kept walking briskly. Luke faced forward, his expression determined, as he swept her farther down the sidewalk. She noticed that people were looking. Finally, he nearly yanked her into a shop. The door shut behind them, plunging them into the air-conditioned entrance of a small beach art gallery.

Luke let go of her arm, his attention on the door. Callie made eye contact with the salesperson, the woman clearly as surprised as Callie at their entrance.

When it seemed like the coast was clear, Luke stuck

his head in Callie's line of vision. "I'm sorry," he said, his gaze darting back to the door once more before focusing entirely on her.

She'd seen his face in magazine photos advertising the area for tourists. But he didn't live like those tourists. He owned what the articles referred to as a "cottage," but it was more like a castle, a two-million-dollar home that sat on its own acreage, probably a third the size of the entire village, secluded and smack in the sand on the edge of the sea with two pools and a tennis court.

He was tall and perfectly fit, with sandy blond hair falling across his forehead, making him look younger than his age. She'd read that he was only a year older than she was, yet he had an air of experience about him that made him seem so much wiser. He was wearing long, beachy shorts and a casual T-shirt; she could tell by the stitching that they'd cost him a fortune. As he took a small step closer to her, she felt self-conscious. What must she look like right now? Her hair was yanked into a ponytail, her arms still dusted with the soil from the yard. Luke was so impeccably clean and gorgeous as he watched her with those sea-blue eyes of his.

He offered his hand. "Luke Sullivan."

"Callie Weaver," she said, still a little dazed.

Chapter Two

"That guy wants an interview with me, but I'm worried about the way he'll spin what I'm saying, so I refuse to talk to him," Luke said. "He's been following me everywhere. You saved me." He smiled, and Callie had to catch her breath.

She jammed her hands in the pockets of her shorts to both keep herself steady and hide the dirt that was probably still under her fingernails from gardening all day. She blinked, trying not to freak out at the fact that she was actually talking to Luke Sullivan.

He turned his wrist over, that enormous watch swinging into view. "I've kept you," he said. "Let me make it up to you. I'll get you a drink."

"I'm fine, thank you," she said, smiling graciously and then starting toward the door. "It was nice…meeting you." She allowed her gaze to flicker up to his face again, but she quickly turned back to the door. She was hot and sweaty. The very last thing she wanted was to sit too close to Luke Sullivan and have a drink. She needed lunch and a shower.

"Where were you headed?" He reached around her and grabbed the handle, opening the door for her. They walked out into the noise of tourists and the blinding sunshine.

"I'm just grabbing some lunch to take back with me. I'm renovating a bed and breakfast on Sand Dune Road."

He stared ahead as he paced beside her on the sidewalk.

"The Beachcomber Bed and Breakfast," she clarified, but she wasn't surprised when he didn't recognize it. It had been closed to the public for years—Gladys had told them—but she continued, her nerves getting the better of her. "Alice McFarlin's place."

Finally, a spark of recognition. "Oh yeah, I remember her. She was pretty involved in the town when I was growing up. I saw her everywhere..." He trailed off, clearly wondering about something, but he snapped out of it. "Anyway, how about that drink?"

"I've been working outside all morning. I'm tired and dirty," she said, not wanting to be rude and just dismiss his kind offer.

"You have to get lunch anyway, yes? And you're not going to work while you sit and eat it, right?" Those blue eyes were on her, the edges crinkling with his smile. "I just dragged you down a sidewalk and threw you into a shop. Please let me buy you lunch. It's the very least I could do."

His expression was completely gorgeous, but it was also kind.

"I'd like to..." she said calmly. Inside she was a nervous wreck.

Before she could finish, he'd put his hand on her back to guide her across the street. "I'll introduce you to the very best burger on the beach."

He came to a stop at a shiny red truck with a surfboard in the back and opened her door before jogging around to his side.

"This is a nice truck," she said, sliding onto the leather seat and latching her seat belt.

"It isn't mine." Luke started the engine. "I borrowed it to pick up the surfboard." He nodded in the direction of the truck's bed.

"Where are we going?" she asked as he pulled onto the road.

He put his blinker on and rounded the curve, making a sharp left. "Somewhere no one will find us."

She felt her eyes bulging but she was unable to stop herself. She didn't even know this guy—so what if she'd seen a few ads with him around town? She knew nothing about him. He was driving a vehicle that wasn't his, she hadn't told a soul where she was...She set her hand on her thigh, inching toward the cell phone in her pocket in case she needed it. He could be a closet murderer or something. He could be stealing her away only to tie her up against a palm tree and leave her for the...what kind of wild animals roam the beaches in North Carolina? She discreetly twisted around to view his backseat, looking for rope, when he caught her eye, the corner of his mouth turning up in amusement.

"You okay?" he asked, before looking back at the road. "This burger place is amazing. It's small and out of the way, so no *reporters*." His voice hung on that last word as if he'd caught on to her thinking, and her cheeks burned. A tiny huff of laughter escaped from his lips, and he glanced back over at her again.

The rest of the ride was quiet as she flip-flopped between sheer embarrassment that he might have been able to decipher her thoughts and utter panic that she was going on a lunch date with Luke Sullivan with paint down her leg. He pulled the truck to a stop in front of a tiny shack of a building and got out. Callie sneaked a quick look at herself in the side-view mirror but this only made her feel more self-conscious.

"Do you mind if I just pop into the ladies' room for a second?" she asked as he opened the door for her.

She did a little jog toward the bathrooms, leaving Luke with the hostess, and commenced digging in her handbag for her powder and lip-gloss. She hit the tap, the water splashing in the basin, and washed her hands before pulling her ponytail loose and running her fingers through her hair. She looked at herself. Oh well. He'd already seen her like this; she didn't need to worry about it. A toilet flushed and a woman stepped up behind her, waiting her turn at the sink. After a friendly nod, Callie moved aside and quickly texted Olivia that she'd be later than expected, but after waiting a little while and not getting any response, she headed out to the dining area.

The entire back of the building was open to the beach, with a long bar facing the ocean, a thatched roof, and dangling twinkle lights that must come on when the sun goes down. Luke waved from his seat on the other side, daylight on his face, giving him a glow. The hostess opened the door, allowing Callie access to the barstools that ran along the back of the building on wooden decking built over the beach. It was weathered and gritty from the surrounding sand. Luke reached over and pulled one of the seats out from under the bar for her.

"What are we having to drink today?" the bartender asked. He was wearing an old T-shirt with a faded logo, his slightly longer than average hair tucked behind his ears.

Luke waited for her to make her choice, so Callie grabbed a menu and scanned the long list of cocktails. "Um," she said, buying time. It had been quite a while since she'd gotten a drink with someone. "A rum and Coke please," she said, unable to focus on any one of the millions of drink options that were scrawled across the glossy page in electric blue script. This wasn't that kind of date anyway, she thought. Best to keep it simple—and just the one drink.

"Coconut rum?" the bartender asked.

She nodded.

"And you, sir?"

"Just a beer, thanks." He nodded toward some sort of import. Then to Callie, he said, "You mentioned a cottage—The Beachcomber? Are you opening soon?"

"My friend Olivia and I are opening it back up at the end of the summer," she said, relieved at the question. This was a nice, easy topic. She loved talking about The Beachcomber.

Callie hated this part of meeting someone. She much preferred the point when both people felt comfortable enough to sit at a table and eat without needing to fill the silence. She'd always been bad at offering up tidbits of information about her life, preferring to keep all that private.

The bartender slid their drinks toward them. Luke retrieved a couple of loose dollars from his pocket and stuffed them into the tip jar.

"Thanks, man," the bartender said. "Ready to order?"

Callie wasn't ready. She hadn't even looked at the menu yet except for her poor attempt to find a drink. "What do you normally get?" she asked Luke.

"A bacon cheeseburger."

"I'll have the same."

He eyed her inquisitively. "They're really big," he warned, a smile twitching at his lips.

His gaze swallowed her in a way that made her feel like she was the only person on the planet. She cleared her throat and looked down at the menu. "That's fine. I can take the rest home if I don't eat it."

He turned back to the bartender and ordered their burgers. When the bartender left to put in the order, Luke swiveled on his barstool to face her. "If the world ended tomorrow, and I had one last meal, it would be this burger."

"You would choose a burger as your last meal?" she asked, surprised. "I can think of so many things that I'd have over a burger."

"You've never had *this* burger." He tipped his beer up to his lips, and she tried not to watch for fear she'd be goggling at his attractiveness. She liked how easily the conversation was going, how he didn't put her on the spot.

"You're very confident," she said, meaning more by her comment than just his certainty about his choice of last meal.

He took a long look at her before shifting his eyes down to his beer and having another sip from his bottle. "What would you have for your last meal, then?"

"I don't know if I'd be worried about my meal. I'd be too busy trying to do everything I wanted before the end." She sipped her rum and Coke, savoring the coconut flavor. A string of paper lanterns hanging from the thatched roof above the bar rattled as they danced in the wind. With the warm breeze and the hiss of the sea behind them, she felt herself relaxing.

His eyebrows rose in interest. "What do you want to do before you die, then?"

"Learn how to knit."

He laughed. "You could choose the hardest, most unreachable thing in the whole world—bungee jumping, mountain climbing, world travel—and you picked knitting? That's something you could do right now. I'll buy you a how-to-knit book on the way home. Come on, you can do better than that," he teased.

With a grin, she thought some more.

"Meet a world leader?"

Callie shook her head.

"Swim with dolphins?"

"Stop," she giggled. "I'm actually trying to think of something but you keep distracting me."

"So no clowning classes?"

"No! Nothing like that," she laughed.

"Well, what would you really want to happen before you die? Really."

"I'd like to be closer with my mother," she said, immediately feeling fire shoot through her veins at admitting that out loud. She'd never done that before. Luke's easy talking had pulled her in and she didn't know how to do this: get personal with a stranger. The things she wanted to do before she died were very intimate desires, the kinds of things buried so deep down in her heart that she wasn't sure she wanted to share them with anyone. The fuzzy memory of her father leaving—a memory that had almost faded completely with time—filtered into her mind, reminding her of the turning point with her mom. It caused Callie to tense up.

His face softened, and she realized then that she'd bristled. She noticed that her knees had moved slightly away from him, her arms folded across her body. She straightened them out, channeling that moment of calm before his question and let her shoulders drop. She leaned back toward him again, grabbing her drink to have something to do with her hands, stirring it with the little black straw in the glass.

"Why aren't you close with your mom?" he asked gently, turning toward the sea, as if the gesture would make the heaviness of the conversation go away. The bright sunlight made the water shimmer like diamonds on the horizon. When he didn't get a response, he turned to her. "You can tell me," he said with a shrug. "I'm an outsider. What would it matter if I knew?"

The answers bubbled up in her mind. She took another drink of her rum and Coke. Her mom hadn't really been there for her since her dad left when she was eight. Callie wanted to know if her mother wished she hadn't been so distant with her after her father left; if she wondered why Callie couldn't just turn off the hurt like her mother obviously could; if she missed her. She opened her mouth to say it, but then she clammed up, choking the answers back. "What do *you* want to do before you die?" she said, steering the subject away from herself.

"I'd like to have a family, kids," he said with a smile. "Travel."

She was surprised by his answers. Lots of people wanted those things, but here was a single guy with his whole life in front of him, and the first thing he'd said was family. Not to mention, kids were a huge investment— emotionally, financially, time-wise. In all the relationships she'd been in, not one of the men had mentioned children, and she'd never felt the need to press them on it. She didn't take marriage and children lightly.

"Where would you travel?" she asked, sticking to the easier side of the conversation.

"Malta, maybe. Belize…Somewhere exotic." He smiled at her.

"They're both by the water," she noted, comforted that he wasn't trying to get anything more out of her. He was easy to talk to; it was as if he sensed when to pull back and push forward, and just as she felt uneasy, he made it all better.

"I could never live away from the water. I love it too much."

"Me too. I used to look forward to my visits here as a kid. I couldn't wait to feel the sting on my face from too much sun and the salt in my hair. It's fantastic."

"When I've been surfing all day, that night when I lie in bed and close my eyes, I feel like I'm still on the swells of the waves."

Callie knew that sensation. She got it too.

He smiled and said, "My mother used to tell me that feeling was the ocean soaking into my soul."

"Mmm, I love that," she said, feeling the tension leaving her.

The bartender arrived with two plates, setting them in front of Luke and Callie. He grabbed a few paper napkins from behind him, folded the wad in half, and set them on the table between them.

Callie looked down at the massive burger.

"You were warned," Luke said.

"I underestimated what you meant by *'big.'*"

"You get a T-shirt if you finish it." He pointed to an array of pastel garments pinned to the slant in the ceiling above the bar, all reading *I survived the Beach Bum Burger Bash* with a line drawing of the burger in front of her.

"Enticing," she said, holding back her grin.

"You're considered royalty if you have one of those shirts."

"Do you have one?"

He looked at her as if her question were ridiculous. "Of course I have one! That's my picture right there on the wall of fame." He nodded toward a small bulletin board with five photos pinned to it. Luke was wearing the navy blue T-shirt over an Oxford button-up with the sleeves rolled, smiling an enormous smile.

"Quite an achievement," she teased.

"Don't make light of it. I'm one of five people on the Outer Banks who can eat the whole thing."

"Now you're just showing off," she giggled. "It can't be that hard."

He flung her a challenging look. "I've only been able to do it once. But I'm throwing down the gauntlet: One of us is leaving with a T-shirt...And we know who that is."

Callie rolled her eyes. Peering down at the small paper napkin she'd put in her lap, certain it was insufficient in this instance, she slid her thumbs under the enormous sandwich, barely able to stretch her fingers around it to lift it to her mouth. She had no utensils, or she'd have cut it into eighths. Assessing the task at hand, she attempted to devise a strategy to get a bite that had bread, meat, cheese, bacon, lettuce, tomato, and onion without the condiments squirting all over Luke when she tried to eat it. With some effort, she managed to strategically squeeze the burger while widening her mouth to reach from top to bottom, and took a bite. Her mouth full, her cheeks like a chipmunk with its stash, she watched to see if Luke could be successful with his effort.

With entertainment clear on his face, he took a bite and chewed.

"It's delicious," she admitted, once she'd finally been able to swallow. She blotted her mouth with her napkin before washing the bite down with her drink. Then she turned to Luke and said, "I've so got this."

His eyebrows lifted in surprise. "It's bigger than you are. I think you're bluffing to get me to eat all mine. I had an omelet this morning. I wasn't prepared. You have to eat this on an empty stomach."

"You're just scared," she said, trying to cover her grin with her game-face.

"Of you? Ha!" he said, but there was affection showing in his eyes. He liked this.

"I'm a force to be reckoned with," she said as she took another bite, this one bigger than the last. After she swallowed, she added, "I may look small, but I'm feisty. And I don't like to lose." She squared her shoulders, the burger between both hands.

He smiled, an undecipherable look lingering on his face.

"What?"

"You have ketchup on your shirt."

She looked down and saw, dripping toward her midsection, an enormous glop of red sauce. She was mortified. "That's fine," she said, acting unbothered. "I'll have a new shirt to wear home anyway."

He shook his head and took another bite.

"I'm so surprised I've never heard about this place," she said as she blotted the sauce stain. But then again, it wasn't the usual tourist location. It was hidden from the main road and she couldn't see a single person she thought looked like a vacationer. Gladys probably wouldn't have known about it, since she didn't go out to eat very much. She'd rather do the cooking herself.

There was a group of guys down the bar who seemed as though they'd just gotten off work—their feet bare, their work boots lined up under their chairs with a bag of tools nearby. They were laughing, their beers swinging between their fingers, their elbows on the bar. Another couple inside was talking to the waitress, and she recognized the woman from the bathroom. The waitress had pulled up a chair and was looking at baby pictures. From what Callie could tell, she knew the baby, calling it by name.

"I like it because it's off the beaten path, and it has this view," Luke said, throwing his thumb over his shoulder.

Callie turned around, holding her burger. The beach was completely secluded—not a soul out there except the silhouette of a sailboat in the distance. The white, powdery sand stretched, untainted, as far as she could see.

"The beach is private; it belongs to the owner of this restaurant." Luke stood for a moment, gesturing for Callie to follow. She set her napkin on the bar and leaned forward with Luke to view a small home sitting in the sand beside the bar. "He lives right there." Luke sat back down, wrapping his hand around his beer and lifting it to his lips. The breeze blew off the ocean, the sound of the waves mixing with the steel drum that was playing over the speakers. "Certain times of year, the beach is closed off. It's a turtle breeding ground."

Callie smiled at that. "I love animals." She got comfortable again on her barstool, and took another bite of her burger. After she finished her bite, she asked, "Do you have any pets?"

"I wish I did, but I'm never home. I'd hate to have an animal waiting for me day in and day out when I could only show up in the evenings to give it any attention."

She went in for another bite of burger.

"If I did have a pet, it would be a dog," he said. "A beachside game of fetch might be tricky with a cat."

She laughed. Here she was, a complete mess, eating a

burger the size of a dinner plate, and talking like she'd known this guy for ages. The more she thought about it, the more it unnerved her. In a weird way, those awkward first dates, while annoying, comforted her—she hadn't ever had to open up and she felt safe that way; it was like a learned formula of conversation. With Luke, she was in unfamiliar territory.

She looked down at her half-eaten burger, her tummy getting very full.

"Reconsidering your bravado now?" he laughed, his teasing light-hearted.

She nodded. "And I was so hoping for us to have matching T-shirts."

"You've given it a good effort," he said with a grin. "Would you believe, I brought my grandmother here and she almost finished one?"

"What?" Callie laughed. "I don't know what's more interesting: the fact that you took your grandmother to a burger shop or that she almost ate this whole thing!"

"She was a funny lady." He wiped his hands on his napkin and took a swig of his beer. "She passed away at eighty-seven, and until then, she called me every day."

"Really?" Callie thought about her own grandmother, and the empty spot still there without her. She had been the rock that had held Callie's family together. Especially after her father left. Callie had so many memories of her; spending whole weekends at her house, taking long walks, baking—her grandmother had even started to show her how to knit, but Callie had never had a chance to practice with her, and she still couldn't do it. Callie missed her terribly.

"Yep. She said that I couldn't get into too much trouble if I had to answer to my grandmother every day. I enjoyed her calls," he said with a chuckle, then took another few bites, following them with his beer. "When she passed away, my mom took over for her."

"That's really sweet. I wish my mom would call me more." As the words left her mouth, she wanted to chase them and pull them back, in disbelief that she'd even uttered them, but she could relate to his comment so much. Her issue with her mother had always been the one thing she wished she could fix, but she just didn't know how.

"That's twice you've mentioned your mom." He didn't say anything else, and she wondered if he could sense her regret in uttering the comment. The breeze blew in, rustling a napkin by her plate. She set her drink down on it.

"I should probably go soon," she said. "I have a lot of work to do on the house."

Luke looked surprised, and Callie wondered if she'd been rude. Maybe he'd wanted to stay, have a few more drinks, but she hadn't planned on all this—any of it: the lunch, the talking, meeting him. She needed to go.

Luke flagged the bartender.

When he came over, Luke asked for the bill and one of the navy shirts from the ceiling, to Callie's complete astonishment, holding up his empty plate. "I couldn't let you leave without getting that matching shirt," he said with a wink. The bartender grabbed a shirt and handed it to her.

"Thank you," she said to Luke with a smile.

Once the bill was delivered, Callie packed the rest of her burger into a "to go" box. "I'm going to put in an order for my housemate and her son before we go, if that's okay. They asked me to get dinner for them tonight," she said, reaching across the bar and snagging a menu.

Luke stood up, a line forming between his eyes as he rooted around in his pockets. He peered down under the barstool before looking up at her with mortification consuming his face. "I don't have my wallet."

"What?" she said over her menu.

"Let me just run out to the truck. Be right back."

She ordered two burgers to go, as she waited for Luke to return. She'd actually enjoyed herself today with Luke, and she couldn't wait to get back to tell Olivia all about it. She'd never believe that Callie had ended up having lunch with the guy from the cover of *Outer Banks Sports Magazine*.

Luke came jogging back over, looking uncertain.

"What's wrong?" she asked.

"My wallet isn't in the truck. I just called the surfboard shop—I left it there when that reporter came in and distracted me."

"Thank God. At least it isn't lost," she said with relief.

"Well, yes, but I can't pay for our lunch."

"Oh!" she laughed. "No worries." Callie reached into her handbag for her wallet as she peered down at the total. "Will you just add this to my bill for the 'to go' order?" she told the bartender as she handed him her credit card.

"I'm so sorry. I feel terrible."

"Don't feel bad," she said.

"I do! I asked you to lunch and then made you pay. This might be an all-time low here for dates."

"It's not a date," she said quickly.

He regarded her curiously. "Let me make it up to you. I'll take you out again. A do-over."

A little hum of excitement rang in her ears. "You don't have to do that." The bartender brought her the bill and she wrote in the tip and signed her name.

"Let me."

Callie had a lot of work to complete on the house. She couldn't just leave Olivia to do it all. And they were already pressed for time, trying to get The Beachcomber open by the autumn. She really didn't need this kind of distraction.

"You can't let me leave you on this note. Please allow me to redeem myself." He was grinning at her in that way of his that made her heart patter.

She swallowed and cleared her throat, inwardly scolding herself for what she was about to say. She'd sworn off dating. She was too busy. "Okay."

His grin widened. "Fantastic. How about tomorrow night?" He pulled his phone from his pocket. "Let me get your address and your cell number. You're at…The Beachcomber?"

She gave him her contact information, and he typed it into his phone.

"I'll pick you up at seven."

"You really don't have to go to all that trouble. I can just meet you somewhere."

"It's fine," he said, as if picking up a girl he'd only just met was something he did every day. But maybe he did. He grabbed her "to go" boxes. "I'll take you back to your car," he said as he led her toward the door.

Chapter Three

"There's some extra wood paneling stacked in the closet of one of the upstairs bedrooms," Olivia said, clapping the dust off her hands as Callie came in through the front door with the boxes of burgers and the T-shirt draped over her arm.

Callie lumped the T-shirt on the side table and went into the kitchen to put the food in the cooler they were using until the new refrigerator was delivered.

"Would you help me pull it all out tomorrow so we can take it to the dump?"

"Yes," Callie said, her mind still on Luke. She walked back into the family room, where Olivia was wiping down the etched glass globes from the new chandelier they were putting up in the dining area.

"You okay?" Olivia said, stopping to look at her. "What took you so long?"

"I went out to lunch," she said. "I didn't have time to get into it on my text to you—everything went so fast and there was a lady in the restroom rushing me..."

Excitement swelled in Olivia's face and she set the globe down next to the T-shirt on the only small table in the room. The rest of the furniture hadn't been delivered. "I know that look. You're all rosy-cheeked and flustered," she said. She cocked her head to the side and studied her friend.

"I went to lunch *with* someone. You'll never guess with whom," Callie said, the sound of it still surreal as she rolled the name over in her mind. She and Olivia had shared many conversations like this over the years as they'd grown up, but never had she had an answer like this one.

"Who?"

"Luke Sullivan." She said the name slowly for emphasis.

Olivia's mouth dropped open and she covered it with her white paint-splattered hands, the dust rag still entwined in her fingers, before running across the room and snagging a newspaper that they'd been using to protect the hardwoods from falling paint. "This guy?" She pointed to a photo of him, wearing swim trunks and no shirt, standing next to a bikini-clad model of a girl, aboard an enormous luxury boat.

Callie nodded. "He got me this." She grabbed the T-shirt and held it out to Olivia. They traded the paper and the shirt, Callie studying the photo of Luke and trying not to stare at his perfectly shaped chest as Olivia frowned, attempting to make sense of what was in her hands.

The subtitle of the article read: *Luke Sullivan to take over Sullivan Enterprises. What could this mean for the Outer Banks' largest real estate company?*

With the shirt still in her hands, Olivia pulled the two beach chairs they'd been using for makeshift seating over, setting them up in the center of the nearly empty room—their usual spot for meals. Once the shock had left Olivia's face, she set the shirt in her lap and pulled her hair out of the rubber band, shaking it free, her long, red ringlets falling across her thin shoulders. "How did you manage to go on a date with Luke Sullivan when you were just running out to get sandwiches?"

Callie was struggling to answer her friend; she was too busy scanning the article. *Luke Sullivan, local playboy slated to take over…Father and founder of Sullivan empire Edward Sullivan having second thoughts about retirement…speculation regarding the motivations of his son, Luke. Does he have the drive to take on a company of this magnitude?*

Playboy? she thought, confused. What had all that family talk been about then? Had he been just saying things to make conversation? Or had he been saying what he thought she might want to hear?

"Hello-o?" Olivia smacked her leg playfully from her perch on the floor.

"Sorry." Callie folded the paper and set it on the floor, dropping down into the chair next to Olivia. She only noticed then that Olivia had picked up a few magazines from the stack of mail they'd been gathering on the side table and set them in her lap. They stayed closed as Callie started to tell her the story. The more detail she gave, however, the more unreal it all sounded, and, after seeing the article, she wondered about Luke's motivations. "He wants to take me out again tomorrow at seven." She looked back over at the paper, staring at the woman in the bikini until the picture blurred in front of her.

Wyatt came in and sat down beside them, having heard some of the story. "Are you nervous?" he asked.

Callie smiled.

"I'm nervous about starting third grade here. I don't know anybody," he admitted, picking at the edge of his flip-flop. "I'd be glad if I met someone."

His candor warmed Callie's heart. She wanted to tell him that Luke wasn't someone she thought could be her new friend. She let her eyes fall onto the photo of him in the paper again, suddenly wondering why she was even wasting her time having dinner with someone when she should be spending that hour or two on The Beachcomber. But she'd committed.

"I know you haven't had a chance to meet any kids yet, but there's a whole class of them waiting. You only have a few weeks left!" She raised her eyebrows and stretched her face into an excited smile for his benefit. Truthfully, she and Olivia both wished he'd had other kids around during the summer, but he'd been a great sport through all this, and she assured Olivia that, in time, he'd find his place.

Olivia had tried very hard to entertain him. She'd had kitchen dance parties, she'd made an entire ice cream bar with twenty different toppings, and she'd even had a tie-dye day, where they dyed shirts. When she'd come downstairs the day after that, she'd dyed her hair blue to match her shirt. It washed out, but the whole time, Wyatt had thought she'd used the clothing dye. She didn't tell him until the very end. He came in with blue stripes in his hair later that morning.

"Have you had a chance to try out your new fishing gear today?" Callie asked. Wyatt had been trying to catch fish since they'd gotten there, but sea fishing was quite different from the freshwater fishing he did back home, and he hadn't caught anything yet.

"No, but I want to! Maybe I'll get lucky and catch something! The guy at the shop says fishing and waiting are basically the same thing, but you never know!" he said with pride. Olivia had spent more money than she'd admitted to Callie on fishing gear for Wyatt. She'd gotten him a surf rod with a saltwater spinning reel, circle hooks, a sand spike, and a lesson in surf fishing at the local bait and tackle shop.

"Maybe you could set it up and show me and your mom what you learned in your lesson." She looked over at Olivia and, in that unspoken language they'd used since they were kids, she told her that the house could wait just a little while. Olivia smiled and took in a heavy breath.

Over the years, Callie had witnessed how hard it had been for Olivia as a single mom, and she knew the internal struggle Olivia was having over being a great mom and still taking risks that could give him a different life.

"Okay!" Wyatt said excitedly, jumping up and down. "Let me set it up. I know how! Then I'll come get you when I'm done." He ran down to get his supplies.

While Wyatt was off gathering what he needed, Olivia had opened one of the magazines. "Did you see this article?" She flipped the magazine around, the pages rolled back so that the piece about the Sullivans was in view.

Callie took it from her. The Sullivans, with their many companies, had wealth so abundant that they rarely mixed with the residents and tourists there in Waves. The article claimed they'd lost touch with the locals. Luke was having lavish parties, sailing around with countless different women in luxury boats while the town was known for its eclectic, bohemian beach vibe. The other Sullivans hardly spent any time in North Carolina anymore—Edward spent most of his time in New York; Lillian Sullivan, Luke's mother, who had raised Luke and his sister alone after her divorce from Edward, had left for Florida as soon as her children were out of college. Luke's sister, Juliette, had chased a fashion design career in New York. So the local press had converged on Luke, and his rise in popularity in the press had caused increased interest in the small village. She read on.

Callie wanted to believe that Luke was as kind as he'd been at lunch but she couldn't clear her mind of the headlines she'd read about his womanizing ways. He'd dated some big movie actress recently, the village in a frenzy as they were spotted out on the waters on his boat. The longtime residents were tiring of the paparazzi that followed her to their town.

"It was really nice of him to take you out," Olivia said as Wyatt called them outside through the open porch window. He was heading to the beach with his two fishing rods in their holders.

Callie slipped her hands into the pockets of her shorts. Although stained with paint from painting the mailbox the other day, they were at least clean, since the only two appliances they had managed to order so far were the new washer and dryer. So while she couldn't keep her drinks cold and was still eating restaurant food, at least she could feel fresh every morning by doing the wash, even if it always looked like she was wearing dirty clothes.

"He forgot his wallet and I had to pay for lunch," she said. "So he invited me to dinner tomorrow night. I don't entirely trust his motives yet. He wouldn't take no for an answer, though. I wonder if he likes the chase."

Olivia squinted her eyes in thought as they exited the back door after Wyatt. "Hard to tell." She stepped over a pile of seashell mulching bags. "But he definitely makes for an easy view." Olivia winked at Callie.

"That, he does." She laughed. "I wasn't prepared for going out. What am I going to wear?" The sand whipped around with the wind, blowing across the old gray boards of the walkway.

"Don't worry. You can borrow that white sundress I bought. I've never worn it, and it cost me a ton. It would be nice for someone to get some use out of it."

Callie had been with Olivia when she'd bought the dress. They'd shared a bottle of champagne, had their nails done, and spent all day shopping—an indulgent girls' day. Olivia hadn't been on a date since she and Wyatt's father had split up. She'd finally agreed to go out with someone, but as she prepared—bought a new dress, got her hair cut and her nails done—she'd chickened out and canceled. Wyatt's father had let them down, and she didn't want it to happen again. Not now that Wyatt's heart could be broken too.

"Are you sure you want me to wear that one?" Callie had loved that dress, and when Olivia bought it, she'd been so glad that her friend had found something so lovely. It tied behind the neck, and flowed down very casually just above the knees. With some strappy sandals and big hoop earrings, it was adorable.

"Yes. I'm more than sure. It's still in the garment bag with the tags on it. I was going to return it, but I just never did."

"You're a life saver," Callie said, not wanting to dwell on the subject. It would only bring them around to Wyatt's father, the whole reason dating was so hard for Olivia. She'd spent so many nights helping Olivia through the tears and the hurt during that time, and she knew her friend didn't want to relive any part of it. They didn't talk about him anymore, never mentioning his name unless he was coming to pick up Wyatt on the odd holiday.

She knew too well what a gaping hole a breakup could cause. Callie had experienced it herself: Things had been going so well. She had bought a loft apartment in Richmond; she'd been promoted to senior manager of accounts at the marketing firm where she worked, and she'd started in a new department. It was there that Callie had met a guy—his name was Kyle; he was a graphic designer. He'd been considerate, mannerly, all the things she might look for, and she'd let herself fall for him.

There was one particular moment when she knew that she'd fallen hard. He'd made her laugh—he always did—but that time as she giggled, she could see a look in his eyes that she thought meant something. They'd dated just long enough for her to start to rethink her future, considering him in her life's choices, when suddenly and completely unexpectedly, he'd broken it off.

He'd said he wasn't ready for a long-term relationship. She thought back to the way he'd kept an extra blanket folded next to the pillow where she slept in his room because she always got cold and how he'd bought a coffee mug to keep in the cabinet just for her—he didn't drink coffee. Callie had pored over every conversation, everything they'd done together, never once feeling that she'd put any pressure on him. They'd just progressed from one stage to another. But the day after he'd ended things, she saw him kissing their co-worker Sheila in the office parking lot, that same look on his face that she'd thought had been only for her. Sick with the weight of betrayal, unable to show up in the office and look them both in the eye, Callie had quit her job that day. She'd just called her boss and resigned.

So when Olivia told her their dream of owning the cottage could actually be a reality, Callie jumped at the chance, leaving her office career behind and investing her time and all her savings in The Beachcomber, where they could meet people from all over, sit out on the back porch with their coffees, and watch the sun rise over the Atlantic.

The Beachcomber was the fresh start she needed.

Chapter Four

Callie woke to the sound of a buzz saw. She checked the clock again—seven o'clock. She'd been tossing and turning for about an hour, the heat and noise creeping in from the construction downstairs. She couldn't wait to get out on the beach and feel the refreshing chill of the sea spray as it caught in the wind and sprinkled her skin.

The saw squealed again, and she was acutely aware of her need for coffee. Delighted that although the kitchen was probably covered in dust from all the work downstairs, it had—as of this week—a working coffee maker, she threw on her clothes and went downstairs. The saw was competing with a loud banging and she covered her ears.

"Sorry!" Olivia said, following her into the kitchen. "The crew for the porches got here early and had to start."

With a groggy nod, Callie took the cream out of the fridge while Olivia retrieved the sugar, setting it beside her with a smile. She was always the early bird. Callie yawned as she filled the coffee maker and got herself a mug. After what seemed like years rather than minutes due to the noise, the coffee finally percolated and she poured herself a cup, offering one to Olivia.

When the sawing tapered off, Callie sent a quiet "thank you" to God as she sat down in silence at the new kitchen table, delivered yesterday evening. The table was a creamy whitewashed color, with the wood grains peeking through in places. It was big enough to fill the large breakfast area that was being widened further to accommodate additional smaller tables and chairs for guests.

* * *

The saws started back up and Callie winced. "I think I'm going to take my coffee outside to wake up a little before I start renovations for the day. Want to come?"

"I woke up really early and just jumped right into it! I'm going to finish the trim in the hallway with Wyatt before I take a break. I'm feeling motivated!" Olivia pumped her fists in the air, making Callie laugh.

"I'll be in to help shortly," Callie said, taking her coffee to the back door and grabbing a magazine from the stack on the way. She needed to buy a book for times like these, but she just hadn't settled into a routine yet, the house still taking nearly every single minute of her time.

While Olivia went back into the hallway Callie let herself out onto the old porch that was being redone. She waved to the crew. They were suspended around the house like a swarm of giant spiders, hammering, sawing, lining up the timber. Next to a giant water cooler, a small radio played Top 40 hits.

She and Olivia had put up a ton of their own money, hiring an architect friend of Olivia's from college, Aiden

Parker, to help with renovations. He'd put his crew on it immediately. He was very well known for his work, and because Olivia was an old friend, he'd given them a good deal, but it was still quite a high price. He was extending the entire back of the old shingled house, giving its three stories their own covered porches facing the coast. The house itself sat right on the shore, but it was back just far enough to be safe at high tide when the waves would eat up the beach, gurgling their way toward them. Once Aiden had the porches built, Callie imagined rows of wicker chairs and hanging flowers dotting the electric blue view of the ocean. It was going to be magnificent.

She took her coffee past the area where they'd been knocking the old wood off the porch and descended the long staircase to the original walkway they'd also be replacing soon, a long expanse of slatted wood that led straight to the ocean. Right now, the wood was puckered in places from years of withstanding the elements, sea grasses peeking up through the slats. She stepped carefully, as she carried her coffee in one hand, and slung her old beach chair over her arm.

The sea air pushed against her, refreshing and crisp in the morning light, the buzzing of the saws nearly drowned out by the surf. A tiny shadow bobbed along the waves, a surfer up for an early ride, and there was a couple walking hand in hand, the water running over their feet relentlessly. Without a free hand herself, Callie held up her coffee in greeting and they waved in return, calling out, "Good morning!"

The shore, an endless breadth of white, looked as though it had been sifted clean this morning, the weather having been so calm in the last week that the waves hadn't kicked up any debris. Callie set up her chair and took a seat right at the water's edge, digging her toes into the sand as the bubbling water retreated out to sea. It was early morning, yet she could still feel the sting of sun on her skin like she had as a girl.

She slipped on her sunglasses, pushed her cup of coffee into the wet compact sand just enough to keep it from tipping, and opened her magazine. The pages fought against the wind as she scanned the table of contents for an article to read. Her heart did a little jump when she saw yet another article about the Sullivans. *So many features*, she thought. No wonder that reporter had been following Luke. She opened to page forty-seven.

She lifted her mug, her coffee soothing her along with the rush of air in her ears and the warmth of sun on her shoulders. The bright white magazine page hurt her eyes in the glare of the morning light even with her sunglasses, but she squinted to get a better focus to read. A seagull flew over, casting a momentary shadow on the page.

Callie read about Luke, and how different he was in business from his father, how he spent a lot of time out with various women, traveling, and how he didn't seem to have the drive that his father had when it came to Sullivan Enterprises. The article alluded to him being more of a figurehead of Blue Water Sailing than anything else, just a face to sell the company's boats. And he definitely had the face.

Callie closed the magazine, not wanting to read any more, and wishing again she hadn't spent so much time away from The Beachcomber to have lunch with him. Now, in light of all she'd read, she wasn't entirely sure she wanted to go to dinner tonight. She didn't have that kind of time to waste. The summer was slipping away from them, and they needed to get The Beachcomber open for business.

She'd had a professional photographer take photos as parts of the house were finished so she could send them out to prospective vacationers. Callie had spoken with another bed and breakfast in the area. They'd booked up through September, and they'd been sending people her way to get information. She'd promised an opening of no later than the end of August, and she was taking reservations.

She finished her coffee and went back inside.

* * *

Callie didn't waste any time after her coffee. She went straight up to clear the extra paneling Olivia had mentioned out of the closet. With a grunt, she opened the door and lifted the large pieces, her hands sweaty and losing their grip. Because of the paint fumes, they'd kept the windows open, the sea breeze their only relief. The cry of gulls and the shushing of the ocean made it feel like the shore was right inside the room.

She grabbed the final piece of paneling, straining to move it. When she pulled it out, there was a small *smack* and she peered into the closet to see what had made the noise. It was a compact, leather-bound book, the edges water stained and yellowed. Callie leaned the paneling against the wall and picked up the book, flipping it open. It looked like a journal; the name Alice McFarlin on the inside, the first entry written in scratchy cursive blue ink and there was no date on it.

She read:

If I don't write every day, I'll explode. No one will listen to me, so, my dear journal, perhaps I will find

*comfort in your silence as you hear all the things I
have to say. God didn't see it in His will to give me
children, and I have to trust that, but He did give me
the thoughts and emotions that I possess at this moment, and I find it very difficult not to act on them…*

Callie shut the book and turned it over in her hand,
inspecting the cover inside and out. Wiping her hands
on her shorts, she took the journal downstairs to show
Olivia.

"Look what I found," she said as she met Olivia in
the hallway. Her friend was covered in dust, the powdery
substance making her cough and sticking to her perspiration. Callie handed her the journal and Olivia flipped
through it.

"Would it be awful to read it?" Olivia asked.

"Technically, it's ours," Callie said. "We bought the
house and the book was in it, so it belongs to us." She
grinned at her friend. "Do you want to be nosy?"

Olivia plopped down on the top step and set the journal
in her lap.

Callie sat one step down and looked up at her friend.

"We'll probably just find her old shopping lists,"
Olivia said with disappointment, handing the journal back
to Callie.

"Maybe not." Callie took it, opening to that first entry
she'd read and turning it so Olivia could read.

Olivia scanned the words. "Oh," she said. "Very dramatic." They both giggled excitedly.

"We should be ashamed of ourselves," Callie said, her
face dropping to a frown, suddenly feeling bad. "These
might be Alice's deepest thoughts. We should treat them
carefully." The idea of sharing her innermost feelings in a

private journal only to have strangers read them was terrifying, and the silliness drained right out of her.

Olivia sobered. "Yes, you're right."

Callie didn't even know if she wanted to read it anymore. "I'll put it in a safe place," she said, not sure what she wanted to do with it. She felt protective of it all of a sudden.

Chapter Five

Callie and Olivia had worked all day, and Callie had barely finished the closets and painting in time to be ready by seven. She'd almost missed the sound of the Range Rover through the window. The guys were finishing up on the walkway before quitting for the night. Olivia had turned on music downstairs and brought up a glass of wine for her that was not quite as chilled as it should have been, since it was still in the beach cooler they'd brought with them when they'd moved, and the ice was melting.

Callie took the last sip of wine and set the empty glass on the bathroom counter, then peered at herself in the mirror. She had on Olivia's white sundress, showing off the tan she had newly acquired from working outside. It had been a long time since she'd spent this much effort on herself, and as she viewed her reflection, she thought about how nice it was to get dressed up, have a nice meal and good conversation. Slipping on her sandals and a silver bangle to match her earrings, she grabbed the empty wine glass and headed downstairs.

She hadn't had time to get nervous until that moment, but as soon as she saw Luke Sullivan standing in the doorway, looking like some sort of movie star, she had to catch her breath, the jitters swarming her. She couldn't stop looking at the flecks of gray in his blue eyes, his easy smile, the gentle swing of his strong arms. She felt herself blushing and looked away. Wyatt had come in for dinner. He had let Luke in and run off, calling for Olivia, who had jumped in the shower earlier to get the heat off her.

"Hey," Luke said, as if he knew her better than he did. "Ready?"

"Yes," she said, hoping she didn't come off too nervous. All those things she'd read about him were clouding her thoughts. "Let me just say goodbye to my friend Olivia. What time should she expect us back?"

"I don't know," he said with a laugh as if the question was ridiculous, but that curiosity in his eyes had returned, and it was intoxicating.

She'd wanted to make sure Olivia knew when to expect her, since she was going out with someone she'd only just met—he was still practically a stranger. But then again, maybe it wasn't out of the ordinary for Luke. Maybe he was hoping if things went well, she might not come home at all. The outrage of this settled in her chest before she convinced herself that she was jumping to conclusions. Yes, the papers had all painted him as a playboy. But the Sullivans were a family that the locals loved to hate. The drama kept things interesting in that small town.

"Hello," Olivia said, shuffling up next to them, goggling as she took the empty wine glass from Callie. She'd done her hair and changed her clothes. "Olivia Dixon."

She held out her other hand, now clean and smooth, toward Luke, glancing over at Callie, who had to hide her smirk. Olivia obviously wanted to say something more but she didn't. Usually full of words, she seemed to have lost them all.

"Luke Sullivan." Luke shook her hand.

He glanced around but then his gaze returned to Callie. Perhaps he was being polite and didn't want to pry. She wished she could've whipped the place up into better shape before having a millionaire come through its doors, but there was no use getting stressed out about it. There was nothing she could do now.

"We should probably get going," he said.

Olivia offered Callie a smile that was riddled with questions and *Oh my Gods*, but Callie tried not to look at her for fear she'd get too nervous. Olivia stepped back, allowing Callie and Luke to leave. As they walked out into the heat of the sunshine, Callie slipped her sunglasses on, after debating whether or not to just hold them and squint so she'd have something to occupy her hands.

Luke opened the passenger side door of the Range Rover for her, the car purring as he climbed in behind the wheel.

"I thought we could have dinner on my boat tonight."

Callie's mind immediately went back to that bikini model in the photo and she suddenly felt like nothing special. She'd spent extra time on herself, scrubbing away all the dirt and paint, applying her makeup and adding shimmery lip-gloss when she usually wouldn't. She'd worn Olivia's white dress.

When she didn't respond, he said, "I don't want the press to think I'm cheating on Ashley. That's why I thought we could have dinner somewhere secluded."

Her pulse throbbed in her ears, and she felt the prickle of heat beneath her cheeks. Did he say *cheating*? And who was Ashley? He was asking Callie out to dinner when he had a girlfriend? She stared at that smug face, trying to keep her eyes from noticeably narrowing. There was no way she was going to stoop so low.

"You have a girlfriend?" she asked as calmly as she could, immediately regretting it because now it might look like she was hoping he didn't, when she wasn't. After all, this wasn't really a date, was it? It was only a kind gesture to repay her. She just didn't want to get in the middle of things.

She must've looked horrified because it seemed to take him off guard. After a moment, he tipped his head back and laughed. "You look concerned," he said, still grinning. "I haven't dated Ashley in about four months but her manager thinks it would be best with her upcoming movie release to keep it quiet so as not to take the focus off the premiere."

The way he could read her was unsettling. "I'm sorry," she said. How terrible that he'd broken up with his girlfriend months ago and he couldn't even feel comfortable taking someone to dinner for fear it would get back to the tabloids.

"About what?"

Not wanting to go into her opinions about his lifestyle and the press, she said simply, "I'm sorry that you and your girlfriend broke up."

"Oh. Well, we weren't even exclusively dating, but when the media sees you out more than once, they hunker down for the proposal shot."

"My God," she said, realizing how totally different their lives were.

Chapter Six

After a few minutes' drive down the road, Luke pulled into the parking lot of a nearby marina and shut off the engine.

He started typing on his phone. "Okay, I'm just putting in our order with the chef. I figured for dinner, we could both get a lobster frittata. I like caviar on mine. How does that sound?" His head popped up when he'd finished typing.

A lobster *what?* She wasn't sure how to answer. Her idea of fancy food was getting a side salad instead of fries.

She'd assumed they were going to sit in a beachside tiki bar somewhere like they had for lunch and sip on piña coladas while reggae music played around them. But now she had visions of her hair pulling out of her clip as the wind tore through her on some boat while she held on to a lobster something or other for dear life. He glanced at her briefly, obviously waiting for an answer.

"I've never had that before," she said honestly. "So I don't know."

It seemed as if understanding dawned on him, and she thought back to the article that had said how the Sullivans were out of touch with the average person. He typed something else on his phone and then looked at her. "If you could have your favorite seafood, what would it be?"

"I always get a crab cake. Maybe some shrimp on the side." Quickly, worried he might be judging her choices in some way, to make it sound better, she added, "With a side salad."

"Done. I've put in the order." He smiled as he finished typing on that phone of his. Then he put it in his pocket and led the way to the massive docks. She followed along beside him, waiting to see what kind of gorgeous boat he had.

Nothing prepared her for what she saw, as they approached a man in a navy sailing uniform. He greeted Luke, addressing him as Mr. Sullivan, and introduced himself to her as the captain as he stepped aside, ushering them aboard the white luxury boat. The floors were a glossy hardwood, the seats all white leather with accent lighting pulling her eyes in every direction. The normally dark blue water looked like a turquoise stripe through the windows of the ship, matching the coordinating throw pillows. The indoor and outdoor spaces were open to each other, connected by a towering arch. Luke walked her over to the compact mahogany bar, where one of the staff was ready to pour a drink from the endless supply of beer and spirits that glistened on the wall behind him. He patted the barstool, indicating for her to take a seat.

"What would you like?" Luke asked her. His demeanor drove home how normal this was for him, making Callie feel very out of place. She took her sunglasses off and set them on the highly lacquered bar to get a better look, as the boat's engine grumbled below. She kept waiting to wake up in her dusty bedroom, the ocean having lulled her to sleep through the open window, but it was clear as Luke put his hand on her back and leaned forward to take a look at his own choices that this was no dream. When she didn't answer, he said, "How about a mojito? It's got white rum, mint, and lime."

"That sounds amazing," she said, still somewhat at a loss for words.

"Two mojitos please," he said to the bartender.

The colossal vessel began to move, its horn blowing as it pulled away from the marina. By the time they'd gotten their drinks—frosty glasses, the concoction as sweet as nectar and surrounded by rounds of lime, mint leaves, and ice—they were already picking up speed in the harbor, heading toward the open water. The breeze blowing in was just the right temperature to cool the sun's relentless rays, and it seemed to be taking its time to dip below the horizon. She'd been glad to have daylight until around nine o'clock each night so they could work on the bed and breakfast, but the heat could be exhausting. Not on board this boat. With the salty air around her and a cold drink in her hand the temperature was perfect.

"I've never been on a boat like this before," she said, trying to make conversation and suddenly struggling when she thought about those articles. She didn't want to admit that the only boat she'd ever been on was her grandfather's little fishing boat. Until now, she hadn't really spent much time at the beach. She'd been too busy working the nine to five that really ended up being more like eight to seven-thirty. But that was all going to change. Being at the beach house would allow her to be closer to Olivia and Wyatt, and to figure out what she really wanted in her own life.

"Grab your drink," he said with a grin, standing up. "Let's go to the stern." She followed his lead.

They sat down on a long leather bench that extended along the back of the boat, and she ran her fingers down the puckered details where leather buttons were sewn into the seat. Luke plopped down, not seeming to notice her admiring the upholstery. He took a long swig of his mojito, his hair blowing in the breeze.

"Look at that," he said, as if he'd seen it a hundred times and it was The Thing to show people whenever he had them aboard.

Callie followed his line of sight out to sea where a pod of dolphins was jumping and swimming together. "Oh! That's amazing," she said, her excitement not tempered by his delivery. She sipped her drink for a little while before asking, "Where are we going?"

"Just for a ride." He smiled, his arm stretched along the seat behind her, his ankle resting on the knee of his other leg, as he slipped on a pair of designer sunglasses. His presence, their surroundings, her fancy dress—it all seemed so surreal. She wondered now more than ever if he'd just been trying to make her comfortable by taking her to that casual burger place yesterday.

She took a nervous sip of her drink. "What have you been up to today?" she asked, trying again to make conversation.

"Buying properties," he said. "A group of waterfront hotels."

"A group of them?" Was that an average day for him?

"My father's had his eye on them for quite some time. I thought it would be a good investment and it would be nice to surprise him."

How kind, she thought. "What does he want to do with them?"

"Sell them. Eventually." He said it as if the answer were obvious.

Hiding her tension, she took another sip of her drink, the sweet lime flavor crisp on her lips.

"Mr. Sullivan," a man said, as he appeared out of nowhere. "Your dinner is ready, sir. Will you be dining on deck or in the dining area?"

"We'll take it at the table here on deck. Thank you, James," Luke said. He stood and held out his hand to help her up. The boat was considerably large—enough not to be bumpy—but she had a sensation of tilting slightly as she stood up, and the mojito was hitting, so she was glad for his offer. She took his hand.

On the starboard side of the boat, along another expanse of cream-colored leather benches, was a dark wood table, four chairs on each side. Luke pulled out a seat for her and, again, she noticed how the gesture didn't seem intentional; it was as if he'd been taught to do it from childhood. It was interesting to see how he behaved in his own environment. It was a far cry from oversized burgers eaten while sitting on sandy barstools. She reminded herself that this was how he lived every day, not that. He went around and sat across from her as a member of the staff set a glass of water, cloth napkins, and silverware in front of them.

Callie was served first, and then one of the staff set down Luke's dish.

His plate held a mass of eggs with a tiny pile of lobster on top. "I'd hate to offer you something that you didn't like," he said, clearly noticing her curiosity. "This, by the way, is lobster frittata. Hand me your fork. I'll let you try a bite." He smiled at her and she fumbled a little as she picked up her utensil. She handed it over and he scooped some onto it, the caviar sitting precariously on top of the bite.

Callie took it from him, peering down at it first before she even thought about putting it into her mouth. She threw a glance over to her mojito, to be sure she had enough left to wash it down if she didn't like it. She was a picky eater, and it didn't look appetizing, but, as the old saying went: *When in Rome...*

"What's the matter?" he asked with a chuckle. It seemed that her deliberation was amusing him. She'd made him curious again. She remembered that look; he was enjoying this.

"Um...I'm afraid I won't like it."

He took off his sunglasses and set them on the table as if he wanted to get a better view of her. He was still smiling, his eyes squinting in an adorable way. He leaned on his forearms. "I've never seen anyone look as worried as you did just now," he said with another huff of amusement. "Try it." He nodded toward her fork.

Callie took a deep breath and then plunged the fork into her mouth. The caviar popped on her tongue as she chewed, the taste overwhelming her senses, filling up her mouth, and the texture of it against the spongy egg gave her a shiver. She swallowed quickly and took an enormous drink of her mojito, the rum sour against the sweetness of the caviar.

Luke threw his head back and laughed. "This is fun," he said, his eyes roaming her face.

"Thank you for that taste," she said, happy to finally see some of his actual personality coming through again. His light-heartedness calmed her a little. "I'll have my crab cake now." She stabbed a bite with her fork.

"Want to know something? I've never had a crab cake," he said.

"What?" She held her fork mid-bite, contorting her face into a dramatic look of disbelief. *What resident of the Outer Banks hasn't eaten a crab cake?* "I tried yours. You have to try a bite." She reached out for his fork and scraped a bite across the plate, handing it back to him.

He put it in his mouth and chewed, his eyebrows rising in response. "That's not bad," he said with a nod.

"Not bad? It's only my favorite food of all time."

He smiled again, his eyes on her.

"So tell me more about The Beachcomber," he said. "How did you end up in Waves?"

As they ate, she told him a little about how she and Olivia had admired the house over the years and how Gladys had told them the minute it was on the market, but she hadn't gotten into a whole lot of detail. There was no need, really, for him to become invested in her story because it was clear after seeing all this that Callie wasn't someone whom he could ever get serious about. Her line of vision narrowed on the long bench at the bow of the boat, thinking that it looked a lot like the spot where that bikini model had been in the photo.

"It's nice, I'm sure, to work for yourself, to create something from the ground up," he said, picking at the last few bites on his plate. "I still sort of work for my father. Well, it's my father's company, but eventually, I'm taking over." She noticed a slight wobble of uncertainty in his eyes when he said it. It was just subtle enough for her to question whether or not she'd actually seen something, but she swore she had.

"Do you want to take over the company?" she asked, unable to stop herself.

"Yes," he said a little too quickly.

She stared at him a moment, trying to figure him out.

"What?" he said, his shoulders tensing.

"Nothing." Her words came out softly, surprising her. She felt bad for rattling him. She hadn't meant to. But as she watched him, he visibly relaxed, clearly trying to regain his composure.

"You looked at me disbelievingly," he said much more calmly, and she was taken aback yet again. Most of her relationships had ended because she'd been closed off and her boyfriends always complained that they could never tell what she was thinking.

"I didn't mean to," she said, trying to cover up her shock. "How could I disbelieve anything you say when I've only just met you?" Perhaps she'd misinterpreted his body language.

He smiled, but there was a little uncertainty behind his eyes and she wondered again if her hunch had been right in the first place. But there was no need to press it. What he did with his life was completely his business.

Just as they'd finished eating, the boat was docking, the motors slowing as they reached land, and he stood up. "Getting you another mojito. I'll be right back." Before the captain had completely steadied the large vessel, Luke was at the bar getting two more drinks.

Callie looked around. Sleek, dark wood sailboats bobbed in the water beside them, their vast, white sails tied up, their decks empty. She noticed the very large cottages that dotted the coast. They seemed to stretch as far as she could see, their Caribbean colors making them look like a string of beads, walls of windows overlooking the ocean, and she wondered if the boats belonged to those residents.

As a kid, on the summers when she'd visited the Outer

Banks with Olivia and her family, they'd come to Avon, to visit its one-screen movie theater on rainy days. The landscape was much more rural then; it had grown up so much, and now, while there were still pockets of that simpler lifestyle along the Outer Banks—Waves being one of them—the clientele had certainly changed.

A pang of worry struck her as she hoped that there were still enough people who would embrace more modest accommodations. Restoring The Beachcomber was the biggest risk she'd ever taken in her life, and while she'd never felt freer, she knew that in the end, she had to make a living. There was a part of her that considered going back to the security of a nine to five job, but she recognized her fear and pushed forward whenever the thought crept in.

Luke came back and handed her another mojito. "Want to take a little walk?"

"Sure. Thank you," she said, standing up with her drink. The captain had lowered the ladder so she could exit easily.

Callie stepped onto the weathered wood of the dock that led to walking paths along the beach, careful to keep hold of her glass as she made her way over to a patch of wildflowers growing in the sandy soil nearby. Luke came up behind her. The sun's rays were still strong despite the evening hour. She strolled along the dock beside Luke, admiring the gaillardia that lined it. Its blossoms were like bursts of sunshine: The daisy-style petals were burnt orange with yellow tips, making the flowers seem as though they were little blooms of fire against the sand-colored sea oats surrounding them. She resisted picking herself a bouquet, knowing there wasn't anywhere to put it on the boat.

She turned to Luke. He looked like a poster boy for

some sort of beach fashion ad. The shirttail of his nautical button-down was untucked in a casual but perfectly executed way, his sunglasses dangling from his fingers. He grinned at her, the lines from so many days in the sun showing around his eyes.

She reached over and delicately slipped the stem of a gaillardia between her fingers, cupping the bloom in her hand. "Aren't these beautiful? They're so vibrant."

"I've never noticed them. Are they weeds?" He bent down to take a look.

"No," she said. "They're wildflowers." She indulged herself and picked one off, threading it through her hair just above her ear.

That curiosity appeared on his face again. "Ah. It looks much prettier now that I get a better look at it." He flashed a flirty smile, and she thought back to his laughter while they were eating their burgers yesterday, before she'd really understood who he was. Seeing all this tonight had changed her perception.

"Want to walk to the beach over there?" he asked. A sailboat bobbed on the horizon, the waves fizzing up the shore, beckoning her.

"Sure."

To her surprise, Luke held out his hand to lead her down the few steps to the grassy area winding toward the shore. She took it, feeling the warmth of his grip, the softness of his touch, and the stillness in his fingers. While the gesture was just friendly, it felt so intimate that Callie found herself trying to hold her fingers casually when it would be so easy to intertwine them with his.

"We used to make bonfires on this beach as kids," he said as they walked. "On any given night there would be at least fifteen teenagers all sitting around a giant fire. After school on Fridays, we'd throw our beach chairs in the back of our trucks and drive over here."

Callie imagined a flock of privileged teenagers in their polo shirts and pressed shorts, laughing behind their designer sunglasses. "So you're an old pro at bringing girls here then," she teased.

"Of course," he played along. "But now I've stepped up my game. I offer mojitos instead of strawberry wine in paper cups."

"I used to drink strawberry wine too!" she giggled. "We'd sneak it into our friends' houses. One of them had an older sister who would buy it for us." She shook her head at the memory. "There was nothing like a bag of Doritos and a paper cup of strawberry wine to get a night going."

"I might have some Doritos on the boat," he said, pretending to turn back just as they reached the sand.

She laughed, pulling him toward the beach.

They walked down to where the waves were breaking and sat in the dry sand just close enough to get their feet wet when the tide came in. She slipped her sandals off and set them beside her.

"Yeah... I haven't been to this beach in a long time," he admitted.

"Who was the last person you were here with?"

Luke pursed his lips as he sifted through the memories. Then that crooked grin spread across his face. "Sally Johansen. I was eighteen." He laughed and then turned to Callie. "Sally Johansen is married with six children—all a year apart."

"Wow." She let that sink in for a moment. "Just think, that could be you!"

"I want a big family, but I can't imagine having six

children, all that close in age. My God, that would be a lot of work."

"Yes, it would."

"It would be fun, though," he said, and she noticed that he'd moved his foot nearer to hers, only a small strip of sand between them.

"To be married to Sally Johansen?"

"No," he said, with a burst of laughter. "Having a bunch of kids. That would be enough children to start our own beach volleyball team."

Callie shared in his amusement before they settled into a happy moment of quiet.

"I was an only child," she said, looking over at him. "I always wanted a sister or brother. It was really lonely sometimes."

"Mmm." Luke nodded. "I have a sister and I'm really close with her now, but growing up we were always at each other—I used to chase her around the house trying to tickle her even though I knew she hated it. Why do kids do things like that?"

Callie smiled. "I don't know," she said. "But I'll bet it's a funny memory now. I wish I had someone to share that kind of thing with. Olivia, my best friend, and I are sort of like that."

"Did you ever do anything funny to her?"

She looked out at the sea and tried to think of something. "I froze her bra once as a prank. I filled a baggie with water and shoved it in there. It was a block of ice in the morning."

They both laughed.

Then his eyes met hers. He leaned toward her, and to her horror, she realized by the look on his face that he might try to kiss her or something. The headlines flashing in her mind like an old movie reel, she realized she'd let her guard down. She leaned back, her mojito nearly sloshing out of her glass.

Luke stopped, clearly surprised at her response, but he covered it well. He seemed almost confused, and she wondered if he'd ever had to work for a girl's affection in his life. She wasn't going to throw herself at him just because he had a cool boat and a pair of sunglasses that cost more than her rent back in the city. By his expression, he hadn't meant any harm, and he almost looked a little mortified.

Callie smiled to reassure him, trying to hide the fact that while she was totally annoyed that he thought she might be so easily willing to surrender to his charm, she kind of liked taking him out of his comfort zone.

"What are you doing tomorrow?" he asked, a new interest showing behind his eyes.

"I'm working on the house."

His gaze dropped down to the sand but he quickly recovered and smiled. She wondered if he thought she was rejecting his possible suggestion to see her again, but she'd only been responding truthfully.

His eyes met hers, his head tilted to the side as he noticeably tried to gain footing in this new territory. "I'd like to help," he said, to her surprise.

Was he just bluffing, dared by her resistance to his advances? "Olivia and I have it covered, but thank you." There was no need to waste anyone's time. She'd already spent far more than she should have aboard this boat, playing his little flirty games. "And we get started *very* early."

Clearly ignoring her last suggestion that he couldn't get himself up and ready in time, he said, "I'm serious."

She smiled kindly so as not to upset him—he'd done

nothing wrong. But she said, "So am I," her words direct and clear.

"We'd better get back to the boat," he said, looking over Callie's shoulder. "Looks like a photographer." Luke stood up and turned away from a man with a large camera, wearing trousers and a two-button shirt—clearly not an outfit for swimming. Was it always like this for Luke—being hounded in his private moments?

Chapter Seven

"He said what?" Olivia asked as she climbed down from the ladder in the center of the room. She'd been up early this morning, having already been in bed when Callie got home.

Callie looked up at the glass-beaded sand dollar chandelier they'd found at a shop in Manteo on their way into town. They'd had an electrician install it yesterday, and Olivia had been cleaning the fingerprints off the glass. She'd said she had waited until Callie got home because she didn't want to climb the tall ladder without someone to keep it steady, since she had to step on the top rung to reach the fixture. The chandelier shimmered as it illuminated the bedroom and Callie could just imagine the white gauzy fabrics and the sand-colored accents that would complement its light green color.

"I think some sea green throw pillows would look good in here once we get the bedding in. Maybe have a wicker chair in the corner... Yeah, Luke asked to come over and help us with renovations."

"That's what I thought you said." Olivia had her hands on her hips, a wide-eyed look on her face. "How are we supposed to look hot and desirable when we're all sweaty and covered in dust and paint?"

"I don't care how I look in front of him. I told him no anyway, though," Callie said, nearly rolling her eyes. She proceeded to tell Olivia about the possible kiss debacle. The more she'd thought about it, the more she'd convinced herself that he'd thought she was just like all those other girls who probably threw themselves at him. Well, she wasn't.

Olivia pressed her lips together as if she were trying to hold in some thought.

"What? Just say it."

"Luke Sullivan tried to kiss you and you didn't kiss him? Are you crazy?" She took Callie by the shoulders and shook her playfully. "That's worth investigating just to see what all those models and actresses are after when they date him. I'm so disappointed in you."

"I only *think* he was trying to kiss me. And, anyway, celebrity or not, there's no way I'm going to let some hothead who thinks he can swoon me with his fancy boat trips kiss me."

Olivia shook her head. "Why didn't I go out instead of you to get lunch yesterday? I'd have totally kissed him."

Callie laughed and clicked off the light. A streak of dark blue rippled across the wall, the reflection of the sunlight through a stained glass sun catcher they'd gotten from Gladys. "You have no shame."

"You're right. I have no shame. But! I can always say that because I took initiative, I actually dated Tony Reemos."

"You were twelve!" Callie said, bursting into laughter.

Olivia had run home that night and called Callie to tell her that she'd met Tony Reemos at the mall and that they'd held hands and exchanged phone numbers. Callie had lain on her bedroom floor, the phone to her ear for an hour, while Olivia told her all the details about this gorgeous boy she'd spent the day with after her mom had dropped her off to go shopping.

"Doesn't matter. I've dated someone famous."

Callie doubled over. "I'd forgotten about that—he isn't famous. He's a barely known actor. That's not to say that it isn't awesome, but I'd hardly call him famous."

"He was in the background of that tissue ad and it was a national commercial!"

Callie laughed again. They headed downstairs together. Callie had a big project in front of her today. She was going to strip old wallpaper off the formal living room walls and paint them a light blue. She'd hoped to hire someone to paint a mural on one of the walls, just something subtle, so she could make it a beachy sitting room.

* * *

With no window treatments, the bright sun filtered into the formal living room, leaving large rectangular patches of light on the hardwoods, which was good, since the workers had cut the power to wire the new porches and Callie had to prepare for taking down the wallpaper. It was an enormous undertaking, so big that it was a little daunting, but when they'd divvied up the tasks, one of them had to take it, so Callie had volunteered, to Olivia's complete relief.

In return, Olivia had promised to do the cooking for the first month once the appliances were installed to pay her back, but Callie assured her it was really fine. Then she told her all her favorite dishes—obviously teasing. Callie loved to cook, and said she'd do both the wallpaper and the cooking without a flinch.

Alone with her thoughts, Callie tried not to dwell on the length of the task at hand, allowing her mind to drift as she laid out the drop cloths. The wooden floor was dusty, quite a contrast to that gleaming boat she'd been on yesterday with Luke. His wealth had made her nervous, but he'd relaxed her so easily. As she dragged the cloth farther down the floor with her foot until it covered the corner, she caught herself thinking about his smile when he was talking about the strawberry wine. The way his forehead wrinkled a little when his eyebrows rose, the lift in his cheekbones when that crooked smile emerged...

"I mixed up the solution for you. It's down in the driveway—I could hardly get that heavy bucket across the street, let alone up all those stairs," Gladys said, startling her as she dumped herself down dramatically into the only chair in the room. Callie had left the chair for her because Gladys was going to walk her through the process. Gladys had insisted on making the wallpaper stripper instead of just buying it, swearing that good old water and liquid fabric softener would do the trick. "We could've mixed it over here, but then I'd have had to cart a zillion bottles of fabric softener over. I didn't know which was worse, so I opted for the one bucket."

"Oh, you should've texted me to help you. I'd have carried it."

Gladys was always helping. When The Beachcomber had come up for sale, Olivia had confided in Callie that she just didn't have the money to put down on it. Callie had wanted to help, but she didn't have enough to cover the whole down payment *and* all that would go into the purchase and restoration of the house. Olivia had fretted over it for ages before finally telling Gladys she didn't think it would be possible to purchase the property.

Gladys had invited them both to come down and have a look at it anyway, claiming they could really just come for a visit. Over dinner that night, Gladys had slid a check across the table from her savings account—half the down payment. She'd told Olivia it was her inheritance, and that best she use it while the moment was right.

It was spending time at Olivia's where Callie learned how family took care of each other, and this was another example. Everything rested on this for Olivia and Callie, but the money didn't affect them as much as Gladys's gesture.

"I can't stand wallpaper," Gladys said, getting back up and straightening one of the drop cloths Callie had put down to protect the floor. "It's more trouble than it's worth." She peered up disapprovingly at the old floral pattern. "When you're tired of it, you can't just change it without a major event."

Callie smiled at her. "We're sticking to paint," she said in agreement.

"Do you have an electric sander? That glue wreaks havoc on drywall."

"Yep." She removed the last of the switch plates and set it down in the pile in the center of the room. "I'll just get the bucket. Be right back."

"Where's Wyatt today?" Gladys asked as Callie hauled in the giant painter's bucket and set it with a slosh on one of the drop cloths.

"Olivia's bought him a new kite. She's outside getting him started."

"Bless her. I know it's hard to keep him entertained. I'll go out and help her after I get you started and rest my legs for a minute."

With a grin, Callie picked up the scorer and started dragging it across the wall in little circles.

"You two are going to be tired tonight after all this work. I think you need to put your feet up and relax. Why don't you let me make you some dinner and we'll spend the evening together?" Gladys asked, shifting to get comfortable. She was smiling, waiting for an answer with that familiar look of motherly concern in her eyes.

"Check with Olivia, but that sounds amazing to me!" Callie picked at a piece of loose wallpaper and then scored some more. "Don't go to too much trouble for us, though."

"Keep scoring that spot. And it's never any trouble. How's the patio out back? There's still a table out there, right? We could eat outside tonight; I hear the weather is going to be just glorious all day." Gladys sat for a few minutes more, offering pointers before going out to help Olivia with Wyatt.

* * *

Callie clapped her hand over her mouth as she walked outside. She couldn't believe what Gladys had done while she was in the shower. Her shoulders ached and her arms were weak from stripping wallpaper all day, but she'd gotten almost all of it off in one day, barely even stopping to eat. The wind cool against her wet hair, she looked over at Olivia, who was smiling in one of Gladys's rocking chairs.

"Y'all have been working so hard. I just thought you needed this."

Gladys had draped the pergola above the patio with a

couple of strands of white lights, she'd brought over three rocking chairs, and she'd cleaned the old rectangular picnic table, covered it in a blue and white gingham cloth, and filled it with candles down the middle. Callie took a step toward the table to admire the enormous centerpiece.

"It was easy," Gladys said. "My favorite way to decorate a table outside. It's just a bunch of glass mason jars and vases. I fill them with sand about a third and plop a candle right in. I like white candles for the beach—it's dramatic." She winked at Callie and started pulling covered dishes out of warming bags. "Sit down in the rocking chair, Wyatt and I will take it from here."

Wyatt, his chest filled with pride, stood with a seashell-design oven mitt on each hand, ready to set the dishes on the table.

"You sure you don't need any help?" Callie offered, taking a seat in one of the rocking chairs. The sand gritted beneath it as she rocked.

"Wyatt's got it all under control."

Olivia pulled a bottle of wine from a bucket of ice by her feet. "My sweet grandmother has thought of everything," she said, holding it up. "Want a glass?"

"Absolutely!" Callie said with a laugh, scooting the rocking chair beside her friend while Olivia tipped the bottle over one of the glasses Gladys had brought from inside. "Did you know she was doing all this?" Callie asked, taking the glass from Olivia with a nod of thanks.

"No. Apparently, she and Wyatt were up to this while we were working today. He's earned twenty bucks already."

"She paid him?" Callie said with a giggle.

"Of course I did," Gladys piped up. "Young man's got to earn that new fishing equipment he wants at the bait and tackle shop." She set the last dish onto the table while Wyatt got out plates and silverware, setting them down gently. "Now, you know I really brought that wine for myself, right? Better pour me a glass before you two drink it all," she teased. "I've got more." She clicked on a small radio and turned it up before sitting down.

Olivia handed her a glass.

"Wyatt, I hear you have a magazine with all that fishing gear you want in it. Why don't you run get it and show me what my twenty dollars is going to buy you?"

"Okay, Gram!" Wyatt slid off the mitts and set them neatly by the warming bags at the edge of the patio before running off to his room to get the magazine.

"That boy helped me cook all day, did you know that?" she said with an affectionate shake of her head. "It probably didn't hurt that we baked dessert first and he got to nibble on chocolate chip cookies the whole time."

"Gram, you spoil him," Olivia said. "But I'm so thankful for it. What would we do without you?"

Gladys raised her glass. "To family," she said, the late evening sun making her cheeks rosy. Olivia and Callie joined in the toast.

Callie was so thankful for Gladys. When her own grandmother had passed away, there'd been a hole in Callie's life, an empty spot that used to be filled with old stories and gentle laughter. Her grandmother was the grounding force in her life that held everything together, and when she was gone, it seemed like the pieces of Callie's life and her family just floated away, all going in haphazard directions.

She could still remember the first time it had hit her that Gladys could fill that void. Callie was only about nine. She was running up the walk to Gladys's house when she tripped and fell, skinning her knee. Gladys took her inside and sat her on a chair in her kitchen. As she bandaged it up, Callie thanked her. Without a flinch, Gladys said, "But that's what family does; we take care of each other." With the loss of her own grandmother still fresh, those words had been a welcome relief for Callie, her little heart aching for someone who could take care of her.

Even now that they were grown, Gladys still managed to take care of them.

* * *

They were on their third bottle of wine, amidst empty plates with remnants of shrimp and sausages, bacon, wrapped asparagus, and homemade crusty bread, Wyatt's fishing magazine held down with the wine bucket so it wouldn't blow away. Callie leaned her chin sleepily on her hand, her elbow on the table, the soft lull of the ocean and the wine making it difficult to keep her eyes open. Wyatt was fiddling with the radio while the three women sat chatting at the table.

"Oh!" Gladys said, holding out a hand to Wyatt. "Stop there."

Wyatt stilled his hand on the tuning knob.

"Turn it up. That's Ella Fitzgerald and Louis Armstrong." Gladys closed her eyes and swayed to the song. "It's one of my favorites: 'Dream a Little Dream of Me'; do you know it?"

Callie nodded. Armstrong's raspy voice and Ella Fitzgerald's sailing pitch were powerful, taking her away, the music consuming her. A gust of wind wrapped around her, rippling the gingham tablecloth, the heavy plates holding it in place.

"I met her in an airport once," Gladys said, her nearly empty glass of wine swinging between her fingers. "Did

you know she was born in Virginia? I miss Virginia sometimes, but the magic of this place always calls my thoughts
right back. How could anything be lovelier than this?"

"We should look for stardust," Wyatt said, perking up.

"Looks like it's all out at sea tonight." Gladys pointed
to the glistening Atlantic, where the moonlight danced off
the ocean, making it sparkle.

The sun had gone down; the candles were dripping onto
the sand in their vases, the white lights twinkling around
them. The old wood from the pergola was hidden in the
darkness of night.

Wyatt, still sitting by the radio, was starting to look
bored.

"What's the matter?" Gladys said with a grin, tipping
her head unsteadily in his direction. She'd had a little too
much wine, but she'd said earlier that everyone needed to
let loose every now and again so they didn't explode. "Life
is in these moments," she'd said. "The moments we don't
think about or plan."

"How can anyone dance to this song?" Wyatt asked,
pursing his lips in confusion.

Gladys set her wine on the table and walked over to
him, pulling him up by his hands. "Like this." She put his
little hand on her side and held his other, swaying back and
forth. He looked uninterested until she whipped him out
and spun him around, making him laugh. He broke free
and asked if he could go inside and play with his Legos.
She let him go and sat down by Olivia and Callie.

"I'm delighted y'all live so close now," she said. "I've
been so lonesome here by myself. Alice was a lovely
neighbor, but nothing compared to this."

Gladys's comment reminded Callie of Alice McFarlin and
the journal. "I wonder if Alice McFarlin was lonely here?"

"She had a brother—Frederick. He used to live in the little cottage next to mine but moved decades ago. His house has sat vacant since—no renters. I assume he still owns it, but I'm not sure."

Olivia set her wine down on the table. "Do you know where he is now?"

Gladys shook her head and placed her hands on her knees, her legs crossed at the ankle. "I haven't seen him in ages. He used to be around all the time and then one day, he just up and left. Alice avoided the question when I tried to ask, so I left it alone. It was odd, since he and Alice always seemed close."

"I found a journal of Alice's," Callie said. "I wonder if her brother would like to have it."

"Oh?"

"We haven't read it—well, just one entry," Olivia said, pouring more wine into her glass.

Callie pulled out her phone. "I'm going to search for his name right now. Maybe we can find him to give it to him." The wine having relaxed her a little too much, she squinted to see the tiny keys on the screen as she typed and hit search. With a huff, she looked up. "There are two hundred forty-three Frederick McFarlins."

Olivia rubbed her face, the gesture making her skin red. "Wonder if there's any information in that journal that might tell us where he is."

Her buzz making her sentimental, Callie was willing to take the chance. "I'll go get it," she said, getting up slowly and going inside.

Wyatt was nearly asleep on the sofa, a gigantic tower of Legos beside him on the floor. She smiled and asked if he wanted to come back out with them but he yawned and shook his head, telling her Olivia had said he could sleep on the sofa until they came in for the night.

Callie grabbed the journal off her dresser and headed back downstairs, opening it to the next entry. When she joined the others, they looked on with interest as she sat down in the rocking chair, more oldies playing on the radio. The reception wasn't perfect, static breaking up the song, so she twisted the antenna just a little. Then she skimmed the diary entries for any indication of Frederick's whereabouts, stopping when she saw his name. "Okay, this might be something." She read: "*Frederick should've never spoken to that woman.*" She looked up and they all shared a dramatic moment before Gladys urged her to keep reading. "*She's caused him nothing but heartbreak since the moment they met. I tried to tell him, but he wouldn't listen. He has stars in his eyes. But that's Frederick, isn't it? He told me he loved her. I can't believe it. He's never told me that about any woman before, and yet the one woman he shouldn't love, he does. Isn't that the way of it?*"

"Do you know the woman he's talking about, Gram?" Olivia asked, her eyes wide.

Gladys shook her head, baffled.

Callie didn't feel right reading any more aloud to Olivia and Gladys, the heaviness of the situation sobering her, but they were pressing her to tell them what it said. "We'll keep her secrets," Olivia promised, immediately recognizing Callie's fears. "You know we will."

Callie saw the understanding in Olivia's eyes. Olivia knew how Callie was about sharing personal things; she knew it made her very uncomfortable. But Callie could tell by both Olivia's and Gladys's faces that they were sincere. Slowly, she started to read the rest of the entry.

"*Frederick has been down lately and I just can't stand to see it. I had him over for dinner tonight to cheer him up.*

We watched old movies like we did as kids, and we played cards. He beat me two to one. I didn't tell him I let him win that last game. He seemed so happy in the moment; I dared not bring him down. I love him so much. I just want to see him happy."

They all sat quietly around the table for a moment. The moonlight was so bright in the inky black of night it cast shadows on the sand.

"Alice was a lovely woman," Gladys said, breaking the silence.

Callie nodded, closing the journal and holding it against her, no closer to finding Frederick, but feeling like she knew Alice just a little better. She was happy that Alice's home had become hers.

Chapter Eight

A tapping noise interrupted the cries of seagulls and the sound of the crashing waves from Callie's open window. She rolled over on the portable air mattress she'd been using until the furniture was delivered, her mouth dry and her head slightly pulsing.

Tap, tap, tap.

She put the pillow over her head and tried to focus on the sound of the waves but from under her pillow, the tapping became more of a loud knocking, and she worried that whatever it was would wake Olivia and Wyatt, so she sat up. She spent a second getting oriented and peered at her watch that was on the floor—six oh-two.

Knock, knock, knock.

Callie sprung out of bed and padded quickly down the stairs to the front door, her energy depleting from just that little burst of activity. She opened it and only then did she remember she was in nothing but a long T-shirt, the weather too hot for anything else. She hid behind the door and peeked around it.

"You said you started early. I figured we'd want a little breakfast first."

She blinked over and over to make sure she was seeing correctly. Luke was in the doorway, holding a cardboard tray with three coffees in one hand and a large paper sack in the other. He held it up. "Breakfast," he said with a smirk. "May I come in?"

"I'm not presentable," Callie said, as heat crept into her face and slid down her neck. She wanted to look nice, to feel good about herself, but she also wanted to see that smile of his again.

"You're plenty presentable," he said, walking in past her. "You don't need a bit of makeup and you're wearing more clothing than most of the people I hang out with. We're at the beach. No biggie. Where's the kitchen?" He carried on into the room and down the hallway.

Callie shut the door and followed behind him, unsuccessfully tugging on her T-shirt to try to make it longer. "Do you always just burst into other people's houses?" she asked quietly as they entered the kitchen.

She had no idea about the state of her hair but she couldn't comb it with her fingers or her T-shirt would ride up. When he turned to look at her, she squared her shoulders proudly as if she didn't care a thing about how she looked. Why should she anyway? But then she wondered if anyone had followed him. The paparazzi might be taking photos of them right now through the window. She'd be the scandalous Other Woman in a feature about that actress girlfriend of his or something. She yanked her shirt down again.

"I didn't burst in," he said. "I knocked. You opened the door." He handed her a paper cup of coffee. "It's a caramel macchiato." He started rooting around in the bag that he'd set in the only clear area on the counter, paint supplies and extra floor tiles taking nearly all of the space.

"How do you know I like caramel macchiatos?" She did, but she wasn't going to let him have the satisfaction of knowing that right away. He was too smug.

He didn't look up. "All girls like caramel macchiatos."

She gasped in disbelief at his generalization. Just because all the girls *he* knew liked them—

But before she could say anything, he redeemed himself a little. "But if you didn't like it, I was going to offer my vanilla latte." He handed her a breakfast sandwich wrapped in paper. "This is a buttermilk biscuit with eggs, cheese, and bacon. Is it safe to say that you like this?"

"Yes." She took it from him and allowed herself a little smile.

"And just so you know, the barista told me that all women like caramel macchiatos. I've never been to the coffee shop before. I have someone who cooks for me usually. I went there because I thought you'd like it."

She stood still for just a tick, letting his gesture sink in. "What made you think I'd like it?" she asked, trying to will the flutter from her chest. He'd surprised her.

"Because I asked a few people on the street to tell me where to get the best breakfast in town, and they said it was the best. And when I got there, I saw their lunch menu had crab cake sandwiches, so I thought it was a good sign." He grinned at her, his smugness now taking on a new light. He wasn't being arrogant, he was proud of himself for following a hunch and getting it right. She had to drink her coffee to keep the silly smile off her face. He was thoughtful.

"Do I smell coffee?" Olivia said from down the hallway.

She entered the kitchen in her thin nightgown. "Oh!" She crossed her arms, her panic-stricken gaze flying over to Callie's bare legs and then back to Luke before questions filled her eyes.

Luke handed her the other caramel macchiato.

Clutching her coffee to her chest, still trying to cover herself, Olivia smiled nervously. "Thank you for the coffee."

"It's a caramel macchiato," he said with a nod.

"Oh, that's my favorite!"

Luke and Callie shared a glance and she shook her head with a grin.

* * *

"So he just…came over?" Olivia whispered to Callie as they finished getting dressed.

Callie nodded. "He seems to do what he wants, doesn't he?"

"I'm sure he doesn't mean any harm. Maybe he really wants to help out."

Callie squinted her eyes at Olivia in doubt. She led the way downstairs, her long hair pulled up into a high ponytail, no makeup on purpose. She wasn't going to do anything special just for Luke Sullivan. In fact, she wanted him to see how average folks got things done when they didn't have a staff to do it for them.

Callie grabbed Olivia's arm, stopping her as they entered the large living room. They hung back, Callie watching to see how Luke handled himself. Wyatt—still in his Spider-Man pajamas, his red curls in a tangle on top of his head—was going through his Matchbox car collection. Luke, holding one of the cars in his hand, was smiling and had squatted down to Wyatt's level.

"I made a ramp outside yesterday," Wyatt said. "It's still there. Wanna see it? We could try it out."

"Absolutely."

"Wyatt, honey, Luke brought breakfast," Olivia said as she and Callie came into the room. "Maybe you can show him after."

Callie took Luke outside through the back door while Olivia got Wyatt the breakfast he'd brought. She stood, facing the view, her hands on her hips, wondering why he'd come today but not wanting to ask. It was early still, and the sun had just risen over the horizon—a glorious bright orange orb floating above the glistening sea as the waves crept ashore, the powdery sand soaking up their foam. The wind tickled her face with wisps of hair that had fallen loose from her ponytail. She pushed them behind her ear. Callie was glad that most of the work on the front of the house was nearly done. She wouldn't mind working with this breeze at all.

Luke looked over at her and smiled before turning back toward the shore. "There's nothing better than this, is there?" he asked.

"It is a great view," she agreed. "We're going to have porches that stretch across the back of the house here." She pointed to the top of the cottage where the construction had begun. "Each level will have its own double doors that open onto it."

"That sounds nice." His shirt rippled in the wind, pressing against his body, revealing the shape of his chest, and erasing any doubt about whether or not he worked out. She noticed the round of his bicep as he lifted his arm to run his hand through his blowing hair.

Callie dragged her eyes away and focused on the house. "I'm going to paint the trim on the side of the house over there." She pointed to a small section with a bay window allowing a view of Wyatt and Olivia in the kitchen. "I figured I could do that first before it gets too hot, then I've got a little bit of sanding and painting to do where I took wallpaper off in the living room. Since you're here, I might as well put you to work."

"Sounds good." He had his game-face on, that air of challenge returning, but a flirty look in his eye. She ignored it. He was easy to like, and while he hadn't listened when she'd told him not to come, she admired his perseverance. Maybe he really did want to get to know her better.

"Why don't you go around front and get the ladders. They're leaning on the house by the porch. I'll pour the paint for the trim."

Luke nodded and headed around the house. She tipped three gallon-sized cans of white exterior paint into a large bucket she'd bought at the home improvement store and grabbed two brushes from the nearby plastic carrier bag that still had supplies from her last shopping trip. Luke brought the first ladder over and set it against the house, disappearing around the corner again as he retrieved the second.

When he returned, he leaned the other ladder next to the first, side by side against the old "shakes" as they were called—the shingles that covered the house. Since they were made of cedar, the newer ones offered a spicy, wooden smell up close. Used for ages along the coast here, they were popular because they were naturally resistant to rot, and they could withstand storms as well as wind and sand abrasion. They always started out a light tan but as they aged, they turned the most gorgeous dark brown color, and the white paint on the trim acted as a defining outline, leaving the blue of the sea and sky to paint the landscape while the house sat quietly behind.

Callie climbed up the ladder, awkwardly holding the heavy bucket, her arms working overtime to steady herself with the weight of it. Luke had looked as though he was going to extend a hand to help, but she kept climbing until she'd nearly reached the top. She hooked the bucket on the ladder hook. *No damsel in distress here, Luke Sullivan*, she thought. Luke grabbed his brush and climbed up beside her, the bucket swinging between them.

With confidence in her actions, Callie dipped her brush into the bucket. "You want to get the brush full enough with paint that it can last you a few strokes, but not too much or it will drip on the siding and that's difficult to get off."

She scraped her brush gently on the side of the bucket and held it up to demonstrate as a couple of seagulls flew overhead, pulling Luke's attention their way. She had to stifle a huff. Was he going to pay attention or not? He was supposedly there to help, and he needed to realize that life wasn't all bikinis and yachts. If he didn't focus, he could mess up the coat of paint.

"Leaning against a stilted house makes me feel like I'm swaying," Luke said, applying paint to his brush as she watched anxiously. He observed her strokes for a moment politely before he started painting. Then, surprisingly, he painted a seamless coat onto the trim, and once he got going he was meticulous, the paint a perfect thickness on the old wood.

"You're good at this," she said, trying to hide her shock. He'd surprised her again.

He grinned but didn't say anything.

As she painted quietly beside him, she wondered if she'd been so worried about him making assumptions about her that she'd failed to notice she was doing the same. Maybe it was because she was broken in some way, unable to give herself wholeheartedly to someone else, always worried about the intentions of others and closing up. She *had* opened up completely with Olivia and Gladys. But then again, she'd known them her whole life. She'd met her friend during the innocence of childhood, when every human being is naturally untainted by life, just before her father had left. In the back of Callie's mind, she'd always wondered if she'd inherited her mother's guardedness. It just felt a whole lot safer that way.

Her father's leaving had blindsided both Callie and her mother. Callie's mother wasn't great after he left, becoming distant at times. She wondered now if she'd just been overwhelmed. Her mother had tried to make an effort, but by that time Callie was already in high school, and too hurt to accept her mother's late response. Callie's father passed away before she ever had a chance to find him and ask him why he'd left. So she was left to wonder.

She moved her arm back and forth, the brush gliding along the wet surface. "Have you ever painted before?" she asked.

Luke was quiet as he worked. Finally, not taking his eyes off the house, he said, "A little." The hesitation in his response made her wonder if there was more behind those words than he was letting on. Already feeling pretty awful for having judged him, she didn't press him on it.

"Have you always lived in Waves?" she asked.

He smiled at her, sending her heart pattering. The sun, now at its spot high in the sky, was hidden behind a cloud, offering some much-needed relief from the heat.

"I've lived here and at my house in Florida. I also have an apartment in New York, but I tend to stay around the coast."

"Which is your favorite?" A breeze blew against her neck, cooling her briefly. She put more paint on her brush while steadying herself against the ladder.

"The Outer Banks is my favorite." He reached his arm out to paint a spot farther down the trim.

Callie continued to apply the next coat. "I loved coming here as a kid—I waited all year for it." She caught a runaway drip with her finger and wiped it on her shorts. "I came here every year with Olivia and her family. I spent so much time with them that I feel more like a Dixon than a Weaver," she said.

"So you've known them since you all were kids?" He picked at his brush, removing a piece of dirt before continuing.

"Yeah. Olivia's my best friend. She's the first person I call when I need to talk, and the one who knows everything about me—the good and the bad."

He nodded. "I know that kind of friend. I grew up with a guy named Todd Crowder. He's moved away now; he and his family live in Portland. I fly out to see him once a year. He and I did everything together growing up. We worked at an ice cream parlor one summer just for fun. We wanted a reason to get out of the house."

She smiled. "Were you any good at scooping ice cream?"

"I could swirl the soft serve ice cream about a foot high without it toppling off the cone. We used to make those for our friends until the manager found out we were giving extra large ice creams for the price of a single." He looked over at her and chuckled. "We gave that manager quite a time that summer. Todd and I would write 'Secret Concoction' on the menu—the day's flavors were written new every morning with chalk. Then we'd come up with a recipe based on the person ordering, changing it depending on what we thought the person might be like. The manager had a fit when he noticed that the topping selection had dwindled to barely anything by Wednesday when it was supposed to last until the weekend. He almost fired us, but he liked the idea so much that he let us continue."

"So what would you make for me?"

Luke eyed her, that smile returning before he pursed his lips, squinting his eyes in thought. "Nothing too fussy— maybe a nice vanilla—but sweet and warm, so perhaps a hot fudge drizzle with homemade mint chocolate bark sprinkled on top."

"That actually sounds perfect. My favorite ice cream flavor is mint chocolate chip."

His eyebrows shot up in surprise, causing three lines on his forehead. "Mine too," he said with another grin.

"Whenever I had a bad day, my grandmother would take me out for ice cream," she said. "I used to want to just get chocolate, but she'd say, 'The fun in life comes from risking doing something new. That's how you grow. Look at all the flavors! Pick one you'd like to try. If you hate it, I'll buy you a chocolate one. The point is to try it.' That's how I ended up liking mint chocolate chip."

"I like your grandmother."

"I miss her."

When they'd finished, they were both speckled with paint.

"The hose is here," she said. "If you want to wash up." She noticed Luke's shirt, after he'd carried the paint bucket over to rinse it, and pursed in her lips, trying not to show concern.

"What?" He dropped the brush with a plop into the nearly empty bucket and turned on the water.

Callie ran her hands under the stream and lathered with the old bar of soap she'd left on top of the hose reel since they'd started painting the exterior last week. It had just been easier to leave it outside.

"Look at your shirt," she said. It was covered in sticky, white paint.

He looked down.

"Couldn't you feel that? It's soaked all the way through!" Callie unwound the hose a little more to get the entirety of her arms wet, the cool water refreshing in the intense heat. "For such a neat painter, I'd expect you to be a little cleaner at the end," she teased. She felt the zing of nervous energy, taking a chance by joking with him. "I barely have any on me." Which was good since she hadn't done laundry and this was the last clean outfit.

With a devious gleam in his eye, Luke held out his arms, confusing her. "Thank you for letting me help today. It was fun." He started walking toward her.

"What are you doing?" she said, backing up and putting the spraying hose in between them.

"I just thought I'd give you a hug..." His face was alight with mischief.

"Don't you dare," she said, jabbing the hose in his direction. "I'll spray you!" She put her thumb over the end of the hose, forcing the water out in a hard stream in his direction. He ducked it, darting to the side, quick on his feet. She slung the stream toward him, but he was too fast and she missed, his arms still outstretched and an enormous smile on his face.

"Come here," he taunted her.

She backed up again, nearly stumbling over some loose patio tiles.

Luke put down his arms, that grin still present. "Okay,"

he said in surrender. "I won't get paint on you. But I had to try! May I have the hose to wash up?"

With a dubious look, she handed him the hose, still leaning back, her arm outstretched as far as it would go. "The water feels wonderful in this heat," she said.

"It does feel good," he said, putting his thumb on the end like she had and shooting a geyser into the air above them, the water falling down on them like a rainstorm.

Callie squealed and jumped out of the way, only getting the spray on half her body. "You've got me all wet!" she giggled, unable to be annoyed.

"You're not *all* wet," he said. "This would be *all* wet." He sprayed her again.

"Oh, you are in so much trouble now," she said, completely forgetting she'd just met him and pawing for the hose, but he held it above her, out of reach, drenching them both, the water puddling at their feet in milky, paint-filled pools. Callie jumped for it, missing and stumbling on the uneven pavers again. Luke caught her with his free hand and scooped her up, pulling her close. She felt the thin, wet fabric of their shirts between them, the way his muscle contracted in his bicep as he caught her, the lightness of his fingers at her waist.

She pulled back and her shirt was soggy with water and paint.

"Got ya," he said, his eyes lingering on her longer than usual. Then he broke out in the most gorgeous smile, sending her stomach into somersaults.

Chapter Nine

"I've been waiting for you two to finish ... You're soaking wet!" Olivia said with a grin from the upstairs window, loud music sailing toward them. Her red curls dangled above them, the ringlets naturally perfect since the humidity hadn't set in yet. Usually, by noon, Olivia had it pinned up in wild, unmanageable strands. She was looking at Callie in that way they had when they could tell what the other was thinking. "Could you come inside? I need your help with something."

Callie and Luke went up the steps to the porch. Luke reached around her and opened the old screen door, the hinges creaking out their age, the screen punched out at the bottom. When they got to the family room, he stopped. The room itself was nearly perfect structurally—it had a vaulted ceiling with paddle fans and a large window that stretched up part of the back wall, allowing a panoramic view of the sea. The only change she and Olivia wanted to make in this room was to extend the windows and add

French doors that opened onto the new porches, and they'd wanted to remove the old built-in shelves that were against the wall, separating it from the kitchen.

In the center of the hardwood floor, Wyatt was building an enormous contraption with gears and other pieces in all the primary colors. He dropped a marble into the top, testing the pathway he was making.

Luke bent over him to view it. "What are you building?" he asked.

"It's a double pathway chute. Watch this," Wyatt said, placing another marble on top. As it rolled, he shifted a lever, changing the direction of the marble.

"That's cool," Luke said with a smile that reached his eyes. "May I build something?"

Wyatt's eyes grew round with excitement. "Sure!"

Luke reached into the box and rummaged around, his gaze darting between the box and the track. He unsnapped a few pieces, redirected the original pathway and put in some gears. "Let's see if this works. How many marbles do you have?"

"Four." Wyatt handed them to him.

Luke dropped them onto the track, one after another, the shiny spheres rolling like wildfire until they hit the gears, shooting out in four different directions, all coming out at the end at the same time.

"Whoa!" Wyatt said, impressed. He tipped his head to take a closer look at the new part Luke had put together.

"I have to go help your mom, okay?" Luke said as he stood. He ruffled Wyatt's hair and followed Callie.

When he smiled at her, she had to take in a breath to steady herself. His ease with children made him even more attractive. She cleared her throat. "He hasn't met any other kids here yet," Callie said in a hushed voice as they left the room. "He'll meet people once school starts, but I hate that he's alone most of this summer."

Luke looked thoughtful. Then, as they climbed the stairs, he said, "My nephew is turning eight. He's having a birthday party at my house. Why don't you all come?"

"I was only voicing my concern. I wouldn't want to impose."

"On a bunch of eight-year-olds? I doubt you'd be imposing," he said when they'd reached the top of the steps.

As she led him into the room where Olivia was working, Luke's gaze was on her. It was the kind of look that revealed how his face would rest after laughing or when he'd just been told some good news. It was sincere and sweet.

"I need a little help with measuring," Olivia said through the pencil in her mouth, the music still blaring. She regarded Callie and Luke before her eyes settled on Callie with a grin. She was up on a stepladder, marking spaces on the ceiling. She had the pencil in her mouth to free her hands to measure the next length but she was just short of the distance to reach. She stopped and took the pencil from her lips. "I need someone tall. Luke, can you stand on that box over there? It should hold you."

Callie grabbed the wooden crate that had held some of Olivia's things when they'd first moved in and scooted it across the bare floor toward Luke. This was the room Callie was sleeping in until they'd chosen bedrooms. Her air mattress was pushed against the wall, the blankets still askew from when Luke had woken her up this morning.

There was almost nothing in the room at all—no blinds, no curtains, no furniture except the small dresser she'd found at an antiques shop on the mainland. They'd delivered it the day after she'd bought it. It was a butter cream color, the legs curled outward but the rest of the design quite simple. She imagined the whole room done in yellow and cream with delicate white starfish in lightwood baskets and driftwood artwork on the walls.

Olivia moved the stepladder to a new spot. Luke took the end of the tape measure and stretched it across the ceiling.

"I want to see how many recessed lights we can fit in this room. It's big and not as bright as I'd like with the main light fixture in the center."

They'd talked about recessed lighting for all the guest rooms. They were going to put them on dimmer switches so that guests arriving late could have soft ambience to set the mood. The Beachcomber was going to be about relaxation and getting away from the hustle and bustle of regular life. While it wasn't going to be luxurious and fancy, it was going to be calm and understated—the perfect place to be after a long day at the beach.

"Once I have measurements, maybe we can look at the plans over dinner," Olivia said, her shoulders rising in excitement. "Luke, would you like to join us?" Before he'd even answered, and despite Callie's look of warning, she added, "We'll probably just get a pizza, but you're welcome to stay."

"I'd love to," he said with a wink at Callie.

Callie tried not to think about the distraction he was causing. His little game of cat and mouse was nothing more than that—a game. She was certain. Why else would he be wasting time at her little beach house? That she was getting all fluttery around him was probably just what he wanted.

But then her eyes fell on the journal sitting on her dresser. How alone Alice had been in this house, and how much laughter had been here today. Whatever his motives, it had been good.

"Well, we'd better get the rest of that sanding and painting done then," she said, trying to keep her thoughts from showing.

* * *

"Why in the world did you ask him to dinner?" Callie said, peering out of the window at Luke as he tossed a ball with Wyatt. They'd finished their work for the day and Luke had offered to take Wyatt outside to play, help him catch a few fish, while Callie and Olivia got cleaned up. He'd worn his swimming trunks to the house this morning and he'd taken off his paint-drenched T-shirt. Callie had tried not to focus on his tan skin. Luke threw the ball to Wyatt, a long pass that arced into the air, sailing straight to Wyatt's arms. When Wyatt caught it, Luke raised his hands in celebration.

"He's nice," Olivia said, leaning over Callie's shoulder. "And you need someone nice in your life."

The comment surprised Callie. What was she talking about? "I can make my own choices, thank you very much," she said, her words coming out playful despite the message she was conveying. She knew Olivia was just trying to help, but Callie didn't need it. She'd done just fine on her own.

"He showed up to help, brought you breakfast, painted all day, finished the sanding in the living room... I think he likes you."

Callie spun around. "I think he's just bored. And why would it matter anyway? I'm too busy to bother with all that nonsense. We have a business to run."

Olivia smiled knowingly at Callie, which only frustrated her because she *didn't* know. "Don't be afraid to take another chance," she said. "Even if it's unexpected. And don't be scared to open up. I know that's hard for you to do, but you really should let people in, Callie. I think he'd like it if you did."

Callie chewed on her lip, unsure how to respond.

"You're loads of fun, Callie. You should let people see that." Olivia looked over her shoulder out the window and laughed so loudly she clapped her hand over her mouth to stifle it.

Wyatt was swimming now and Luke was standing on the beach keeping an eye on him. Written in giant letters in the sand were the words *Callie! Come outside!*

Callie pulled back to focus on Olivia's face. "He's a distraction," she said unconvincingly.

Olivia's face was kind. "From what?" Taking Callie by the arm playfully, she said, "Come on, let's go outside." She grabbed three bottles of beer from the cooler and the opener and headed toward the door.

With a deep breath, Callie went out behind her. No matter what Olivia thought was right for her, she'd never put her trust in someone she'd just met who had no real reason to be in her life at all. According to those articles she'd read, Luke had a short attention span, and she wasn't going to get hurt because she wasn't going to let herself.

When they got to the beach, Luke took the bottles from Olivia and opened them for her, sticking the caps in his pocket and handing a bottle to each of them.

"Hi," he said to Callie with a warm smile. "Did you see my message?" He nodded toward the sand.

"Subtle," she said, although he looked so adorable, his smile peeking out from behind his bottle as he took a sip

of his beer, that she had to work to hide her own grin. He
certainly was charming. She had to take a sip of beer herself to be able to take her eyes off him.

"Nice shirt," he said with a smirk.

"I need to do laundry." She looked down at her *I survived the Beach Bum Burger Bash* T-shirt. It was too long,
nearly covering her shorts.

Wyatt came up to them dripping wet. "Mom, did you
see my handstand? I did one before the wave got me."

"I did!" Olivia said with excitement. She grabbed a
towel from the beach bag Luke must have brought down
with them and wrapped it around Wyatt, but he took it off.
"Come down to the water and watch me."

"Okay," Olivia said with a grin toward Callie and Luke.
She took the towel to the shore and laid it on the sand, sitting down, her back to them.

"Thank you for letting me stay for dinner," Luke said,
the bottle of beer swaying between his fingers by his side.
"I've had a lot of fun today."

"I'm surprised you didn't have work to do with that big
company of yours," Callie said, wondering how he'd had
the time to spend all day with them, given what she'd read
about the size of the Sullivan empire and his father's work
ethic. She remembered what she'd read: . . . *speculation regarding the motivations of his son, Luke. Does he have the
drive to take on a company of this magnitude?*

"I'm on vacation at the moment. Well, I was supposed
to be, but I got a call that the lawyer wanted to meet with
me about a few properties so I canceled my trip and I've
just been popping in to put out the biggest fires." But before she could respond, he added, "But my dad works
every single day of the week, no matter what." His face
had dropped to a frown. "He thinks that's how you make a

million, working all hours. I suppose I should believe him because he's definitely proven that fact. I work differently from how he does, but I work hard too."

"I wasn't implying you didn't," she said, feeling guilty. She'd thought he'd just say something cute and be his usual flirty self, but then she remembered his reaction on the boat the other day.

He took a swig of his beer and then looked over at hers, that smile returning, to her relief. "Your beer's going to get hot," he said.

She tipped it up and took a long drink.

Then he said more calmly, "Work's good, though. I don't want to make it sound like it isn't. I love what I do."

"What's an average day like for you?" Callie asked. Wyatt and Olivia came back up, Wyatt out of breath from all his swimming. He was busy drying himself off while Olivia joined in the conversation, her beer half finished.

"I usually go for an early run or something and then I start work at around eight in the morning. I take a long lunch, and then come back to it at around three o'clock, working into the night when I need to. I finish up the day's business, and after that, if there's time, I do whatever— surfing, parties…"

"I like parties!" Wyatt said with a smile as he walked over.

"Yeah, they're fun," Luke said, visibly glad to talk to him. He was great with Wyatt. "If it's okay with your mom, I'd like to have you come to my nephew's birthday party tomorrow evening. Would you like to do that?"

Wyatt turned toward Olivia, with a wide-eyed smile. "Can I, Mom?"

Probably because she'd only just heard of the party, Olivia, blinking and visibly processing all at once, said,

"Tomorrow? I . . . Uh . . . Sure. If it's okay with Luke and his family."

"Totally fine, I'm certain, but I'll check with my sister."

Callie always knew what Olivia was thinking and, right now, she could tell by the look in her eyes that she had a dozen thoughts going through her mind. Callie could guess them: *What will I wear? What will Wyatt wear? What kind of present will we get a rich kid who has everything?*

* * *

There was a knock at the door. Callie, expecting the pizza any minute, opened it to find Gladys instead, hugging an enormous turquoise pot with yellow and purple painted flowers·that matched the purple of the tall, stalky plant in the pot.

"I brought you something," she said as Callie reached out to help her set it down on the porch, the weight of it causing a thud. "And I stopped by to see Wyatt," she added. "He texted me earlier and said that I had to come over and watch him swim against the waves. He says he's a pro now."

"Did you walk all the way across the street with this pot?" Callie asked.

"A girl's gotta get her cardio in somehow!" Gladys said with a wink, coming inside the doorway. "Hi, Wyatt! . . . Oh!" She coughed and straightened her shirt as Luke walked up beside Callie.

"Luke Sullivan," he said, holding out his hand.

Gladys shook it, surveying him inquisitively.

"I didn't mean to interrupt," he said. "I was just coming to help Callie get the pizza. I thought you were the delivery guy."

Gladys's head slowly turned to Callie and her eyebrow rose ever so subtly before she spoke to Luke. "I'm terribly sorry," she said, "But Callie didn't tell me she'd made any friends around here. You surprised me. Glad to see some new blood in the house." She'd gotten over her shock, but her loaded glances told Callie she'd have some explaining to do. By her reaction, it was pretty clear that Gladys knew who Luke was.

Luke stepped onto the porch and bent down to look at the pot. "This is nice," he said, running his fingers over the colors on the front of it. "Did you paint it?"

Gladys nodded.

"I like the shadows you've added along the petals."

"Well, it was just something I did for fun," Gladys said, brushing it off, clearly as affected by Luke's interest as Callie was. "This plant I have here attracts butterflies and if you get really close to it, it smells like licorice."

Wyatt leaned in to test the scent.

"What's all the fuss up here?" Olivia said, joining them. "Oh! That pot is gorgeous."

"Thank you, dear. Glad you like it." Gladys reached over and pressed the soil down around the flowering plant to keep it firm after the journey across the street and then clapped the excess off her hands over the pot. "I planted four for myself, and thought I'd do one up for you two. It's delicate. If the rain decides to grace us with its presence, you might want to bring it in if it gets too windy."

They'd been pretty lucky since they'd first arrived at The Beachcomber, but Gladys had warned them, and Callie knew it was only a matter of time before they'd have to deal with the late afternoon thunderstorms that rolled in after the high heat of the day.

"Well, I won't stay if you have company. I just wanted

to stop by and give you that. Wyatt, I can see you swim another time."

"You can stay if you'd like," Olivia said. "We've got pizza coming and there's plenty."

"Oh no," she said. "Y'all enjoy your supper. I've got a mess to clean up on my back deck and it might rain." She turned to Wyatt. "I can see that trick tomorrow, dear." She opened the door herself and walked out onto the porch.

"Please, may I show her, Mom?" Wyatt asked.

"No one's out there, Wyatt. It's not safe—the surf is really rough right now. Why don't we show her tomorrow?"

"I can go out with him," Luke said.

"Thank you, Luke, but I wouldn't want to trouble you. It's dinnertime, Wyatt. Let's wait."

Wyatt's face dropped but he nodded in understanding.

"Really," Luke said. "It's fine. I'll take him out to show his grandmother. We'll be five minutes, right Wyatt?" He winked at him.

"Okay," she relented. "Five minutes. But then you need to come in. Don't make Luke stay out there all night."

"You and Luke go get ready, Wyatt," Gladys told him with a smile. "I'll be out in just a second."

"Yes, ma'am!" Wyatt walked beside Luke to the back door, talking the whole way.

"I really wish he wouldn't go out so far," Olivia said. "He has no fear sometimes. It's so worrying."

"He knows better than to swim alone," Gladys said. She always tried to set Olivia's mind at ease. "He told me he couldn't go into the water without an adult. For an eight-year-old, that's pretty responsible."

"That's good. I just don't want him to misread the distance from shore and get too far out. He's never lived near the ocean before."

"You're a good mom." Gladys always supported Olivia, helping her in any way she could after Wyatt's dad left. Olivia had worried aloud on occasion that Wyatt would grow up without any male role models. It bothered her. How much easier it would be to have a man in his life that could take him out to the beach, swim out with him, lift him up if a wave toppled him over, toss him in the air and play with him.

Over the years, Olivia had been honest about it, but she never wanted any pity, so she didn't let on that she needed anything. But Gladys was always right there. She'd told Olivia not to hide the past from Wyatt, and to answer any questions he might have because, as Gladys always said, "The truth will set you free."

"It's nice having her so close," Olivia admitted, once Gladys had gone outside. "It'll be good for Wyatt to have family nearby with the two of us working all the time. Luke being around is helping too. He's good with kids."

Callie nodded. "Things will settle down. We've had a lot to do with the house and once we get into the swing of things, it should get easier. But you're right. Having Gladys here does help. And whenever she came to visit us, I missed her every time she left." Callie smiled at the memory.

* * *

Callie got Luke another beer, the empty pizza box still on the table outside between their plates. She gathered them up to take them into the house, but Luke asked her to leave them. She set it all down in a pile at the end of the table. Olivia had taken Wyatt in for a bath and bedtime, and the rain still hadn't materialized, so they'd stayed outside, lit a candle, and continued talking.

"It's humid," Callie said, tilting her head back to feel the wind on her face. "It reminds me of one night when I was young. I'd gotten a telescope for my birthday and I'd waited until well past my bedtime for it to get dark so I could see the stars and the moon. Mom had called me inside a couple of times, but I only barely heard her, completely transfixed on that telescope."

Luke was leaning on his elbow, his hand in his chin, those eyes alight with interest.

"I'd focused in on a beautiful crater on the moon when I heard her swishing through the grass." She could still remember: The only light was the small porch light that was swarming with insects, the air breezy as it was now. "When I heard her coming, I braced myself because it finally registered that she'd been calling me and I thought she was going to be really angry. But she wasn't. She was smiling. She came up behind me and pulled my hair off my neck before speaking into my ear. 'What do you see?' she asked."

Luke was smiling as if a thought had just occurred to him, and it took her out of the story. "What?" she asked.

"I'm imagining what your mother saw," he said. "She probably looked out of the window and watched you tinkering with the telescope, all serious and engrossed. I saw that same face when you were painting. That's why she didn't get mad. I'll bet she could tell you weren't ignoring her."

With a punch of nostalgia, Callie said, "You're probably right. I'd never really thought about it until now. I just remember that smile and I feel so lucky to have that memory. She didn't smile a whole lot after my dad left, and I tried not to forget what it looked like. I showed her the moon and we stayed outside for ages that night looking at the stars, taking our time. I can't remember a lot of what I saw through that lens—it was so long ago—but I can still remember her smile."

"That's a great story," he said.

A lull of silence fell between them as the sea roared. "The ocean looks rough tonight," Callie finally said, turning toward it. She held her beer but didn't drink it, worried that she'd had just enough to make her a bit too honest, and that after spending this evening with him, she might let him know how great she thought he was.

"It's perfect for surfing," he said, the fire from the candle dancing in his eyes. The air was thick with heat, the sky black, without a hint of light; the clouds were rolling in. He took a drink of his beer and set it on the table, those blue eyes now on her. "Have you ever been surfing?"

Callie shook her head, her attention again on the ocean, unable to look into his eyes for fear she'd feel that familiar buzz of excitement. She knew better than to allow herself to feel that way because she'd only get hurt. But then she turned toward him, thinking how, if this were all a game for him, just a chase, he certainly was a good actor. She didn't want to think about how much experience he'd had courting ladies.

"I'd love to take you surfing. What are you doing tomorrow?"

"Well, if we're going to go to your nephew's birthday party, I'll be shopping for a present and something to wear," she said, steering the topic of conversation elsewhere.

There was a *crack* and then *boom*, startling them both. Only then did she notice dark thunderheads above them, hidden by the blackness of night. The sea roared angrily with disapproval.

After that, it got eerily quiet, the sound of the waves

the only noise. And then there were a few taps on the table around them. Callie stood up, gathering the trash and empty plates, and Luke blew out the candle, as the raindrops started falling faster, getting them wet.

"Quick! Grab those beach towels!" she said, laughing despite the rush, as she pointed to the towels that Olivia had hung over a few chairs to dry after Wyatt had been out swimming. She threw the pizza box in the outside bin, abandoning the plates so she could make a run for it. The taps were followed by a beating rain that made Callie feel like she was inside one of the rain sticks she'd played with as a kid.

With a quick swipe, Luke grabbed the towels, throwing them over his arm.

They ran up to the back door.

"It's locked!" she said in disbelief. "I'll bet Olivia did it out of habit. She always does that," she said, knocking. No one came. "She's probably upstairs with Wyatt. We'll have to go around to the front."

They left the porch, plunging themselves into the pouring rain. It was sheeting down, causing her vision to blur. Callie wasn't familiar enough yet with the landscape to run easily in the dark, and she stumbled on something. But before she could fall, she felt strong arms around her, lifting her up and nearly taking her breath away. Just as she could process it, the sensation was gone and they were running again, but Luke had her hand. As she moved blindly, the sound of the rain and thunder in her ears, her senses were on high alert. Luke's grasp on her hand was strong yet gentle as he guided her through the darkness, making her feel safe despite the surroundings. His breath was short and fast. They got to the front, taking the stairs as quickly as they could, another clap of thunder booming.

As the coastal wind blew harder, the house started to sway. It was designed that way to help it withstand the storms that the Atlantic threw at it. But that didn't make the feeling any less concerning. Trying not to think about it, she opened the front door and they nearly fell inside.

They stood there, dripping wet. Luke's gaze started to travel down her body, but he seemed to recover himself and drew his focus back to her face and smiled. "I forgot the candle," he said, dumping the towels on the floor, and they laughed quietly, both of them still a little winded.

"It's fine," she said. She grabbed a beach towel from the basket where they kept them. "Here," she said, holding it out to him. "Use it to keep your seat dry on the way home. I'll get it back at the birthday party."

When she said that, he looked a little disappointed and she wondered if he might have been hoping to stay longer. Luke moved closer to her, looking down into her eyes. "I had fun tonight," he said, his words heavy with unsaid thoughts. Did he feel like she did—that she'd never felt more alive than she did running through the darkness with him? She leaned in just a little, their bodies so close, wondering if he might try to kiss her again. But did she want that? What if she'd just been swept up in the moment? Callie took a step back.

"Will you be okay driving in this?" she asked.

Looking a little unsure, Luke took in a breath. "Yeah, it's just a storm," he said, toweling his hair. "It'll probably pass before I'm even home."

"Okay," she said with a thoughtful smile. "I'll see you tomorrow night."

Chapter Ten

"Look at this," Olivia said from the other room as the deliverymen finished the appliance installation. She came into the kitchen where Callie was, holding an old lockbox about the size of a shoebox. It was brown with a keyhole on the front, the hinges thick with dust.

Wyatt was beside her with a little hammer, both he and his mother wearing matching safety glasses. "I know this wasn't in the plan for today. I've been working to get rid of those built-in shelves like we'd talked about while the workers are here so they can fill in any missing drywall. I'm doing one and Wyatt's doing the other. Take a look at what we found." She held up the box.

"It was in the bottom of the built-in," Wyatt said.

"Apparently, the bottom of each one—the part that juts out—is hollow and accessible by lifting the last shelf out," Olivia explained with excitement.

"Is it treasure?" Wyatt asked.

"I don't know," Callie said, sitting down at the table

with her coffee. "What's written on that brass tag there?" She pointed just above the keyhole.

Olivia set it down and squinted at the tag, running her finger over it to shine it up. "It looks like 'FM.'"

"Could M be for McFarlin?" Callie took a sip of the coffee. She'd made it while she waited to sign off on the delivery, the warm, creamy liquid melting away her aches from working so hard yesterday. "F for Frederick." Callie jiggled the lock. "I wonder where the key is."

"*I* wonder why it was left here, if it is in fact his. Wouldn't it be of importance to him or Alice? Unless it's empty..." Olivia lifted it to her ear and gave it a shake. "It sounds like something's in it."

Wyatt twisted the latch, but it wouldn't budge.

"They left the lockbox and that journal that you found. Wonder what else they left." The deliverymen quietly interrupted, handing Olivia a clipboard for signature.

"I'm sure Alice had hidden them and, after she died, no one knew they were here."

"The fact that they were hidden makes me wonder what's in them," Olivia said quietly, scrawling her name across the paper on the clipboard, raising her eyebrows in curiosity. "Maybe there are some family secrets," she teased. She put the box on the floor of the pantry and shut the door.

Callie walked over to the oven as Olivia handed the paperwork back to the crew, thanking them. "Oh, oh! We have fire!" she said with excitement. She turned the knobs of the brand new gas stove that had just been delivered, along with the giant refrigerator. They must have been the first delivery of the day because they'd been there right at eight-thirty in the morning.

After the deliverymen left, Callie sat back down. She put her face in her hands. "I shouldn't have let Luke stay so long last night," she said, her heart telling her something else. She wished he were there right now, holding her hand like he had last night. She missed his smile already and couldn't wait to see him tonight.

"No, I think you just let yourself relax, let things come naturally," Olivia said, grinning.

"Now we have this party tonight..." Callie lifted her mug to her lips to keep from smiling.

"It'll be fine. Plus, Wyatt's absolutely thrilled about it." She opened the fridge and freezer, peering inside at the new space.

There was a knock at the front door and they both looked at each other.

Olivia shut the freezer and went to get it while Callie got up, leaving her coffee, not going with her to answer the door just in case it was Luke, but unable to sit with all her nervous energy. Instead, she wiped down the stove and the new granite countertops they'd picked out. They'd chosen them because the light caramel and cream specks on them reminded them of the wet grains of sand on the shore just after the tide went out. She needed something to do to keep her mind off last night.

Last week, they'd painted the kitchen a beachy pink color, the stainless steel appliances coordinating with the silver metallic seashells they'd put up on the wall. They'd also added whitewashed cabinets, demolishing the dark wood ones that had been there since probably the 1970s. With the new tan tiles under her feet, she stood back, admiring the look of it all.

"Callie," Olivia said, entering the kitchen with a man. He had dark hair, a thin build, and a smile that would put any stranger at ease. "This is Aiden Parker. He's finalized the plans for the back porches."

Callie walked over and shook his hand. "It's nice to finally meet you," she said. Olivia had driven up to the cottage the day Aiden had come to survey the property, but Callie was still settling things back in Richmond, and she'd told Olivia to just go with her instincts on the plans. Callie trusted her more than anyone else, and she knew that Olivia would make a perfect choice regarding the back porches. After seeing Aiden's initial plans when she'd first arrived at The Beachcomber, she realized she'd been right.

Callie dried her hands on a towel and stepped over to them to give them her full attention. "Olivia's told me a lot about you."

Aiden cast an amused glance over to Olivia. "That's scary," he said with a grin. "Considering most of our stories have something to do with college parties..."

Olivia and Aiden had gone to college together, and he'd lived in the same apartment building on the floor just under hers. He'd been the first person Olivia had met when she'd gotten to college, which happened to be her birthday. He'd taken her out that night, and every year after until they graduated. With life having pulled them in different directions after graduation, Olivia had said she was glad to have a chance to see him again.

Callie jokingly scolded Olivia with a look to let her know that she'd held out on her. "Well, clearly she wasn't telling me the right stories, then."

Aiden laughed and looked over at Olivia again. When he did, it was clear by the friendliness in his face that their shared experiences were all happy ones. "I'm glad she asked me to do this. I haven't been back to the Outer Banks in ages. I've forgotten how great it is."

"Did you used to vacation here?" Callie asked.

"I lived here for quite a few years." He peeked out the

back window, changing course. "I think adding the back porches will really change this place."

"Thank you for giving us such a deal," Olivia said.

Aiden had done all the plans for free. They were only paying for the crew, which, given their budget, was still a hefty price tag, but the result would be amazing.

"You're welcome," he said. "Anything for a friend." He smiled warmly at her. "Mind if I run out to the car? I'm going to grab my laptop and take a few measurements and photos. When I'm done, I'll be able to show you a mock-up of what it will look like."

"Oh, that'll be wonderful," Callie said with excitement, but before she could say anything more, there was a click and a hum—the most glorious sounding hum ever. She ran over to the floor vent and stood on it, feeling a rush of cool air on her bare feet. "Air's on!" she said to Olivia, unable to control her happiness. The HVAC people had been upgrading the outdoor unit this morning as well. Things were moving right along, and she couldn't be more thrilled.

* * *

After she'd seen the mock-up, Callie left Olivia to tend to Aiden while she got busy working in the formal living room. With all the rough spots sanded, and the painting started, she was just finishing up. She poured light blue paint into the tray and slid her roller through it, rolling it back and forth to get the excess off. Then she pushed it along the wall, the beautiful color transforming the space right in front of her eyes.

Callie had gotten the other half of the room done before Gladys let herself in. She had suggested Gladys come over if she got bored, so they could chat while she worked.

"Oh! It looks nice!" she said, tottering into the room. "It's going to be just lovely. I can hardly take all this excitement with you all across the street, the changes to the house, the thrill of the bed and breakfast and all the delightful visitors it will draw...It's all just wonderful!" She dropped herself down into the chair.

"This house has been very quiet for a long time after Alice closed the bed and breakfast. But I understood. She was aging, you know. Her hips didn't work like they used to, and she just couldn't do all that running around anymore."

"We found something else of hers," Callie said as she climbed down the small ladder she'd been using to paint up near the trim at the ceiling. "We think. It's an old lockbox."

Gladys frowned. "Really? Anything in it?"

Callie shook her head and went to get the box from the kitchen pantry, where they'd stowed it away.

"Look," she said, coming back in with it. She sat down in a chair and scooted closer to Gladys, turning the box around. "It says 'FM.' That could be her brother."

Gladys rubbed her hands together, thinking. "It would make sense. Frederick McFarlin."

"We should get it back to him," Callie said, moving closer and wiping the initials to try to clear the old brass again, but she was unsuccessful. The metal had aged with time, the shiny finish she kept striving to get, gone. "But there were so many Frederick McFarlins when we looked the other night, remember?"

Gladys tucked her hair back behind her ear dramatically. "I might know someone who could get us in touch with him."

"Oh?" Callie had picked up the roller again to paint but set it back down.

"I have coffee with some ladies in town and one of them, Adelaide Foster, might know him. She used to do business with him, I believe, but it's been quite a while. He was a handyman. I'll see if she still has his number."

"That would be great." Callie felt so good knowing that the lockbox might be returned. While there was probably nothing of worth inside it—or surely Frederick would've kept it—it still had an air of mystery around it, since it had obviously been hidden away in that built-in. "Maybe we could give him the journal too, since it was his sister's."

"Have you peeked inside it any more?"

"No."

Gladys nodded with understanding, probably knowing how private Callie was. She'd feel guilty prying. "I didn't mean to disturb you," she said, fluttering her hands in the air. "Paint, paint!" She set the lockbox down beside her chair while Callie resumed her work. "So tell me while you work. You're spending some time with that young man, Luke Sullivan?"

"He's just a friend," Callie said, the prickle of emotion causing a flutter and making her cheeks burn as she pushed the roller up the wall.

When Gladys didn't say anything, she turned around.

"You didn't sound very convincing," Gladys said with a smirk.

"Well, my tone was by accident then. I barely know him."

Gladys nodded. "He certainly seemed interested in you—I could tell by the way he looked at you."

"Do you think?" She took in a breath and resumed painting, trying to keep the ridiculous smile off her face. With her focus still on the wall, she asked, as coolly and collectedly as she could, "What do you know about him?"

"I don't know him," she said. "But I saw him do something really nice once."

"Oh?" She looked over, unable to hide her interest.

"I was in a restaurant—it's closed now—but he was eating with a group of friends. An older lady at a nearby table left and forgot her purse beside her plate after she'd paid. He noticed and grabbed it, running after her. I watched through the large window as he ran full speed down the street after her car, all the way to the stoplight where he finally flagged her down and handed it to her through her window."

"How thoughtful," she said, realizing that she'd completely turned around toward Gladys, the paint roller at her side.

Gladys smiled. "You like him."

Callie rolled her eyes and turned around to resume painting.

Gladys must have sensed Callie's unwillingness to discuss it because she moved on to another topic. "Olivia mentioned a birthday party."

"Yes, it's tonight."

"At Mr. Sullivan's?"

Well, she *thought* Gladys had changed topics.

"Yes." Callie swiveled around and set the roller down again, her focus completely disrupted. She struggled to keep from smiling. "I just don't need any interruptions to my life at the moment, Gladys," she said.

"Mmm." Gladys nodded. She never had to actually say anything to let Callie know her opinion.

Callie shook her head and started painting again. She didn't *need* distractions, but did that mean she didn't want them?

* * *

Callie unpinned her hair, which now resembled a bent hanger, since it had dried in the clip she'd put it in after her shower this afternoon. She set the clip down on top of Alice's journal and shook her hair out with her fingers, but it didn't help. Gladys was still there, puttering around the kitchen downstairs with Olivia and Wyatt. Only moments before, Gladys had run home and returned with a jug of lemonade and a key lime pie.

Just as Callie was starting to worry about what to wear to the party, her phone lit up and she recognized that new number. It was Luke.

"People will be in and out all day. What time should I tell Julie you're coming?" he asked after a quick hello.

She could only assume he meant his sister, Juliette Sullivan, who she'd read had moved to New York to start her own casual wear fashion line. A few of the boutiques in town had her pieces on display. According to local legend, the line was started entirely with her daddy's money, and she'd yet to make the millions she'd promised him she would. But Callie had also read that a few big designers had taken notice and Juliette's line had made it into a couple of department stores in New York, so she might still redeem herself.

Callie was about to go to the Sullivan mansion for a birthday party. She'd already worn the most expensive dress in the cottage on their date. What were she and Olivia supposed to wear today? They hadn't even had time to go shopping for a gift, let alone an outfit, and he wanted a time. She looked at the clock.

"Why are you so quiet?" he asked.

"Umm…" Callie panicked, flopping down onto the air

mattress, unsure of how to answer. She peered into the open closet. Most of their clothes were still in storage.

"What?" he asked, and she was surprised by the gentle sound in his voice, as if he really wanted to know, almost like he was worried about her.

She picked at the light blue paint that remained in the ridge of her fingernail and tried to figure out how to explain it to him. What was frustrating her was the fact that he'd probably never worried about something like this in his life. What if he thought she was making excuses and she didn't want to go? That wasn't true at all, because she'd love to give Wyatt a fun night out. And, if she was honest, she wanted to see Luke. Dropping her hand into her lap, she decided to just come out with it. "I don't have any clothes nice enough for a party at your house."

"That's what you're so quiet about? I don't care what you wear. Wear whatever you want," he said with a chuckle.

"Luke…" She took in a breath and lay back on her air mattress, running her fingers through her crooked curls. "Olivia and Wyatt don't have anything either. In fact, I don't even know the dress code. What do people wear to things like this? My few outfits are covered in paint, and the dress I wore for drinks with you is dirty."

"Just wear something casual."

Callie groaned. "There's casual and then there's bag lady attire. I'm not joking, Luke. I think I have to go shopping."

"I like the bag lady look. I think you can pull it off."

She rolled her eyes and sucked in her smile even though he couldn't see it. "No. I've got to go anyway to get a present for the birthday boy. So be straight with me, are we talking dresses or shorts and T-shirts?"

"I'll come with you. I promised Julie I'd pick up some balloons anyway."

"You don't have to."

"I don't? Okay, never mind then," he teased.

Callie sat silently on the end of the phone. She wanted him to come. She wanted to see him.

"I'll be there in an hour."

She couldn't stop herself from grinning.

* * *

Sherry's was the name of a boutique that had only recently opened, the retail market being quite limited in Waves. Most of the shopping was farther north in the villages of Nags Head and Duck. As advertised, Sherry's had Juliette's line in the window. It was situated in the center of the one small, renovated strip mall in town. Callie wasn't sure they could afford anything from the shop but she figured she could have a look and maybe get some ideas, then move on to the next. It was quiet today—no reporters. Luke opened the door and allowed them to enter first, Wyatt trailing behind Callie and Olivia. They'd promised him an ice cream cone if he could endure all the clothes shopping. He was giving it his best effort, they could tell.

While Olivia thumbed through a rack of tank tops, Callie turned to Luke. "So what would you pick out?" she asked. He was wearing a perfectly worn, pale blue T-shirt with a stylishly faded boating logo on the front and a pair of shorts, and he looked more like a surfer than a millionaire, his bronze skin and bleached streaks in his hair revealing long days on the beach. She wondered what it would be like to run her fingers down his arm. She pulled her eyes away. When had she last felt like this? Had she ever?

He stared at her, clearly out of his comfort zone but

trying to come up with something. Perhaps he'd been expecting to just weigh in on her choices rather than being
asked to pick something at random.

"This isn't hard," she said. "Look around. Think about
any girl you know, and imagine what she might be wearing
at your party." She pulled a top from one of the racks and
held it up. "Would she wear this to the party?"

He looked into her eyes and then his gaze moved
around her face. "No," he said with a smile.

She hung it back with the others. "How about this?"

He shook his head.

"Okay, then. Find me something she'd wear."

Luke glanced over at Wyatt for help but Wyatt, who'd
located a chair, was trying to solve two sides on his Rubik's
cube. He made eye contact and shrugged.

"You're no help," Luke told him with a smirk. Then he
began to walk around the shop, tugging on the sleeves of
shirts to view them and then letting them drop, the garments swinging back into position on the rack.

Wyatt sniggered.

Olivia, who'd already told her she'd planned to splurge
today if she found something wonderful, had two silky
tops and a pair of linen trousers draped over her arm while
Callie followed Luke with her eyes. He was concentrating,
the skin adorably wrinkled between his eyes as he looked
through a row of mint green tops. Then he caught sight of
something and moved over to another rack.

"This," he said, pulling out a flowing sundress and
holding it up. The dress was soft and feminine with pale
flowers in various shades of pink and salmon. It had
spaghetti straps and the hem looked like it would fall
just above her knees. The almond-colored wedge sandals
she'd seen in the window at the front of the shop and a

brown pair of Jackie O–style sunglasses would look great with it.

"I'll try it on," she said, taking it from him. She couldn't help but smile—he'd picked out something that was just her personality without even knowing it.

After asking the sales lady to get her size in the wedge sandals, Callie slipped into the dressing room and tried it on. She turned around and saw her reflection. It was perfect. She peered down at the tag to view the price and held her breath for a second. It was a hundred and fifty dollars. But more concerning than that was the fact that the brand was Coastal Pop. That was Juliette Sullivan's brand. She couldn't show up to the party wearing Juliette's dress! She'd look like she was trying too hard.

Callie came out of the dressing room and Luke's face lit up. "That looks great," he said.

Olivia had chosen an outfit from the sale section and was looking through the children's clothes for Wyatt. She gave her a very happy thumbs up.

"I like it too, but I can't buy it. It's your sister's line."

"You know my sister's clothing brand?" He was almost cautious as he asked.

Olivia had lumped a few things on the counter and was counting with her fingers as she mentally added up the total. Callie wondered if she was just as shocked at the prices. This was the only boutique like it in the area, and Callie knew they did have a clientele—those people who rented the enormous new cottages that stretched across the beach, eating up the coastline as fast as the contractors could build them.

"Of course we know your sister's line," said Olivia. "You're a Sullivan, a local celebrity." She laughed. "Okay, we have to admit it, we may have paid more attention to certain articles in certain local publications than we might have a few months ago."

Callie bit her lip. She got the sense that Luke didn't like reporters, and he wasn't too keen on what they wrote about him. Luke wasn't smiling.

"Olivia, he's going to think we're stalking him!" She turned to Luke. "But we can't help but know who you are. I think I first heard your last name when I was around twelve. And when I told Olivia about getting a burger with you that day we met, we had a few magazines lying around so we read the articles."

Luke looked startled. "So you think you know everything there is to know about the Sullivans?"

Callie shook her head. "No!" She felt awful—imagine if someone had access to all kinds of information about her. It made her want to squirm.

Luke opened his mouth to speak, but didn't.

"Really, we know better than to believe everything we read in the papers."

He nodded slowly, then narrowed his eyes, but his lips were starting to smile again. "What's my mother's name?"

"Oh!" said Olivia. "I know this! Lillian!"

"Olivia!" Callie said, shaking her head and grinning.

Luke's eyebrows shot up. "What's my favorite color?"

Olivia's face crumpled in thought. "Blue? No, red?"

"She doesn't know," Callie said. "*We* don't know."

"Good." Luke grinned. And as Olivia walked toward the counter, laughing, he leaned forward and whispered in Callie's ear, "My favorite color is green," sending a shiver down her arm.

She felt a thrill shoot right through her chest. It was like he'd given her something.

Chapter Eleven

"I can't believe I actually bought his sister's dress," Callie said as they parked the car.

Taking a large step onto the pavement to avoid sand in her new sandals, she was momentarily distracted as she took in the castle-like structure in front of her—a perfectly manicured lawn, palm trees meticulously placed in the exquisitely landscaped yard, and the house itself: all skylights and balconies. They'd parked behind more luxury cars than Callie could count, at the end of the huge, circular drive made entirely of aggregate. Down the street, she noticed what looked like a news van. A man was getting out, and aiming a camera at the house. Callie looked away, wondering if she'd read about the party in the local paper tomorrow. She focused on Olivia and Wyatt.

"He said his sister would be delighted, remember?"

Olivia opened the back door to let Wyatt out. He was wearing a two-button navy polo shirt and seersucker shorts with a new pair of loafers, his red curls combed to the side.

Callie had hidden her grin when he'd first come downstairs. She hadn't wanted to embarrass him, but he was adorable. She'd never seen him all dressed up like that before. He'd tugged at the collar of his shirt, and he seemed a bit uncomfortable, but, in the end, it was clear he'd endure anything if it meant meeting someone his own age.

"Juliette will think you're wearing it for her!" Olivia said, pulling the gift from the backseat. They'd settled on a dinosaur excavating kit, complete with sand trays, picks, hammers, and dinosaur bones. Luke had said he'd like it. "Can you believe we're actually going to meet Juliette Sullivan? She does runway shows on TV!"

"It's definitely weird," Callie said as they reached the door. The man with the camera had moved closer and she could hear him snap a photo. She smoothed her dress.

Luke opened the door and greeted them before they'd rung the bell. He was holding a beer in his hand. "Come in." He leaned down toward Wyatt. "Mitchell's out back. That's my nephew's name. He's wearing a light blue shirt and white shorts. Go tell him I sent you." Then, he seemed to notice the man as well, shaking his head as they entered. He shut the door.

Wyatt seemed a little shy as he walked through the crowd of people, across the gigantic open space, the kitchen, den, and dining area all sharing the same flawlessly glossed hardwoods. White columns were the only structures separating the rooms, stretching two stories high to the balcony, where the second floor overlooked the large bay window facing the ocean.

"I'll just walk Wyatt out," Luke said. "Get yourselves a drink." He pointed toward the spacious kitchen, where a bartender was standing behind a bar that took up one whole wall. "Or you can go outside. There's more out there."

"We'll follow you outside," Callie suggested, just dying for fresh air and sunshine to calm her nerves. She caught the eye of a group of women dressed like fashion models who were chattering loudly and laughing, their perfectly manicured hands wrapped around glasses of champagne. With a quick assessment of her dress, it seemed, they smiled briefly and went back to their conversation. Callie wondered if they'd noticed it was Juliette's. She felt self-conscious.

Luke noticed Wyatt struggling to get through the crowd of people. He squatted down and whispered something to Wyatt, who nodded. Then, he scooped up Wyatt and gave him a piggyback ride across the room.

He led them through the two towering double doors that were propped open and tied with at least thirty silver Mylar balloons. Callie stepped onto the most magnificent deck—it was bigger than the whole of the downstairs at The Beachcomber. On either end there was a bar with a working bartender, crowds gathered around as both were tossing liquor bottles into the air and catching them. Between the bars were tables with turquoise umbrellas, hundreds of fresh flowers, chaise lounges, and wicker seating—all done up with matching cushions and throw pillows. Circular stone structures held fire pits that were roaring with flames resembling the orange sun as it began its slow descent behind the house.

Once Callie could force her vision beyond the deck, she was able to take in the yard below. The sand stretched as far as she could see in both directions—not another cottage in sight—the ocean rolling onto the shore. But close to the house, the yard had been landscaped with grass rivaling the best golf courses she could imagine, countless palm trees, outdoor lighting, patios, more umbrellas, and furniture.

Wyatt had found the other partygoers, Luke introducing him to Mitchell. The kids were piled into two bouncy castles that were as grand as the property itself. There was a clown making balloon animals, an ice cream stand, and a cotton candy machine with a man in a red and white striped suit and a tall white chef's hat at the helm. Happiness flooded her as she saw Wyatt bounce along by the mesh netting. He grabbed the side and doubled over laughing, as another boy jumped toward him and pulled him back into the center.

"Here you are," Luke said, handing her and Olivia each a drink. Callie had been so taken with the view that she hadn't realized he'd made it back up to them. "They're mojitos," he said, allowing a grin.

"Thank you," she said.

"Luke!" a woman said from behind as she draped her thin arm around his shoulder and kissed his cheek.

Callie tried not to gawk when she saw her—Juliette. She looked exactly like she had in the photos; she was just as flawless. Her long brown hair was poker straight and parted perfectly down the middle. She had large hoop earrings, her makeup understated with just a hint of clear lip-gloss, and her dress was amazing—soft pink chiffon, with a high neck that tied around the back in a bow and cascaded down her bare back. Her nude heels gave her a good four inches of height. Callie guessed she wasn't planning to walk in the sand in those shoes.

"Luke!" she said again. "Introduce me to your friends!" She smiled, showing her perfect, white teeth.

"Julie, this is Callie and her friend Olivia. Ladies, my sister, Juliette."

"It's nice to meet you!" She shimmied off her brother and held out a delicate hand. Callie shook it and then

Olivia followed suit. She leaned forward toward Callie and whispered, "I like your dress." Then she gave her a wink. Her face was kind and put Callie at ease.

Callie smiled. "It's a great design," she said.

"You look great in it! You're gorgeous!"

Callie's skin prickled with embarrassment. She'd never really given much thought to her looks more than whether she had broccoli in her teeth or not.

"Isn't she beautiful, Luke?"

"Yes," he said with a contemplative look, and then tipped his beer back, draining it.

"Enjoy the party! Off to celebrate!" She kissed Luke on the cheek again, disappearing into the crowd at the bar.

Olivia waved to Wyatt, who was still jumping in the bouncy castle, his shirttail untucked and his hair a mess. "I'm going to go see him," she said as he beckoned her down. "He looks so cute! I want pictures!" She'd pulled her phone from her handbag and was already taking them from the deck.

"If I could, I'd like to steal Callie away for a moment anyway," Luke said seriously. He set his empty beer bottle on a table and a member of the staff swooped in and scooped it up immediately.

Olivia was already heading down the stairs, still snapping photos. She turned around and threw up her hand with a smile.

"Slip your shoes off," he said, leading Callie down the steps toward the bouncy castle, where Olivia had her hands cupped around her eyes, peering in at Wyatt while he showed her the tricks he could do. "Let's go down to the beach."

She got to the bottom of the steps and took her sandals off, placing them neatly under the deck with one hand, her mojito in the other, and followed Luke down the wooden sidewalk that divided the yard in half and led straight to the ocean.

He walked quietly beside her and she wondered what it was that he had to say.

They walked along the walkway, the lush grass giving way to taller sea oats and wild grasses along sand fences that were all part of the dunes that had been created to prevent erosion on the small barrier islands. Callie stepped down the few steps at the end and put her feet in the sand, immediately responding to the heat of it. The intense sun beating down on it relentlessly made the surface feel like hot coals.

Luke took her hand. "Run," he said, pulling her toward the water.

He took off, and Callie had to work overtime to keep up, his hand gripping hers as she pushed herself full speed along the powdery beach, trying to hold her drink steady, her feet feeling like fire, until they reached the wet gritty shoreline. A wave broke, fizzing and bubbling its way toward her, the gurgling spray cooling her feet immediately. Luke dropped her hand and walked closer to the waves, the current sliding up around his ankles. Callie moved beside him. She pushed a runaway strand of hair off her face.

"They're all liars," he said, looking out at the water.

She didn't understand, so she waited for more.

He finally turned to look at her. "Those articles. They aren't real. They don't know. None of them know." Any trace of sarcasm or arrogance was gone. He looked exposed, vulnerable. "They say I'm shallow, that I date models and actresses just so I can have a pretty face to look at...I date them because they understand. Their lives are even more in the spotlight than mine. I own a sailing company. Who am I? But this town has made me into someone; they've built me up into this character—for what? To increase tourism? To give people something to talk about? They say that I don't understand the locals. It's not that I don't understand them. It's that I can't just be. I always see a judging eye, someone who has some opinion about my life's choices. So I keep to myself."

"I'm sorry," she said. "I had no idea."

He turned back to the ocean again as if it held answers somewhere far off in the distance.

Callie didn't talk. With the wind in her ears and the whooshing of the ocean, she let the silence settle between them. He seemed like he'd wanted to get that out, and she was glad he'd confided in her.

"I've never told anyone that."

"Really?"

"I've never felt the need to." He picked up a shell and chucked it into a breaking wave. "But when I'd heard you'd read some of those awful things about me, it frustrated me and I wanted you to know."

He'd surprised her again. And she couldn't help the flutter in her chest at the thought that he'd wanted her to know the real him, but it scared her as well. She wasn't ready for things to get real. He'd trusted her with his thoughts. She wasn't the best person at relationships and, while they weren't in one yet, this was how they usually started.

She mustered all the strength she had to respond to him. She didn't want to do this wrong; she wasn't any good at it. "I'm glad you trust me," she said, her words feeling flimsy as they came out of her mouth. But the concern he seemed to have at making sure she understood him made her let go of her worries and speak from her heart. "I don't believe those articles," she said, watching the bubbles rise in her mojito, the ice melting in the heat. She looked up. "I guess I kind of did, when you took me on that big boat of yours and ordered that lobster what's-it-called. I thought maybe the guy in the burger joint was just an act to appeal to me. But I know now that's not true. Not at all."

He let out a breath as if he'd been holding it in and smiled at her—a genuine smile, one that gave away how thrilled he was with her comment—and she knew she'd said just the right thing. And she hadn't even had to try. She'd just done what had come naturally.

Chapter Twelve

"Look at these two," Olivia said with a giggle, pointing into the bouncy castle, as Luke and Callie walked up from the beach. Mitchell and Wyatt were still bouncing and they were going up and down with each other, doing some sort of gymnastics routine they'd created while the other kids bounded around inside. The two of them jumped up and did a toe touch before bouncing again and doing a flip. Both Olivia and Juliette took photos, laughing together.

"Looks like fun," Luke said, crawling in. He barely fit through the small door.

When he stood up, the boys squealed at his arrival.

Luke's weight, as he bounced, made both children soar into the air with uproarious laughter. Callie couldn't help herself—she was laughing right alongside them while Luke jumped up to do a toe touch like the boys, both of them doubling over, heaving with giggles.

"Come in!" Luke said, bouncing to the side and putting

his face right up to Callie's, only the mesh netting between them. "You know you want to."

Callie shook her head. "I have a dress on." *A very expensive dress.*

"I dare you."

"Go on," Olivia urged.

"I'll go easy. We'll just jump—no funny business." He made a face at the boys, causing them to cackle again. A few of the other kids were now watching with interest.

She deliberated. There was absolutely no reason for her to get in there and jump. She wasn't dressed for it. She'd spent too much time on her hair to have it go all a mess...

"Please, Callie," Wyatt said, an enormous grin on his face, those little eyes pleading.

He'd sat quietly so many days while they'd worked, he'd trudged along beside them as they ran errands for the house, he'd never once complained.

"Okay," she said to the cheers of Luke, Wyatt, and Mitchell. Handing her mojito to a grinning Olivia, she slipped off her sandals and carefully climbed through the precariously small entry onto the wriggling, unsteady floor of the bouncy castle.

Luke took her hands and held her steady as she stood up, his grip more affectionate than she'd expected. That confident smile had returned, sending her heart racing. Slowly, still holding her hands, he bounced up and down just enough to put a little air between her feet and the floor.

"Higher!" Wyatt called.

"Hang on. I'm getting her used to it," Luke said over his shoulder.

As they bounced, still holding hands, she started to feel stable, relaxing into the movement of the floor beneath her as the other kids jumped. Luke must have sensed it, because he did a giant jump, shooting her into the air. She let go of his hands and grabbed her dress, coming back down and having to grab on to him to stay on her feet. She gave him a playful but cautionary look.

"Sorry," he said, chewing on a smile. She was holding the top of his arms still, his face too close to hers as he looked down at her. She pulled away and straightened her dress.

"Do it again!" Wyatt said, his smile spread from ear to ear. He bounced around in a circle, clapping his hands.

"I got a photo!" Olivia called in.

"Awesome," Callie said, laughing.

Luke bounced again, sending her up. When she came back down, Callie gave him a light-hearted push, at which he dramatically fell into a back roll before looking at the boys with wide eyes. "She's really strong," he said with mock seriousness and Wyatt could hardly catch his breath, he was laughing so hard.

He righted himself and stepped over to Callie. "We'll let you two work on your routine some more. I'm going to take Callie back to solid ground again."

Mitchell and Wyatt both booed him before bouncing off into the other kids.

Callie climbed out carefully, put her sandals back on, and ran her fingers through her hair. She pretended to be put out, but she knew Luke could see through it. He handed her the mojito with a devious grin. Then he tipped his head toward the bouncy castle. "Look."

Olivia and Juliette were climbing in. Callie laughed, covering her mouth. When she turned back to Luke, he looked pensive. "I want to show you something," he said, as if he'd just decided right then. "Come with me."

Callie looked around at all the people. "Shouldn't we

stay at the party?" She didn't want to monopolize all his attention.

"I think they'll all survive without me," he teased.

Luke headed around the house toward the private tennis court. It was hidden from view by landscaping. They carried on down the path until they reached a large garage. It was the size of a barn; four towering sets of double doors faced the ocean. They were open. He gestured for Callie to enter. She walked into the garage and found herself speechless as she took in the walls, plastered with surfboards—all with brightly painted artwork on them: floral designs, geometrics, waves, and sea creatures.

"These are amazing, Luke," she said. "What is all this?"

"I painted them," he said, and she only noticed just then that his eyes were on her. "Have a look around."

She ran her hand along one that was still on the workhorses, the colors so vibrant and beautiful that they almost took her breath away. A wave crashing on the shore in electric blue with perfect shadows and shading to make it look so real that she could almost feel its spray.

"How come no one has written an article about *this*? It's fantastic." She took in the boards hanging from the rafters, more climbing every surface of the walls, others lying on the floor.

"Because no one knows I paint them. I created a brand name called Salty Tides, but I haven't done anything with it. See the logo there? I designed it." He tapped just under the picture on the board, zeroing her in on the scratchy two-line lettering spelling *Salty Tides* with the *i* in *Tides* as a little wave.

"Why haven't you done anything with it?" Unable to keep her curiosity at bay, she walked over to another board, the slick surface like glass under fingertips.

He took in a deep breath. "My dad thinks it's a waste of time when I've got millions riding on real estate. I spend most of my time learning how he manages the company so I can take over when I'm ready. It's better not to be distracted, so I keep this little hobby from the public."

She couldn't imagine keeping this a secret. His talent was so clear to her that the possibilities for this were coming at her one after another. She didn't know the surfboard industry but there was no doubt in her mind that these would sell. The artwork alone was just incredible. "Do you *have* to take over the company?"

"I want to. Like I said, I want to prove that I can be trusted." Before she could challenge him, he took her hand, leading her over to a worktable. "Look at this," he said, showing her a large pencil drawing. "It's that flower you put in your hair when we had dinner on my boat. I'm going to make a stencil out of it so I can paint it on one of the boards."

She smiled. "It's called a gaillardia," she said, feeling like that day was ages ago. So much had happened since then, and she would never have thought in a million years that she'd be standing here with him, feeling the way she did every time he looked at her.

The wind picked up, sending a gust into the garage, the drawing paper lifting off the table and flying into the air. He caught it and set a paint can on top of it. Luke had the doors open on both sides of the building, most likely to vent the place while he painted, but it was starting to cause a wind tunnel, a constant stream of air blowing against them.

Her hair blew into her eyes and she thought Luke was going to put it behind her ear, but instead, he cupped his hand around her face, looking down at her with those blue eyes as if he wanted to kiss her. After last time, she worried he might not try. She wanted to kiss him, but things were moving along faster than she could process them, and she still didn't know if she was ready. She was concerned with what would happen if she let him. She feared that she might not be able to recover if he broke her heart. Callie looked into his eyes, wanting to tell him all this, but instead, she looked away, and he let the moment go. She noticed she was smiling and when she looked at him, he was too.

"We should probably get back to the party," she said.

"Yeah."

As they walked up, the bouncy castle was still abuzz with children's laughter. Olivia walked toward them, her stride almost a skip, an excited expression on her face. "Look who I found!" she called out. She was on Aiden Parker's arm.

"You know each other?" Luke asked. They were standing by the juggler, who was tossing bowling pins for a crowd of kids and parents while riding a unicycle. They moved aside to be out of the way of the performance.

"Olivia and I went to college together," Aiden explained to Luke. "I'm mixing a little business and pleasure while I'm here for Mitchell's party."

"He's the architect who's working on The Beachcomber," Olivia added. "How long have you two known each other?"

"A lifetime. Aiden's my cousin." Luke clapped him on the back. "Did you just get here? Let's all have a drink."

Chapter Thirteen

When Callie and Luke got up on the deck with Aiden and Olivia to get their drinks, the thump of live music echoed in Callie's chest and she peeked inside the house to see that a group of musicians had set up and begun to play in the corner of the great living room.

Juliette appeared, a glass of white perched delicately in her fingers. "Don't you just love this? I got a band!" she said dramatically, a delightful grin on her face. "I rented out a string of small cottages for everyone here, since they're all from out of town. I have a shuttle running the whole night. I figured that once the kids get tired, the daddies can take them home and the mommies can party into the night."

"Fun for the daddies," Aiden laughed.

Juliette gave him a light-hearted eye roll. "These women are my good friends. The men are lovely, don't get me wrong. But we girls need some time to let loose too, don't you think?" Aiden opened his mouth to speak, but Juliette gasped, cutting him off, clearly a little chattier after a few drinks. "You and Callie should stay late with us tonight," she said to Olivia. "And Mom! Where is she? We need to get her a drink!"

"Speaking of drinks," Aiden said. "What would you ladies like? Another...Is that a mojito?"

They both nodded.

"Great. Luke and I will get you one."

After Juliette had run off into the crowd, Olivia turned to Callie. "I'm having so much fun," she said. "We should stay. Maybe Gram can watch Wyatt for us—she's always asking for him to stay over. If I text her, and she says yes, would you stay?"

Callie chewed on her nail.

"Don't think so much," Olivia said, that sisterly look in her eyes. Callie and Olivia had shared so many moments together that they might as well be sisters.

"Okay," she relented. Olivia rarely got time to herself and if she wanted to stay, then Callie should put her own confusion aside and stay with her.

Looking deliriously happy, Olivia pulled out her phone and started texting madly. "Thank you," she said, looking up for a moment before turning her attention back to her phone.

Luke and Aiden came back with more than their drinks. Juliette was with them, but also another woman walked beside Luke: An older woman, she was thin, with salt-and-pepper hair styled just so, fanning across her forehead, and diamond earrings the size of small buttons in her ears. Her demeanor seemed slightly stiff, given the party going on; her expression was serious, yet gentle. Luke leaned down to say something to her, and she smiled warmly at him before the sober expression returned.

As they got closer, Callie could see the woman's complexion; clearly she'd spent a lot of time and money to keep her skin looking flawless for her age, but her eyes told a different story. There was something behind them—they looked tired, or maybe sad. She couldn't tell.

"Callie," Luke said, stepping forward and handing her a new, ice-cold glass. He moved to the side to allow the woman to take the spot directly in front of Callie. "This is my mother. Mom, this is Callie."

"Lillian Sullivan," she said, giving her an appraising once-over, making Callie feel as if she were just another girl Luke brought to the house.

While the others fell into conversation, sitting down on the deck chairs, Lillian turned to her son. "Where have you been, dear? I've been looking for you all night."

"I was showing Callie my work in the garage."

Lillian was motionless for an instant, the comment noticeably affecting her. "Oh?" she said, before turning slowly and looking at Callie as if she'd only just now seen her. She smiled at her, and Callie had to work to keep her breath from coming out like a popped balloon. Lillian Sullivan could certainly be intimidating. But when she softened, it was like she was a totally different person.

"Have you seen Luke surf? I love to watch him surf." She looked up at the sky and shook her head as if the memory was right there, before her gaze landed back on Callie.

"I haven't," she answered, nervously taking a sip of her drink.

Luke piped up, "I tried to get her to go surfing with me, but she wouldn't go."

"I didn't say I wouldn't go. You asked me to go today and the party was today."

"So you would go?" He was grinning at her as he lifted his drink to his lips. What was it—whiskey and coke? She knew he was baiting her.

"Yes, I'd go."

Amusement swelled in Luke's features. "Are you nervous about surfing?"

"No." What she couldn't say out loud was that she was nervous about being with him. She was finding it harder to push her feelings away; unable to control how her body responded to Luke. Her skin felt all tingly and alive just looking at him.

"Callie," Olivia called from the sofa. When she leaned around Luke to see her friend, she was surprised to find Aiden with his arm stretched out behind Olivia. They sure did look cozy. Olivia waved her phone in the air. "Gram's coming to get Wyatt later. We can stay."

"Yay!" Juliette said, coming back over after being sidetracked by a few of her friends.

Luke shook his head. "I'll be helping Mitchell to bed tonight, I can tell." He chuckled. "Julie isn't always like this, but she deserves to have a night out. She's only recently divorced," he said quietly. "And she's had a rough go of things for the last few years. I'm glad to see her finally happy."

"Divorce is a messy endeavor," Lillian said. "I know from experience." She'd gotten a glass of wine from one of the waiters and was holding it with both hands, her diamond rings swinging around her finger with the weight of the stones. "It was devastating when I had to go through it, and I'm so sad Juliette has to go through the same thing."

"Me too," Luke said, putting his arm around his mother and kissing the top of her head. Then, switching gears in an obvious attempt to lighten his mother's mood, he said, "I think you need to hang out with us tonight."

She looked lovingly up at her son. "I'd never manage. I'll be asleep before you all have even started."

"Nonsense. Aiden and I will keep you going."

Callie sat down. She was taken with Luke's relationship with his mother.

He shook his mother's shoulders playfully. "Come on..." he coaxed.

"Stop it," she scolded with a laugh. "You're going to make me spill my wine." When he let her go, she added, "You can't stay up too late if you're going to take Callie surfing anyway. You don't want to sleep all day."

"Did you hear that, Callie?" Luke said, plopping down beside her on the sofa. "Mom says we're going surfing tomorrow. I never argue with my mother." He winked at Lillian.

Callie didn't argue either.

* * *

Wyatt, exhausted, climbed into the back of Gladys's car and covered up with the beach towel that Luke had returned as promised—all clean and freshly laundered. Callie had gone with Olivia to meet Gladys out front of the Sullivans' so she could wish him goodnight before Gladys took him home. She noticed the news van had gone.

"I painted a few wine glasses tonight for fun with Adelaide." Gladys opened her car door but stood just beside it, carrying on their conversation. "It was Adelaide." Gladys opened her car door but stood just beside it, carrying on their conversation. "It was Adelaide Foster, Callie," she said.

Callie tried to recollect the name—it sounded familiar.

"Oh! Yes. The lockbox. Did she give you Frederick McFarlin's contact information?"

Gladys frowned. "No. I'm sorry. She couldn't find it."

"Aw, that's too bad," she said, shaking her head. "Well, we tried." As Gladys climbed into the driver's seat, they said a quick goodbye to Wyatt and headed inside.

When they entered the house, Aiden met them in the entryway. "Luke said to go upstairs and get him when you're back in. He's putting Mitchell to bed," he told Callie.

Olivia followed Aiden into the living room while Callie took the steps carefully, the drinks she'd had making her just relaxed enough that she felt the need to hold the railing.

When she found the room, Luke was on the floor, leaning against a large, four-poster bed, reading to Mitchell from a chapter book. Something he'd read had made Mitchell laugh and Callie could see Luke's smile emerge just before he turned to look at her.

"Hi," he said, looking so content that she had to catch her breath. Images of him as a father flashed through her head, questions about what he'd be like years down the road came flooding in. She willed herself to stop.

He ruffled Mitchell's hair. "That's it for tonight, buddy. Happy birthday."

Mitchell smiled and yawned, turning over in his bed, exhaustion winning out.

Luke nodded toward the door.

When they got downstairs, Olivia had already settled in beside Aiden in the living room. He had his arm around her in a way that could be just friendly but Callie had to wonder.

"I'll get us a drink," Luke said, leaving her to have a seat on her own. She went over next to Olivia.

"Aiden has always had great business sense," Lillian was telling Olivia when Callie joined them mid-conversation. "Edward, his uncle, dotes on him any chance he gets." Lillian smiled, clearly glad to be able to speak highly of her nephew.

"Oh, my gosh, I know," Juliette said, her eyes heavy. "Dad just loves Aiden."

Luke appeared, handing Callie some sort of pink drink with a wedge of pineapple and a maraschino cherry, his gaze lingering on Aiden.

Callie took a sip of her drink. The band started playing again, and Juliette popped up. "Oh! They're playing 'Brown Eyed Girl'!" Her feet were bare, her heels on their sides under the large window. Her glass of wine sloshed as she started to dance. "Luke, get out here and dance!" Juliette swayed before resuming her dancing.

"I think *you* need to dance, Mom," Luke said, standing up. He turned to Callie. "The next song is yours, I promise." He flashed that smile that sent her stomach whirring, so she took another sip of her drink to try to squash it.

Luke gently took his mother's wine and set it on the table beside her. Then he took her by the hands and led her out to the dance floor. The minute they got out there, he dipped her dramatically, making her giggle. When he set her back up, she gave him a displeased look but she had a hard time keeping it on her face, her smile emerging again.

"Luke's always been a mama's boy," Aiden said, his tone lighthearted. "He's a one of a kind—so laid back, full of life."

"I like that," Callie heard herself saying and then realized the thought had actually come out. She looked down at her drink, blaming the alcohol but really, it was true. She couldn't take her eyes off him.

She resumed drinking her fruity concoction, not wanting to speak again for fear she might spout off about all of Luke's wonderful qualities. When she raised her head from her drink, Luke was standing in front of her. "Want to dance?" The music was slow, the kind that made her feel like putting her head on his shoulder.

"Get out here right now!" Juliette called from her group of friends.

"What's in this drink?" Callie asked, feeling the weight in her legs as she stood up. She used all her focus to get the glass onto the table. When she righted herself, she took hold of his arm to keep herself steady.

"A couple of different kinds of rum," he said. "We don't have to dance. I'll get you a water. Sit back down."

"No." She smiled up at him. "I'm okay. It just hit me hard, that's all." She could feel the firmness in his grip on her as if he were making sure she wouldn't fall. "Let's dance."

She put her arms around his neck and made eye contact. "I'm having so much fun," she admitted.

The corners of his eyes wrinkled just slightly with his grin. "I'm glad," he said. "I can tell that drink has hit you. Sure you don't want some water?"

"I don't need any water," she said, feeling his hands on her hips.

"Okay." He smiled again.

"What?"

"Tell me, what have you liked most about tonight?"

She reached up a little more and clasped her hands behind his neck, pulling their bodies closer. "I liked seeing your surfboards, hearing you talk about them." She blinked, willing her eyes to open again. "I liked talking on the beach when we got here and I liked watching you put Mitchell to bed. I like this."

He chuckled. "Let's definitely get you some water."

She stared at him alarmed. "Why do you keep telling me I need water?"

"Because you haven't opened up so easily since I've met you. I can see how hard it is when you tell me about yourself. I like this version of you. Keep it. But without the alcohol." He leaned down, his lips so close to her ear that she got a shiver. "I think you might actually like me." He pulled back, grinning that crooked grin, those eyes like sapphires.

"You just like the chase," she said, her thoughts still pouring out, and the sting on his face surprised her, making her doubt her ability to think rationally. Guilt swelled in her stomach for a moment, but then she faltered. What if he was playing her right now? "I'm probably the first girl who wouldn't kiss you on command. Well, I don't do that," she said, the words coming out softly, giving away her uncertainty.

His gaze was intense, and their feet had almost stopped moving entirely. She could read him perfectly in that moment and he was telling her that she was wrong about him. Neither of them made a move. Finally, he said, "And what if I kissed you now?"

Everything in her body wanted to kiss him, but she didn't trust her judgment. Things would be different once the alcohol wore off, she was sure of it. She mustered all the courage she had. "I said I won't kiss you on command."

The intensity faded and he looked away, contemplative. He nodded, pulling her closer, and they danced.

Chapter Fourteen

Callie rolled over on her air mattress, her head feeling like it was being hit with a million bowling balls and her mouth bone dry. She grimaced. The shuttle had taken them home well after midnight and both Olivia and Callie had fallen into bed in their respective rooms without even a word to each other. They were both completely exhausted. Wyatt had stayed at Gladys's, and she wondered if he was still there. She tried to open her eyes, the sunlight making the pounding worse. Beside her was a glass of water and a note that read, *Luke's staff brought the car home this morning. I didn't wake you. I'm going to Gram's to be nursed back to life. Thought you'd like a quiet house. O.*

Callie took a big drink from the water glass, her stomach rumbling but the pain in her head preventing her from moving to get herself something to eat. The night was coming back to her in bits and pieces—she could recall leaving the car keys, dancing...She chewed on her lip, remembering her conversation with Luke. The thing was, even without the alcohol, she might have told him those things.

With a yawn, she slowly stood, the room moving with her. She took another drink of water and got her bearings. Her eye caught Alice's journal on her dresser and she remembered Gladys telling her about Adelaide. It was a shame that Adelaide didn't have Frederick's contact details. Callie felt a renewed prickle of interest in the idea of finding him to return the journal and the lockbox. Perhaps the journal would contain Frederick's business name, and she could find him that way. It would be a good distraction from the thoughts she had about last night, about Luke. She took it with her and went to make some coffee.

With the sound of the coffee machine percolating and an empty mug waiting to be filled, Callie opened the journal, thumbing through, looking for Frederick's name when she stopped on the word "brother." She read:

> *I've always been cautious with my own choices, and sometimes, I wonder if I've been a little too cautious. My whole life, I was so afraid of getting hurt that now I sit here alone, under this lamp, writing to you, my dear journal, my quiet companion. But my brother is the complete opposite. He allows his heart to lead him, he's too honest, and he jumps before he realizes the consequences. Because of that, he had a child who will never know who his father is.*

A child? Callie pursed her lips, shocked. Callie could relate to this entry so much. She, too, had been cautious about getting close to people. She stared at the words, wondering if she'd be alone at the end, with only a journal to keep her company. Callie didn't blame her mother for her difficulty letting people in, but she'd had a part in it. She pondered whether her mother thought about her, if she was ever curious about what she'd been up to. Would she come to The Beachcomber if Callie asked her?

Thinking back to the journal, Callie wondered what it would be like to not have known her father at all. She might have chosen the question mark over the hurt of his absence. Maybe Frederick was doing his kid a favor. But maybe not. Did he sit somewhere missing his child? Did he feel like he'd abandoned his baby? She'd often wondered, growing up, if her dad had missed her, and sometimes she'd considered trying to find him, but her apprehension had prevented it. It was only after he died and one of his friends had called to let them know, with no personal message to her or her mother, and no attempt to reach out prior to his death, that her fears were confirmed.

As she poured her coffee, she heard a knock at the door. Callie squeezed her eyes shut, to alleviate the pounding in her head. Setting the mug onto the counter, she walked to the front door to answer it.

Luke, looking all alert and carefree, was grinning at her from the other side of the door. "Hey," he said, his eyes moving down to her bare feet and back up. "Still answering the door in your T-shirts?" He grinned.

She moved out of the way to allow him to enter. She didn't bother covering herself this time, her throbbing headache preventing her from caring. "My head is killing me."

Luke came in and shut the door. "You need water."

"I'm making coffee."

"No, I mean ocean water. The sun and the movement of the sea will help."

The faint memory of their surfing date feathered its way into her consciousness. "It might make me nauseous."

He laughed quietly, his eyes on her.

She poured her coffee and added sugar and cream. "Want some?"

Luke shook his head, pulling out a kitchen chair and sitting down. "No, thank you." He looked out at the sea a moment through the window before turning back to her as she sat down beside him with her mug.

"Last night was fun," he said. "How much did you drink?"

"I lost count." She closed her eyes and took a long sip of coffee. She was okay, as long as she didn't talk . . .

"I shouldn't have made you that drink at the end. It had too much rum in it. I'm sorry. I just thought you might like it."

"I did. And how were you to know?"

He leaned forward. "At least it got you dancing."

She narrowed her eyes at him but only half seriously. "Maybe you did know what it might do then."

She expected some witty response about trying to get her to talk or something, but instead he said, "You know what I think? I think you're relying on those articles you read about me because you can't face the fact that you're scared."

"What?" What was he talking about? Had she missed something?

"You heard me. You're scared to death to feel something for someone, to let someone in." He scooted closer. "But I'm telling you right now that you don't have to be scared. I wouldn't knowingly give you too much to drink. I'm not playing any games. There's no hidden agenda. I want to hang out with you . . ." His knee started bouncing under the table and he looked as though he didn't want to finish his sentence, but then he became still and looked into her eyes. "Because I think you're amazing, and when I leave you, I can't wait to see you again."

She looked down into her mug, the brown liquid still, the sunlight sending a tiny glare across it. All her thoughts were bumping into one another, and she couldn't speak. She didn't know what to do or how to react because her own feelings for him were muddling everything up. How did he know her so well?

"Wanna go surfing?" he asked tenderly, as if he knew how hard it was for her to respond to that kind of admission. She didn't know how to be honest with someone. Where was she supposed to draw the line? Was she supposed to just tell him every single thought she had? She didn't know. But she was thankful that he could sense her uncertainty and he was taking it easy on her. "Well?"

She nodded, afraid to open her mouth for fear she'd blurt out how much what he'd said had affected her, how she couldn't wait to see him either, and how thankful she was that he'd come into her life.

"You up for a drive? It's an hour and a half, but I promise, it's worth it." He nodded toward her mug and stood up. "And I have snacks for the road." He flashed a grin at her, erasing all her worry.

* * *

Callie heard the humming start of an engine as Luke waited downstairs for her to get ready. She had on a bikini, which she hoped would work for surfing, and a tank top with a pair of shorts. She gawked at the incredible SUV she'd never seen him drive before that was parked in front of the house. It was jet black, and looked as though it was brand new. He leaned across the seat. There was a click and the passenger door opened. She put her foot on the silver step and hoisted herself up into the vehicle.

"Where are we going?" she asked as she shut the door and fastened her seat belt.

He smiled like he had the day he'd brought her coffee. "It's a surprise. Somewhere away from possible reporters or people who drive me crazy." He put the windows down and pulled onto the road. "It's a great ride; let's relax and enjoy it."

As he drove, Callie pulled her hair to the side to keep it from blowing into her face, the warm wind calming her. "I like your car," she said, wondering how many he had.

"I don't usually drive this," Luke said, glancing over at her and then back to the road. "It's my father's. He leaves it here for when he visits." She noticed a slight tension in the way he said the word "father." She didn't think he'd meant the intonation, looking at his calm expression, but there was something lurking in that word.

Callie hadn't seen Luke's father at the party, which surprised her. Surely he would've been at his grandson's celebration? "Your dad couldn't make it to Mitchell's birthday party?" she asked.

Luke shook his head, a slight annoyance visible in his eyes. "Nope. He was working. He said he couldn't get away."

"I'm sorry to hear that." She gazed out the window a minute, realizing how little people really knew about this family. The road stretched ahead of them—single lanes, sandy from the dunes that sat right at the edge of the road, the ocean crashing behind them.

He pulled to a stop at a red light. "I'm glad, though. It would've put a lot of pressure on my mom. She feels the need to be peacekeeper between me and my father."

"You aren't close with him?"

He took in a breath and let it out, his grip on the wheel never loosening. "Well, he's my dad. But he and I haven't always seen eye to eye on things when it comes to our family business. I tried to do the right thing, show him how I can run it like he does, and I'm good at it, but he never trusts me." The light turned green and Luke accelerated.

"That's too bad." Callie thought about her own father, wondering if things would've been similar.

"It is," he agreed. "Let's not talk about my family," he said, clicking on the radio. "I don't want to bore you with all the details." He reached around behind his seat, rummaging in a grocery bag. He pulled out a smaller bag and held it up. "Popcorn?" Then he flashed that smile and she was so happy to see it again.

Chapter Fifteen

The road just came to an end.

After all that driving, they'd made it to the town of Corolla and where the road stopped, the beach began. Luke pulled to the side and asked Callie to stay there. They couldn't just park at the end of the road, could they?

He went around the car, bending down on each side, and then he got back in. "I just had to let some air out of the tires," he said. "We're nearly there." Then, to her surprise, he put the SUV in four-wheel drive and started driving on the sand. There weren't a lot of people on the beach as he drove along the track made by other vehicles. A few trucks were parked, their tailgates open, beach chairs set out beside them. He maneuvered around a man throwing a Frisbee to his dog, the large, yellow lab springing into the air to catch it.

"I've never been here before," she told him. Callie leaned her elbow out the open window, taking in the wide shoreline and the smattering of cottages along the dunes.

"How do they get here?" she asked, pointing to one of the cottages.

"By beach," he said, grinning over at her, clearly happy that he could show her something that interested her. "This is the main road."

"The beach?"

"Yep. The only way to get out here is by truck. These cottages are quite expensive to make because all the materials have to be brought across the sand."

"Wow."

"I like it," he said. "I like how secluded it is." He held the wheel tightly as they bumped along the shore. They continued down the beach until the people dwindled and theirs was the only vehicle she could see. "But you know what I like best about it?"

She watched him as he drove.

"That." He pointed down the shore and Callie gasped. Running toward her at full speed were two chocolate brown wild horses, their manes flapping in the wind, their strong leg muscles flexing as their hooves pushed against the sand.

"They're gorgeous," she said, her eyes glued to them. Callie had heard about the wild horses of the Outer Banks, but she'd never seen one before.

"They're believed to be descendants of Spanish mustangs left by explorers," he said. "Been here over five hundred years."

"Look!" She pointed to the dune where a foal was eating next to its mother. "They're so beautiful."

Luke turned the SUV toward the ocean and put it in park. "My mom used to bring me here when I was a kid. Back then, hardly anyone knew this was out here. It was so remote." He opened the door and got out. "I'm glad you like it," he said as she exited on her side.

He opened the back hatch and drew out a blue-and-white beach umbrella, anchoring it in the sand by the vehicle. Another horse walked around them, giving them a large distance, unfazed by the humans in its way. On either side of the umbrella pole, Luke set up two chairs facing the sea and placed a cooler in the center. Callie and Luke were completely secluded—just them and the horses. Callie didn't sit. Instead, she looked out at the ocean, the breeze on her face.

Luke stepped into her view slowly. "Before we surf, I'd like to make something for you," he said, and she noticed an uncertainty in his eyes. He deliberated a second before continuing. "You've done more for me than anyone else has, and I don't think you know you're doing it, but it makes me want to spend time with you...do nice things for you."

"What did I do?" she asked, at a loss for what could have made him feel so utterly comfortable with her.

Callie thought back to all those snapshots she'd seen in the press—him on boats, photos of him holding doors open at elite restaurants for beautiful women, his model-like stance as he leaned against a wall at an airport awaiting the arrival of one of his famous friends. This person in front of her now was not that face. He was a real, live, breathing soul; he was sharing even more of himself with her, and she couldn't wait to hear what he had to say.

"You didn't want anything from me."

"What?"

"When I tried to kiss you when we first met, you didn't let me."

"Nope."

"You were right. You were the first girl who hasn't let me. Most of the girls I've dated wanted something—a trip somewhere, a nice meal, something. I always thought I had to give it to them. But you make me feel like you want to be with me. Just me."

"I'm so sorry I let those articles affect my thinking," she said.

"It's what they want people to think. That's what sells."

He walked around and reached into the back of the SUV, pulling out a small easel and a canvas. He set it up in the sand, pressing the easel down to secure it from getting blown away and clipping the back of the canvas to it. He had a small caddy with paints of every color, an assortment of brushes, and a jug of water for rinsing the brushes.

"I want to paint something for you now. But first!" he said, with a dramatic flair that made her giggle. "Have a seat. Relax."

Another horse walked by as Luke opened the cooler and pulled out a plastic champagne glass. Then he uncorked a bottle and poured some into the flute, along with some orange juice, the liquids fizzing and popping. He handed it to her as she took a seat.

Two horses were now standing at the break in the waves, the spray shooting up around their hooves. "Paint that," she said, pointing to it, the thrill of the moment causing her to forget everything else. She took a drink of her mimosa.

Luke pulled his cell phone from his pocket and snapped a photo. He cupped his hands around the screen, his hair blowing against his forehead in an irresistible way. "In case they move," he said, holding up the phone. By his smile, it was clear that he was delighted by the challenge.

Setting his phone on the easel, he opened a few shades of brown paint, then the black, the green, the blue. He dipped his brush in and, as if it were as easy as breathing, he started to paint in quick, sketchy strokes. She watched the movement of his back, the muscles in his arms as she took another crisp drink of her ice-cold mimosa. She kicked her shoes off and dug her feet under the warm sand. The horses' tails lifted up as if they were posing for their portrait. They were so still, like they knew.

Luke moved a bit to the side to get a different angle, and she noticed the small smear of paint on his hand. There was something electrifying about the gentle movements of his masculine hands while he created this gorgeous picture from nothing. It was as intoxicating as the drink in her hand. His face was set in concentration, his lips resting together gently. She wondered what it would feel like to have those lips on her.

She couldn't take her eyes off Luke or the painting, and the more he painted, the more she realized how incredibly talented he was.

"So, you've taken trips to the Outer Banks as a kid, but you've never seen the horses?"

"No," she said, the glass cool in her hand and the wind in her hair. "We stayed in cottages along the beaches farther south. My favorite memory was getting ice cream after a really hot day at the beach. I still remember how my lips would feel like fire after so many hours in the sun and the ice cream was so cold... We'd sit out on wooden benches with all the other vacationers and I was so small, my feet would swing above the deck. I'd have to lick around the cone to eat it faster than the summer heat could melt it." She took a sip of her drink, still thinking. "I haven't thought about those days in years."

"I know that feeling well," he said, taking his eyes off the canvas long enough to acknowledge her. "Growing up here was a little different. The small things like ice cream aren't isolated memories because they're lumped in with all the other day-to-day things we did. But I do remember making homemade chocolate one summer with my mom. We got it everywhere, trying to take it off the stove before it burned. It sloshed in the pot, spilling over, but we couldn't catch it because it was hot." He was laughing while painting, his face irresistible in that moment. "We let it cool and then ran our fingers through it like finger paint. I still remember licking it off. It was the best chocolate I'd tasted."

One of the horses moved, moseying on down the beach, and Luke kept painting from memory. When he got to the detail on the mane, he picked up his cell phone and stretched the image with his two fingers, cupping his other hand around the screen again to shield it from the glare. Then he painted some more.

He spent a little time stepping back to look at it and then adding details but, every time, the painting was so amazing that she'd thought he was finished. Then he would put in a small highlight and the tiny change would blow her away. She was transfixed.

Finally, he turned around. His hands were covered in paint. "Finished," he said, with the most genuine smile. "Your painting." He waved his hand and presented it to her like a game show host.

Callie set her flute down on the cooler and walked over to get a better look. She shook her head, words escaping her right then. "Thank you," she finally said. She'd never had anyone give her a gift like that. "I love it."

"I'm glad you like it," he said. "I've never painted for anyone before."

"Not even your family?"

He shook his head.

"Why not?"

"Whenever I tried to, my father always steered me toward something else."

Why would his father push him away from talent like this?

"I don't think he meant any harm; he just sees things differently from me." He looked up at the sky. "I've never been like him. Over the years, when Dad would preach to me the importance of carrying on the family business, of taking the necessary courses at school and watching everything he did to learn how to do it 'right,' he never could understand why I didn't see the urgency in it. He hated my art classes. He said they were a waste of time when my path was already plowed by his hard work. He's passionate about his business. He worries constantly that I won't share that passion. And I think the thought of the business crumbling is more than he can bear. He's always seen our differences as a threat instead of what they are: just differences. I'm nothing like him. But I can't change that about myself."

"And you shouldn't."

"I've spent my whole life trying to live up to what my father wanted me to be, competing with Aiden. Dad loves him—Aiden's successful in his own business and I think he would like nothing more than to have the opportunity I have with my father's company. I worry that I've fallen short in my dad's eyes." Luke fell quiet and Callie let the silence hang between them. He added, "Aiden has that same drive for business. He built his architectural firm into a huge success, working all hours. I haven't stopped hearing about it."

Callie moved in front of him, looking up at his face, the hurt showing despite his effort to hide it.

"He wanted to offer Aiden the business. My mother

stopped him. She told him that the papers would have a field day with it and my name would be destroyed. I'd never live it down and it would be devastating for the family and for any future career I had."

Callie noticed that he hadn't said that his mother denied that Aiden would be the better choice. She'd only danced around the issue by mentioning the bad press.

"It was enough, and my dad relented and told her I could take over."

"I'm so sorry, Luke."

"I'm going to prove him wrong," he said. "When I get the company, I'm going to keep the business running and ensure its success."

"I don't doubt that you will. You're amazing."

"You are a breath of fresh air," he said, the spray kicking up over the sand behind them. He took a step closer to her, his eyes locked with hers. It was as if he wanted to kiss her, and she wanted nothing more than to feel his lips on hers. But he didn't.

"We'll leave the painting out while we surf—the wind will dry it quickly so you'll be able to take it home." He held up his paint-splattered hands. "I'm going down to the water for a second. Come with me?"

Callie steadied herself, knowing that he was putting on the brakes for her, but wishing there were something she could've done to let him know it was okay. Despite the paint, Callie took his hand as they walked. Luke was clearly surprised, but he didn't let go. He looked into her eyes, affection bubbling up in his gaze. He felt comfortable with her, and now, she felt pressure not to let him down. It scared her to death. She could just walk away except there was this one hitch: She was happy whenever she was with him and she couldn't get enough of him.

* * *

"Your toes should always touch the back of the board," Luke said, paddling beside Callie as they bobbed over a wave together. She'd only realized that Luke had brought her the board with the gaillardia when he'd unfastened it from the top of the SUV. He smiled fondly at her, slowing down, as she paddled with everything she had to keep up with him.

"Put your hands by your chest and push up when the wave comes," he said as a small one headed their way. He brought one foot forward and stood up on the board, the wave rippling under him and dissipating. "Like that." He turned around as the water thundered behind him. "Here's one." He got back down onto his belly and pushed toward it and Callie followed, the rush of it filling her.

Luke put his hands on his board, so Callie did too. Then he got on his knees. She followed. With a quick movement, he planted his feet and was standing just as the wave swept her off her board, toppling her onto the sand beneath. The water felt like a million icy bubbles on her skin, chilling her sun-warmed face immediately. The rush of the tide as it pulled on her body was a welcome exercise for her stiff muscles, sore from working so much over the past few days. She came up for air and felt a hand grab hers. With her free hand, she wiped the salty water from her eyes before opening them.

"You okay?" Luke asked. His chest was wet, showing off his physique, and Callie had to make herself focus on his face. She was keenly aware that he was still holding her hand.

"Yes," she said with a smile as she pulled out of his grip and bobbed over a wave before it broke on the shore.

"I'll put my board up and come out with you on yours." Before she could say anything he paddled to shore, took the surfboard under his arm, and jogged onto the beach while she bobbed around in the water.

When he got back out to her, she turned around to face him, but he redirected her toward the waves. "Keep your head on a swivel or a wave will wipe us both out." He leaned down onto her board, and she scooted forward. "Stay where you are. I'll paddle us out."

When a wave came in, she watched its white bubbling cap while it built speed, her heart racing as they moved closer to it. Luke shifted behind her but she kept her eye on it like he'd said to do. "On your knees," he said calmly, the wave getting bigger.

The board was turning at Luke's command. "Stand up!" he said with excitement. "Bend your knees." She did, and they were both riding it in!

"Oh!" Callie said, the thrill of it overwhelming her. His hands were on her waist, their bodies close. She turned to look at him, causing both of them to lose their balance and tumble into the surf. She came up through the water and pushed her hair away from her face. "I was up for a second!" she said with a laugh.

"You were awesome! Great job!"

"Thank you," she said. She was still catching her breath. "I think it was you who did all the work, though." She climbed back up onto the surfboard and he sat behind her, the water sliding across its surface as the waves moved in and out.

"I turned us around but you balanced all by yourself."

As they sat together, an airplane with a banner advertising a seafood buffet caused a moment's shadow as it flew between them and the sun. She felt Luke's arms around her and she leaned back, letting the moment happen between them.

"That was fun," he said into her ear. She turned toward him and he touched his lips to hers, taking her breath away. "Stole one," he said with a grin.

She twisted completely around and swung her legs on either side of the board as it bobbed.

"What?" he said innocently, as if he had no idea why she'd turned to look at him. "You said you wouldn't kiss me on command, so that put me in a weird spot, since I wanted to kiss you just then. I figured I'd have to steal one."

Her lips tingled with the words that were about to come out of her mouth. Callie had never let herself be this emotionally exposed before. She debated saying it, but she knew she would anyway because it was a hundred percent true. "You didn't have to steal a kiss. I would've given it to you," she said.

His eyebrows rose at that news. He scooted closer to her, his hands moving to her hips as he steadied them on the board, his blue eyes shimmering in the sunlight.

"I didn't do this right the first time," he said. "Or just now." He leaned in slowly as if asking permission. Her stillness gave him his answer and he put his lips right near hers, his breath making her lightheaded. Then, he wrapped his arms completely around her, swallowing her in his embrace, his salty lips suddenly on hers. She closed her eyes and put her arms around his neck as he steadied them both, the water under them moving in time to their own movements.

She took in his scent—the earthy, warm smell of his skin and the lingering spice from his morning aftershave. The softness of his lips, and the way they fit together perfectly with hers—it all made Callie realize that something had been missing for her. She wanted to know everything about Luke all at once, and she didn't want a single minute to go by when she didn't have this feeling. She'd dated plenty of people before, but nothing she'd ever experienced compared to this moment and she knew that she'd never forget it as long as she lived.

Luke was the first to pull back. He smiled at her, that look that she loved so much returning. It wasn't smug at all—just like when he'd brought her coffee, she'd read it wrong when they'd met; it was his complete satisfaction and happiness with that moment. Looking at him now, she couldn't believe she'd ever read it as anything else.

"Hungry?" he asked, his gaze still devouring her.

"Yes," she said, giving in to the moment. She couldn't tell if she was hungry or not. She could hardly think about anything other than him.

They paddled to shore and he tossed the board gently into the sand next to his. "I have shrimp cocktail, herb and butter crackers made by our chef, and any fruit or veggie you can think of in the back of the truck."

When they got to the chairs, Luke asked her to sit. She watched him going back and forth between the cooler and the vehicle, beads of water on his bare skin, until he finally asked her to come around. When Callie saw what he'd done, she smiled. The entire back of the truck had a spread of food like some sort of beachy buffet, their plates and utensils ready. He'd unfolded a small camping table and two chairs just beside it, and he'd even turned on a portable radio, the music playing above the sound of the wind and sea. "You've thought of everything," she said. "It's a good thing I came today."

"It is a good thing," he said, locking eyes with her, and she knew what he meant.

Something told her that he was in her life to stay—she couldn't imagine not seeing him again. And she could feel how *good* it was.

"Thank you for bringing me here," she said as he placed her glass in front of her, filled it with wine, and took the lid off the shrimp cocktail.

"I'm glad I could show you this. I can't believe you've never been out here to see the horses." He popped a shrimp in his mouth and sat down across from her, the wind blowing his hair off his forehead.

"We always just visited Gladys at her cottage."

"And Gladys is Olivia's grandmother, right?"

"Yeah. I'm glad I spent so much time with Olivia's family growing up."

The sun was on Luke's face, making him squint just a little as he looked at her, but those blue eyes were focused. She told him about her father leaving, about her mother, and how she wished things could be different between them. "My grandmother was the one who could sort of mediate between us. She knew my mother so well that whenever I struggled with the way she was, my grandmother could always help me understand her. It was rocky to begin with but when my grandma passed, my mother and I both just sort of fell apart and our relationship never really recovered."

"I'm so sorry to hear that."

"I think about calling my mom sometimes. I just don't know what to say."

He nodded.

She liked how he listened. Olivia and Gladys were wonderful at supporting her, they were great with her, but Luke didn't try to help her. He just quietly let her talk, and his face told her everything she needed. He was right there, taking it all in, learning about her, and hearing her with no motive other than to just be. There were a lot of things she found attractive about Luke Sullivan, but this was deeper than anything she'd experienced with him, more than she'd experienced with anyone. She was falling fast and hard for this man.

Chapter Sixteen

After spending all day with Luke and then making the long trip home, it was late when Callie got back to the cottage, and Olivia and Wyatt were asleep. She closed the door quietly.

She and Luke had stayed at the beach until dusk, nearly eight-thirty in the evening, and he finally suggested that they go while he could still see the beach to get them home. She couldn't deny having thought that she didn't really care if she made it home; they could always use that blanket in the back. But she'd kept her head on her shoulders and helped him pack the things into the SUV, the painting staying up front with her. She didn't want it out of her sight for a second because today was one of the best memories she'd made so far, and that artwork would always remind her of that.

Callie clicked on the light in her bedroom and leaned the painting against the wall, admiring its beauty. After surfing, packing the SUV, and the drive, she felt exhaustion setting in. She'd had a big day and she had a lot of work ahead of her tomorrow. After a quick shower, it was time to settle into bed.

Her mind was going at warp speed, rehashing her night, questions filling her head one after another: questions about her mom, about her life, her feelings for Luke... With an uncomfortable huff, she turned over, pulling the blanket with her, and lay on her side, her eyes wide. She wanted to turn off her thoughts, but she couldn't, so she got up and clicked on the light. Normally, reading was how she settled her mind, but she had yet to buy a book, having not had any time to read since she'd gotten to The Beachcomber. She grabbed Alice's journal. Maybe searching for information about Frederick would take her mind off everything.

Her eyes aching for sleep but her mind denying it, she opened up to the page where she'd stopped reading last and began.

What if this child doesn't fit into his world? What if the child is supposed to be in our world, my world? I'm his aunt, for God's sake, and he has no idea! This sweet baby boy has been taken from us—his family—stolen. If I allow myself to think about it, it tears me up. When I'm out, I look for him. In every stroller, in every shopping cart, on every street corner, I look, but I don't run into him. I don't get to see him grow up. And neither will Frederick. I don't know how my brother can live with himself.

Baby boy? Callie stared at the black through her window, the journal only adding to the chaos in her head. With a pang of guilt, she shut the book, not feeling relaxed in the slightest by reading it. Callie set the journal down and turned off the light. In the darkness, she tried to relax and not think about anything except what she needed to get done tomorrow.

* * *

"This is beautiful," Olivia said, holding Luke's painting up. She leaned it against the wall and grabbed her coffee from the only side table in the room. "We should put it here in the family room. Where did you get it?"

"Luke painted it."

Olivia's eyes grew round as she cupped her mug with both hands. "Really?" She was standing in a T-shirt, her hair pulled off her face into a clip.

Callie nodded with a smile but she wasn't thinking about the painting. She was thinking about yesterday. She caught herself as the back of her hand brushed her lips, reliving his kiss. She cleared her throat. "I like him," she admitted.

With an excited smile, Olivia said, "I know you do. I can tell." She set her coffee down. "I'm so excited for you!" She put her arms around Callie and gave her a squeeze.

"I more than *like* him, Olivia. He's one of the greatest people I've met. He gets me and he's kind and thoughtful."

"I'm so glad that you're admitting this to yourself. Feel it! Let the fireworks happen because they're amazing."

With a smile, Callie nodded. "You're right."

There was a knock interrupting their moment, and Olivia sent Callie to get it, scurrying upstairs to put on more clothes. But she was back down before Callie had even gotten to the door, having thrown on a pair of shorts, running her fingers through her hair. Callie grinned. She certainly seemed excited.

Aiden stood at the front door, a hard hat in one hand, his computer bag slung over his shoulder, and he was holding a white orchid in a small pot, wrapped in cellophane. "Oh my gosh, Aiden," Olivia said as he handed it to her. "Orchids are my very favorite flower."

"I remember," he said with a grin. "You were the only college student I know who could actually keep plants alive. Most of us could hardly grow that plant that Joe had in the window. The half-dead one. What was it?"

"A philodendron." She laughed.

Callie knew how difficult orchids were to keep, yet somehow Olivia could do it. She watered them with three ice cubes once a week and she always knew the correct placement for proper light. Callie knew that because Olivia was her best friend. But what caught her attention was that Aiden had remembered it. All of a sudden she recalled how close he'd been to Olivia at the party, and his friendliness now definitely seemed like a little more.

"The crew's on the way. They were just behind me, so we'll be able to get going soon. We'll have to cut the power again."

"That's okay," Olivia said. "Let me get you a drink to cool you off. It's going to get pretty hot in here once you get working. What would you like?" She started toward the kitchen and turned around. "I have iced tea, soda, milk, water…"

"Iced tea would be great."

Callie pulled up one of the beach chairs for him and followed Olivia into the kitchen. "I'll help you, Olivia. Have a seat, Aiden, and we'll bring it out." Then she hurried behind her friend.

"Olivia," she whispered with urgency. "Did you notice what I noticed?"

"What's that?" Olivia set the orchid on the counter and pulled a glass from the cabinet, filling it with ice.

Callie leaned into her space to pull her attention toward her. "I think Aiden might have a crush on you," she whispered.

Olivia tipped her head back and laughed as she retrieved the pitcher of iced tea from the newly delivered fridge. "Don't be ridiculous," she said, her words coming out a little less assured than she'd planned, clearly. There was a sparkle of excitement in her eyes before she turned away from Callie.

"He brought you an orchid."

"He was just being nice," she said over her shoulder. "I've known him a long time."

"Let's just say that I don't have guy friends bringing me orchids."

"He's been thoughtful ever since I've known him. He always does nice things for me like that." She returned the pitcher to the fridge.

"Oh really," Callie said suggestively.

Olivia took the glass off the counter. "Please." She pursed her lips, took the glass with her, and left the room, but there was a little spring to her step.

The chair in the family room was empty, Aiden's hard hat and bag leaning against the wall. "Where did he go?" Callie asked. They checked the hallway but it was empty and the bathroom door was open.

Callie heard laughter and went to the front window. Aiden was playing catch with Wyatt. Between catches, he was throwing the ball up and catching it behind his back, making Wyatt laugh. Callie didn't have to say anything for Olivia to understand what she was thinking.

Olivia looked back out the window, pensively. Callie knew how afraid she was of relationships—they weren't easy when a child was involved—but, by the look on her face, Olivia might feel a little something for Aiden as well.

* * *

"Oh, that's perfect!" Olivia said as Callie added the last pillow to the bed upstairs. The furniture had come around ten o'clock and Callie had been working frantically to get the room done, just itching to tick one item off their "to do" list. She felt as though things were coming together as she finished it.

This room was called The Windy Sails Suite, as it had its own bathroom and small sitting area attached. A few days ago, Olivia had painted the walls a light sea-foam green, and they had picked out a whitewashed bedroom set with a matching sunburst mirror that had the same finish for above the bed. The linens were a crisp white and they were complemented by tan and pink throw pillows. Callie arranged three white beach-themed sculptures on the dresser.

She stepped back with pride to view her hard work, thinking of all the people who would enjoy this room, and tugged on her shirt to cool off a little—the air was humid and stuffy. "How's Aiden coming along downstairs?"

"The crew's removed all the windows in the family room so our wonderful air conditioning is off for the moment. They're about to begin demo on the back wall." Aiden had insisted that keeping the same architectural style as the rest of the house with the large windows at the back was the way to go, but to get the greatest view, it would be best to move them a little more than he'd originally thought before adding the French doors. "You know," she said, looking a little too casual, like she had to work at it. "Maybe we could all go out one night or something—you, Luke, Aiden, and me. That might be fun."

"Oh really?" Callie teased.

"As friends!"

With a grin, she let it go. "Maybe." She'd just let whatever was happening happen.

* * *

Callie decided to sit out on the beach to relax after the long day. Before she left the cottage, she grabbed the journal—she still didn't have any quality reading material and her curiosity was winning out. What was the harm in reading it, really? She'd probably never find Frederick anyway. With a glass of wine in one hand, the journal in another, and that now-familiar salty breeze coming off the ocean, she dropped her bag into the sand and sat down in her beach chair.

Callie opened the journal to where she'd left off, letting the late sun warm her face.

I saw him today! He's eight…

That was Wyatt's age.

His birthday was two weeks ago. I know the date by heart: October 20th. His front teeth have grown in—they're too big for him, but they make his face look so much older. His blond hair is lighter than I would've thought, given his daddy's complexion, but there's no denying him. He looks just like Frederick. I walked slowly past him and he dropped his baseball. I picked it up for him before it rolled away. When I handed it back, he said, "Thank you," and my heart almost melted. His mother hurried him along the sidewalk but I stood there and watched him go until he was out of sight. I had a scarf on my head to protect it from the wind today, and my sunglasses on. I wondered if his mother would recognize me, but she was in such a hurry, I don't think she paid me any notice. I was glad for the scarf though. But honestly, I don't know if she'd know me anyway.

Callie felt a connection to this little boy. She wondered what had become of him. Unable to cease her curiosity, she read the next entry.

I keep thinking of all the time I've missed with my nephew. Frederick may have decided against telling him who he was, but I didn't get a choice in the matter, and he's my family too. I would've liked to bake cookies with him or see him unwrap his birthday presents. I could take him on trips to the aquarium; we could build sandcastles together. Seeing him the other day was bittersweet: It was like taking a breath after being held underwater, but now, I just feel emptier. He looks like such a sweet boy. I wish I could know him.

She sat for the longest time, her finger in the journal, marking its place, thinking as the water sparkled on the horizon. Her dad had missed out on all those things too—had he had thoughts like Alice's? What about Frederick? Why would he just leave his child? How could people do that?

As lovely as it was out there, she needed to get up and make dinner—it was her night. The builders were finishing up for the day but coming again tomorrow to complete the walkway that would run from the yard to the ocean, and she still had to put in the order for landscaping with the local garden shop. She stood up, closed the journal, and folded up her chair, then headed toward the house.

* * *

"You'll never believe this," Gladys said over her empty dinner plate. She'd refused to let Callie cook tonight. She'd brought them a whole dinner.

By the look on Gladys's face, she'd clearly been waiting until after the meal to tell Callie and Olivia this news so she could have their undivided attention. Wyatt was fishing on the beach while the three ladies had a glass of wine. Gladys's face was animated as she reached into the pocket of her shorts and pulled out a slip of paper. "Adelaide found Frederick's number." She slid the paper across the table.

Callie clapped a hand over her mouth as she peered down at the handwritten phone number scrawled across the little piece of paper. "Let's call him," she said through her fingers.

"Right now?" Olivia asked, swirling her wine in her

glass with a smile. "This means a lot to you, doesn't it?"

"Yes. I want him to have what's rightfully his. He might not even know Alice had that lockbox. It could have valuable items in it, personal items." She thought back to that baby boy.

Gladys nodded toward the paper. "Call him." The way she said it, her encouragement seemed more rooted in support for Callie than in the excitement of reaching Frederick.

With an air of drama, Callie pulled her phone from her pocket and, a zinging feeling running through her fingers, she dialed the number. After two rings, there was an answer.

"Hello?"

She cleared her throat, setting down her wine and sitting up straight. "Um, my name is Callie Weaver. I'm the new owner of Alice McFarlin's place..." The silence that followed was slightly unsettling, so she plowed on. "I'm looking for her brother, Frederick. Is this him speaking?"

"Yes," he said kindly, causing her to exhale.

She smiled excitedly at Gladys and Olivia.

"Hi," she said a bit too enthusiastically. "We've found a lockbox with your initials on it. I think it might be yours, and I'd like to return it to you."

"Oh. That's very kind of you."

"Yes, well, I didn't know if you were missing it or not." More silence.

"Yes, I've missed it," he said softly. "I know just the box you're talking about. I thought it was gone, but Alice must've kept it. I'm glad she did."

"Can we arrange a day and time to meet so I can give it back?"

"Of course. How about tomorrow?"

"That would be perfect! Maybe around two?"

"Thank you for going out of your way."

"You're welcome." She couldn't believe it; she was going to get the lockbox back to its rightful owner. How lucky was that?

Chapter Seventeen

Callie lay in bed holding the journal in her hands, grinding her teeth, guilt washing over her for just holding it now that she could actually give it back to someone. There was no reason to read it. She'd be delivering it to Frederick tomorrow. She'd only allowed herself to read it before because she was hoping to find him and now she had.

She put it back on the dresser and tried to go to sleep. But, she wondered, who was the man she would encounter tomorrow? What might Alice have said? Callie closed her eyes and rolled over onto her side, away from the dresser. But the more she lay there in the dark, the more she stewed about how Frederick had abandoned his child. Her pulse sped up as she reached up and grabbed the journal. Hoping to understand him a little better, she opened it and read, curling up under her sheet and summer blanket, the tiny lamp by her air mattress giving her enough light to see the words.

I spoke to Frederick. We'd spent a long time talking over coffee and I had waited until just the right moment to mention the topic. See, any talk about Frederick's son is off limits. He closes right up. But this time was different. I'd seen the boy again—I've seen him many times now, and it doesn't make it any easier. He was at the intersection by the new hotel, his car packed to the brim with things, and I wondered if he was going away to college. He'd graduated high school just before the summer. I went to his graduation to watch him walk across the stage and get his diploma. Frederick didn't tell me he was going, but I saw him hanging back behind the crowd. I asked him if he ever wished things were different. He replied, "Well they're not, so why should we bother wishing something that won't happen." He got up and left the room.

Irritation burned inside her and she wanted to go to Frederick right now and shake him. What if his son wondered where he'd gotten his height from or his features? Shouldn't he at least be allowed the choice of knowing? With a huff, she picked up the journal and decided to read on. But she wasn't prepared for what she read next.

The boy has come home! I don't know why I call him "the boy." Maybe saying his name would make the situation too real, and I'd fall apart. He's home from college and he's back in town.
    He's flashy now, like his family.

Callie stopped, her gaze lingering on that last sentence, the wheels in her head turning. She shook it off and kept reading.

He's at that age where he feels invincible, like he could conquer the world. And, given his upbringing and his money, he probably will.

She was unwilling to think the thought that was pushing its way through her mind, her fingers feeling unusually light as she turned the page.

But when I look at him, I still see Frederick's face and the smile of the little boy who dropped his baseball all those years ago. I wish one day he could know that I've been there. I've watched his soccer games and been at his choir performances; I've walked down the beach until it becomes his family's private property and I've seen him building sandcastles. I've watched him grow into the young man he is now, and whenever I can, I try to send him my love in little glances, smiles, whatever the moment will allow. He is my family and I'm there for my family.

When she'd first met Luke, she'd mentioned Alice McFarlin and he'd said, "I saw her everywhere."

An icy cold slithered through her. *Oh my God.*

She got up and went into the kitchen, taking the journal with her. She pulled a knife from the drawer and went over to the lockbox, wedging the point of it into the lock and twisting, but it wouldn't turn. From the look of the box, it didn't seem terribly secure, though; if she tried hard enough, she might just get it open. She grabbed a sharper knife. With a shaky hand, she jabbed it into the lock again and frantically pushed, prodded, twisted. Nothing.

"Whatcha doing?" Wyatt said with a sleepy face as he padded into the kitchen.

Callie jumped, throwing the knives back into a drawer. "Oh, just trying to see if I could open this old thing," she said as calmly as she could, her hands still trembling, her heart pounding. With a little smile put on for Wyatt's benefit, she slid the box back into the pantry. "What are you doing up?"

"I'm thirsty," he said, scratching the back of his neck and yawning.

"I'll get you some water and you can take it up to bed. How does that sound?"

He nodded, gritting his teeth to stifle another yawn.

* * *

The idea was ridiculous. She was just reading into things. But those words from the journal kept shouting at her as she lay in bed the next morning, her eyes burning from a terrible night's sleep. She reached over and twisted her clock around—ten o'clock! She'd slept half the day! She squeezed her eyes shut and tried to clear her head, which felt like it was full of cotton, her capacity for coherent thought completely drained.

She opened the window and took in the morning air, noticing the clouds rolling in. The heat overwhelmed her enough to shut it, and she went downstairs.

"Morning, sleepy head!" Olivia said. She and Gladys were sorting plates and putting them away in the large storage cabinets they'd had installed for guests' dishes. Well, Gladys was mostly chatting while Olivia sorted, but Olivia liked things just so—both Gladys and Callie knew that—which might have been why Gladys was doing more assisting than actual sorting.

"Morning." She pulled a glass from the cabinet and

filled it with orange juice. "I'll help you with that as soon as I get a little food into my system."

"No worries. You should have your breakfast outside before the storm comes. It's hot but the ocean breeze is still nice."

Callie nodded. "I think I will."

"Why don't I join you?" Gladys stood up and pressed against her lower back in a stretch. "It'll give Olivia some peace and quiet. I've been rattling on to her all morning about nothing in particular. You look like you're still tired. Let me make you an egg sandwich," said Gladys. "Go outside and relax; the heat'll push the exhaustion right out of you."

"I don't mind making myself some breakfast." She took a sip of her juice.

"Make an old woman feel useful." Gladys was already pulling a pan out and turning on the gas stove, the little blue flame popping and igniting under the pan.

"Okay," she relented, heading toward the back porch. "Thank you."

"No problem at all."

Callie stepped onto the porch and pushed the screen door open, her juice glass already fogging up in the relentless heat. It was oppressive today, even with the thick cloud cover. She sat down on the edge of the walkway and set her orange juice on one of the boards, the new wood a yellow color. It would take some time to age it but the salt would certainly help things along. The tide pulled and pushed against the shore, the spray exploding angrily with every crash. She looked up at the clouds; thick as they were, they didn't do much to block the brightness, and she wished she'd grabbed her sunglasses.

Gladys had been right. Out here, she felt more alive, the fresh air bringing light to her thoughts. She'd been jumping to conclusions with the journal. It didn't make any sense at all, and she had let the late hour and her sleepy mind play tricks on her. She thought about telling Gladys about it, as she had always been the person she'd talked to over the years about things. She and Olivia were the only ones who knew Callie's real feelings about her mother and their strained relationship after her beloved grandmother had passed.

She could ask Gladys about Frederick...But then again, she was going to see him soon so perhaps she'd have her answers then.

"Phew! The wind is pickin' up, isn't it?" Gladys said as she strode down the walk barefoot, holding a plate with the steaming sandwich. She set it down on Callie's lap as Callie helped her steady it. "Got it?"

Callie nodded.

"You look like you've been through the wringer."

"I think it was just the wine last night," she said before taking a bite of her sandwich and thanking Gladys with a smile.

Gladys sat down next to her. "Could be the storm coming. The barometric pressure makes you feel different sometimes. I'm always my most creative just before a storm." She looked out at the ocean. "I think that's why Olivia's inside nesting. Something about a summer thunderstorm makes a person feel like hunkering down in a cozy spot. I left her organizing a closet upstairs. She'd already finished all those dishes," she said with a grin.

Callie smiled.

"Something's eating at ya," Gladys said. "What is it?"

Callie looked down at her half-eaten sandwich.

"The truth will set you free," Gladys said with a knowing smile.

"I was just wondering about Frederick McFarlin. Did you know him very well?"

Gladys shook her head. "He spent a lot of time to himself, and then when we were young—in our early thirties—he just disappeared. I did ask Alice once, and she just said he'd moved. Alice looked so frazzled over it that I just didn't feel it was my place to ask anything else. She seemed closed off about it."

They sat quietly for a while, and Callie finished her sandwich.

"How's your mama?" Gladys said as if she were changing subjects. Callie didn't want to think about how the question tied to her last comment about being closed off, but she knew it did. Callie didn't argue or have anything against her mother; they'd just sort of drifted apart. The more time Callie spent with Olivia and her family, the closer she got with them and the less she had to think about her mother's unwillingness to communicate.

"She's fine, I guess."

"You guess?" she asked, her words gentle. "You know, I was thinking that maybe you should invite her to the opening of The Beachcomber. I'll bet she'd be really proud of you."

Callie nodded, unable to produce more than that. She'd had the same thought herself. She felt an over-whelming guilt that she couldn't define. She knew she should be keenly aware of how her own mother was doing and want to invite her to things like that, but what little relationship they'd possessed had just slipped away.

Gladys put her hands on her knees, her fingers spreading over them for balance, and pushed herself up. "I should probably head on," she said. "I'm giving the house a good clean today and then I'm going to my daughter's house just in case this storm hits worse than expected." She was good at knowing when to stop the discussion about Callie's mother, and that was what she was doing now, Callie was nearly sure of it.

Callie followed suit, grabbing her empty orange juice glass in one hand, her plate in the other. "I know. It's getting late and I'd like to plant the bushes before it rains. I only have until afternoon and then I'm going to take that lockbox back to Frederick."

* * *

Wyatt smiled, pride filling his face as he came outside. Callie had picked up the bushes she'd called in this morning and now, on her knees, wrist deep in soil, she was nearly done. She looked up from her planting. She'd gotten the whole row of bushes done along the new walkway and the sky had been grumbling the last few minutes.

"Guess what I did," he said. "I got the lock open on the lockbox for you. There's stuff inside."

Callie stared at him, her hands still, all her questions from last night slamming back into the front of her mind. She was suddenly unsure of how she wanted to proceed. She wasn't certain she wanted to pry into Frederick's life now. She knew why: She was really afraid to find out any more about that baby boy. Callie swallowed her worry, took off her gardening gloves, and slowly stood up.

"Come on!" Wyatt grabbed her by the arm, pulling her up the walk.

When she got inside, Callie protectively looked in on the contents of the box, not wanting to disturb anything. Olivia came over and peered down at it curiously before congratulating Wyatt on getting it open. Carefully, Callie pulled out a small sketchpad, setting it delicately on the table. There was a local high school graduation program…She reached into the box again, taking out a stack of newspaper and magazine clippings, and—she stopped breathing—all of them were about the Sullivan family.

Confusion swam across Olivia's face. "That's weird," she said, but her attention was pulled away when Wyatt asked a question. Callie wasn't listening. Slowly, her breath shallow, she set them down and retrieved the sketchpad. She swallowed and opened it. Her heart rose into her throat as she saw drawings. One was of a dog on a street. She turned the page: an ocean landscape. They were so good. "He's an artist," she whispered to herself, still trying to find her breath.

Wyatt wanted to show Olivia something that he'd made. "I'll be right back," she said as he pulled her away.

Callie turned the page and had to hold on to the chair for support. It was a pencil sketch of the wild horses and a woman looking out at the ocean, only her back visible, with a small boy by her side. Callie could still hear Luke's voice when he'd told her about the beach with the horses: *My mom used to bring me here when I was a kid.*

She shut the sketchpad, needing a moment to process all this, her skin cold.

She shoved everything back into the lockbox, and shut it, wriggling the latch until it had closed. She inspected it to make sure it didn't look like anyone had pried into it, and it looked fine. Her heart raced in her chest, her fingertips like ice despite the heat, her mouth dry. She pushed the lockbox back into the pantry and shut the door. Her hands lingered on the knob as if she had to keep the box from escaping. A loud clap of thunder boomed, shaking her to the core.

Chapter Eighteen

Callie's hands were sweaty as she drove the hour-long drive, the lockbox and Alice's journal on her passenger seat. She hadn't told Olivia what she suspected about Luke or what was drawn in the sketchpad.

She'd asked Frederick to come to The Beachcomber, but he'd said he didn't feel like he could. He just wasn't strong enough. He couldn't face the house and all its memories. Now she understood why—it was more than just losing Alice. Callie wrestled with whether or not to mention her suspicions about Luke to Frederick. How would she bring something like that up? Her stomach churned. She could just give him the box and be on her way. But didn't Gladys always say that the truth would set you free? Yet what good could come of this truth?

As Callie drove, the sky was a threatening shade of gray, lightning flashes radiating through the clouds. The forecasters were watching a fast-moving category four hurricane off the coast of Kingston, Jamaica. It was headed for the East Coast, but they weren't sure if it would move off to sea. She didn't want to worry unnecessarily—storms like this were more common in autumn and residents knew how to prepare for them, but it wasn't losing strength as it moved, and being late summer, it was very early in the season to have this type of storm. It was projected that if it made landfall in the U.S., it could hit the Outer Banks directly. While The Beachcomber's porches wouldn't be finished before the hurricane hit, the walls would be completed out back and they'd installed the latest hurricane window shutters throughout to protect the house. It had stood strong in storms for decades.

The rain began to fall on Callie's windshield: First one big drop, then two, then a few more as if the clouds were holding on for dear life, their grasp slipping. Then suddenly a sheeting rain came pouring down, making it difficult to see. Thunder clapped loudly as Callie clicked her windshield wipers on high and turned on the headlights. The rain was coming at a slant and nearly clouding her view completely. She put on her flashers and slowed down, both hands on the wheel.

Worried she'd miss the next turn, since she'd never taken this route before and visibility was low, she decided to pull off for a minute and let the worst of it pass. Callie looked over at the items in her front seat. *What am I doing?* she thought.

Her mind went to Luke. He'd had no say in this matter so far. Did he even have an inkling about any of it? He'd told her how difficult things had been with his father, Edward—surely this would damage that beyond repair. Maybe she should just leave the lockbox on the doorstep and forget she ever knew a thing. Yes. That was probably best. If Frederick wanted to be in Luke's life that was his choice to make, not Callie's.

She was almost there, the rain was already letting up, and yet she sat paralyzed. But then she remembered Alice's words in the journal: *He allows his heart to lead him, he's too honest, and he jumps before he realizes the consequences.* Callie checked for traffic and then pulled off, the air thick with humidity.

She made the last few turns and pulled up outside a small house. It was a brick ranch with a minimal but tidy amount of landscaping. She pulled into the paved drive and parked behind a white sedan. The rain had tapered off to a continuous drizzle. It clouded her windshield as she deliberated one last time. Then, with a deep breath, she gathered the items in the passenger seat and got out of the car, jogging up to the front door and setting the lockbox on the stoop. She placed the journal on top of it, nerves making her stomach uneasy.

The door opened and she jumped, facing a tall man with dark hair graying at the sides, his bright blue eyes inquisitive as he smiled at her with a familiar smile. She'd seen it so many times on Luke's face; this confirmed her suspicions completely. She tried to control her breathing as the panic welled up again.

"Are you Frederick McFarlin?" she asked, although she already knew the answer just by looking at him.

"Yes." His smile faded to a look of trepidation as he focused on the lockbox at her side. Then, as if snapping out of it, he came back up to her face, producing another smile.

"I'm Callie Weaver—"

"Please. Come in."

"Oh no, it's fine. Don't let me trouble you."

"It's no trouble. Let me make you a drink to thank you for coming all this way."

"I shouldn't—I have to be getting back to the house."

"Oh." His face fell a little. "You sure? It's really no trouble."

Callie knew she should leave, but his kind eyes made her relent and she picked up the lockbox and journal, and followed him in. She didn't know why, but she'd expected an artist's studio or something. The décor was eclectic— he had wooden artwork displayed above the sofa, pieces of driftwood carved into waves and fish; there were photos of waterfalls and an aerial one of a shoreline. She walked over to a painting but, judging by what she'd seen of his drawings, it didn't look like one of his—she couldn't really tell, though.

"How about that drink? Would you like coffee? Or water, tea…"

"A glass of water would be nice," she said.

Frederick left the room and Callie looked around, hoping to find some evidence of his life that could give her answers. He had a few framed photos on the wall but they were of places—maybe locations he'd visited. There was a magazine rack in the corner filled with books. The mantel on the small, brick fireplace was empty.

He returned, set a glass of iced water on the coffee table, and sat back down in the recliner, next to the box. "So, you've bought my sister's place."

Callie perched on the sofa opposite him. "I've admired it since I was a little girl."

"You going to open it back up again?" He ran his hands back and forth along the arms of the chair and Callie wondered if it was a nervous gesture.

She nodded. "We plan to. My best friend Olivia Dixon

owns it with me. Did you ever meet her? Gladys Dixon's granddaughter."

"Gladys Dixon?" He was settling into the conversation now, his shoulders falling a little, and Callie could feel her own body relax in response.

"She's lived across the street from Alice for thirty years."

He smiled. "Oh, Gladys! She's a nice lady. I wasn't around the house a lot in those days." His gaze rested on the lockbox.

"Oh, well, I think you'd love what we've done with the place. We've cleaned it all up. We're putting porches on all the back rooms, repainting everything. I'd like to get a mural painted in the front room. I haven't arranged to have anyone come out but I have someone in mind."

He seemed so absorbed by the lockbox, Callie wasn't sure if he'd even heard her. He leaned forward and ran his hand over the lid. "It's open!"

She set her glass down. "Yes—I'm so sorry. Olivia's son, Wyatt, jimmied it open and I didn't have the key to lock it again."

Frederick put the box on the table and stared at the closed lid. "Did you look inside?"

Callie squirmed. "I know I shouldn't have . . . Frederick, I'm so sorry. It was none of my business." Her head pounded. What was she supposed to do now? Tell him she knew Luke? Run away?

Frederick slowly eased the lid open and pulled out the drawings on top. He studied the horses, sketched in perfectly haphazard scribbles, and slid his finger under the edge of the paper, revealing a sketch of just the fingers of a woman's hand on the next sheet. But he didn't turn the page.

Callie could feel her heart rising into her throat. "Are these your drawings?"

He blinked rapidly. "Yes." He looked away.

"Do you still draw?"

"No."

Callie cleared her throat. "I should go. I'm sorry."

He looked up. "Please..." His eyes were wide.

It would be best to go right now, before things got even more complicated, but she couldn't leave him like this— he looked so sad. She lowered herself again. "Why don't you draw anymore?" she asked boldly.

He didn't say anything. She reached out to get her water, hoping that her hand wouldn't shake when she held it. She took a sip to buy herself time. What was she supposed to do? Wasn't it dishonest of her to sit and pretend she didn't know what was going on? And this man, he wasn't a father who didn't care. He was broken by his loss.

She mustered up her energy and said, "It's just...I know an artist, and I was so impressed by him that I feel it would be a great loss if he ever stopped painting." She leaned forward for emphasis. "He painted the horses in Corolla for me. He took me there because he said his mother used to take him as a child." When she said that, Frederick looked as though he'd been punched in the gut, the color draining out of his face.

"Luke?"

She nodded.

Without taking his eyes off her, Frederick turned to the next sketch. He pulled his eyes away finally and his gaze fell onto the page with the woman. He was quiet as his eyes moved over the drawing. Callie allowed the silence. She sipped her water and watched, waiting for the response that was causing him great emotion to produce.

He cleared his throat. "This was my last drawing." He tilted his head back as if to catch the tears that brimmed in his eyes. He blinked them away. "When I'd finished it, I walked up to the woman in the picture. So as not to worry Luke, I simply said, 'It's a beautiful day.' She smiled at me. She'd brought Luke there to play so I could see him. And her." He closed his eyes as if the memory were able to calm him. "I asked her..." He opened his eyes again and looked back at Callie, his shaking hands on his knees. "If she thought there would be more beautiful days like this one in the future. I remember, she pursed her lips and said, simply, 'I don't think so.' She was never going to tell him. She assured me of that. It was the last time I drew her and her son."

"Your son."

Frederick hung his head and without warning, he started to sob. Callie didn't know what to do. She got up, set down her water, and put her arms around him. His back heaved as he cried, and her heart broke for this man. She grabbed a tissue from a box that was on the small table next to them and handed it to him. "He has your smile," she said, but it only made him cry more.

Luke had said his mother *used to* take him to that beach—as in more than once. Had she changed her mind and gone back? Had she been waiting for Frederick and he'd never shown up again? Callie sat down on the floor in front of him to try to get him to look at her. "You love him. Why didn't you ever tell him?" She could feel her own tears rising and she knew that it was because those were the questions she'd had for her own father.

"It's complicated," he said, sitting up and trying unsuccessfully to get himself together.

She reached over and got her water, pushing her own

emotion back down where it had come from. "I meant to give you the box and leave. But I feel like I have to tell you—I already know half your story. I wanted to find out where you were and I thought there might be some clue in your sister's journal, so I read it. I had no idea, at first, that it was about someone I knew."

Frederick looked unsure, but at the same time he seemed as if he'd held this burden all by himself for so many years that he was dying to let someone else help him deal with it.

"It might not change anything, but you wouldn't have to endure it all alone. I know you didn't tell Alice a lot—she wrote about that in her journal."

"That's because she judged me. She was angry with me for giving him up so easily, but she didn't know that I cried myself to sleep every single night. I never married or had kids. I didn't have any will to after losing him and Lillian, because I knew that I had a son and I wasn't allowed to be in his life."

"Said who?"

"Lillian."

"Why was she the only one with a say in this matter?"

"I was the quintessential starving artist. I had nothing to offer. She'd been unfaithful to her husband, and knowledge of that would've caused a messy divorce. She'd have lost everything. But that aside, she told me she regretted it. She felt terribly guilty, and said she would spend the rest of her life being the perfect wife to make it up to him. We agreed to keep it quiet and Luke would have a wonderful life, a life grander than anything I could've offered. He went to top schools, he had the best upbringing money could buy. And now look at him."

She sat there, letting this information sink in. But at the same time, she felt like Luke should know.

"You said he paints?" Frederick asked, interest on his face.

She nodded. "He's amazing."

He put his fingers to his lips and lifted his eyes up toward the ceiling, all that pain welling up again. The anguish seemed so great that all she wanted to do was help him. She thought about Luke and his passion for art, how he lit up whenever he talked about painting, how thrilled he was as he painted the horses for her. She couldn't imagine the pain that must have caused Frederick to put a halt to that kind of passion.

"So he painted for you? The horses?" he asked, pulling her out of her thoughts. He had life behind those aging eyes all of a sudden.

She nodded.

"I painted them for Lillian." He stretched his wrinkled fingers out and inspected them as if he'd still see the paint under his nails all these years later. "I wonder what she did with the painting." His mouth turned down, uncertainty showing.

What *had* she done with it? Had she hidden it somewhere, thrown it out, or was it on display to remind her...?

"I sometimes think about painting again," he said. "It's a delicate thing, though, creativity. Art is a manifestation of our feelings, our soul, and my expression was of love and happiness. Without those two things, I couldn't do it anymore. After she and Luke had left my life, I stared at a blank canvas for days, paint dripping from my brush onto my boots, and nothing would come from my hand. So I stopped."

Callie eyed the lockbox sitting on the floor. "Did you keep all those articles in there? Or did Alice?"

Frederick looked up and rubbed the scruff on his face with his dry hands, making a scraping sound.

He shook his head as if it didn't matter. "I clipped all those, yes. I miss the Outer Banks so much. I miss my art. And I miss seeing Luke. I wish I could be strong enough to be near him, but the older we both get, the harder it becomes because there are so many lost years between us." The tears started brimming again, his nose red, his cheeks flushed. He looked away, his lip beginning to quiver. All those years were welling up to the surface and spilling over, and it was breaking Callie's heart to watch it. He'd held himself away from his home, from Luke, from Alice, from his passion...

"Would you paint the mural for me at The Beach-comber?" she heard herself ask, the final word coming out before she snapped her mouth shut. What was she saying? She shouldn't have said it, but she knew why she had: He could come back to the place he loved and be with the boy he'd lost. If it could only be that easy...

"I'm sorry," he said. "I just couldn't."

Callie nodded, feeling like a complete idiot for even asking. How would she have explained herself to Luke if Frederick had been there and it had all come out? How would she have ever answered to the fact that she had actually invited him there? She was so relieved he'd said no.

After she left and all the way home, flashes of her conversation with Frederick filled her mind, like rapid-fire clips, making her second-guess everything she'd said and done. She shouldn't have interfered. She might ruin Luke's life, not to mention Lillian's, if this got out. Could it? Hopefully not. She promised herself she'd never utter a word of it. She wouldn't tell Olivia anything, which was causing her anxiety because she told her best friend everything. But with Olivia's ties to Aiden, she just couldn't risk it. She worried about how she'd ever face Luke again. How could she look at him, knowing what she knew, and not tell him? The more she drove, the more upset she became, the thoughts eating away at her, making her wish she'd never found that box and journal.

* * *

"So, did you meet him?" Olivia said as she poured them both a glass of wine and peered out the window into the darkness to try to see if there were any changes in the weather. The radio was spitting out the latest report; the storm was gaining speed instead of losing steam as they'd hoped.

Callie only realized just then that Aiden was there. She focused on the large, circular clock they'd put up over the table, her heartbeats winning in the race against the second hand. He'd just come in to get settled and was looking on, drinking his own glass of wine. She smiled at him, trying to keep her thoughts to herself. Had Olivia told him about the box and all the articles about the Sullivans? Olivia was whistling—actually whistling—while making their dinner: lemon chicken casserole with her famous bread crumble.

"So?" Olivia looked over her shoulder. "Did you meet Frederick?" she asked again.

"Yes," Callie said.

"And what was all that stuff he had in the box?"

Callie smiled nervously. "Turns out the contents of the lockbox were nothing too important." She felt terrible telling her friend that, but she knew that with Aiden there, she couldn't risk telling Olivia the truth, even if she wanted to.

"Did he say anything about his son?"

Callie wished she'd never mentioned what she'd read to Olivia, but in her curiosity the other day, she had.

Aiden was watching her from behind his glass, completely oblivious to the reaction going on in her body. Her shoulders were pinching, heat sliding up her neck.

"No, I didn't think it was my business," she said calmly.

She gazed out the window at the things left by the workers, who had finished hours ago. Because of the vaulted ceilings, they'd hired painters for the family room. More furniture was also coming—she'd gotten the call for the delivery—and Aiden's guys were finishing the small back expansion and the porches.

"Luke called," Olivia said. "He couldn't get you on your phone, so he called Aiden to see if you were here."

Any attempt Callie had made to get the prior conversation out of her mind dissolved in that one word: Luke. He was going to ask her where she had been. Had Olivia told him? This was all getting too crazy. She needed to take a step away from it, give it time. Suddenly aware that Olivia was watching her, she checked her phone. Two missed calls. His number.

"Call him back," Olivia said. "He seemed like he wanted to tell you something."

"Okay," Callie said, pushing a smile to her lips.

* * *

"Go out with me tomorrow," Luke said. His voice was light and carefree like it had always been. "I want to see you."

Callie lay on her back, sprawled on her air mattress, her hair fanned out over her pillow. She wanted to see him too, but she was so afraid she'd tell him something she shouldn't. She was worried she'd let something slip. "I can't," she said. "I've got a ton of work on the cottage."

"It'll all still be there when we get back," he urged. "What's a couple of hours?"

"I'm sorry. I just can't."

"Well, I'll help then."

"No, Luke," she said, trying to keep herself from sounding desperate. "I need to focus, and you distract me."

She heard a huff and could feel his smile on the other end. "I distract you?" His voice was smooth like silk, and she rolled over in frustration, burying her face in her pillow.

She finally flipped over to answer him. "Yes. You distract me. Now let me work!" Before she could be persuaded, she got off the phone, claiming her work was going to take half the night and all day tomorrow. Her hands trembling, Callie shook her head, wondering how she'd ever get through this.

Chapter Nineteen

"I'm smitten with Aiden," Olivia said the next morning, sitting beside Callie at the kitchen table, her eyebrows bouncing up and down as she held her cup of coffee in front of her face as if she were hiding behind it, the mere thought of Aiden making her cheeks rosy. But then her face dropped. "But I'm worried," she said before Callie could get excited for her.

"About what?" Callie scooted her chair closer and then stirred her coffee. She set the spoon down beside her mug, her eyes on Olivia.

"He's a wonderful man. I've known him for ages..."

"I know he really likes you, Olivia. It isn't hard to tell."

Olivia nodded. "But what if I let myself fall for him and then it doesn't work out? What would that do to Wyatt? He doesn't have a great experience with men already because of his dad, and I know he'll love Aiden. I wouldn't want to take that away if something happened between us. It could cause a rift between me and Wyatt, and I don't know if

I could live with that." She took in a deep breath and let it out, her elbows on the table. "It's almost not worth the risk, you know?"

Callie put her hand on Olivia's arm. "You're a great mother," she said. "You look out for Wyatt, and you do everything for him that you can. But you can't foresee every obstacle. What if you denied him someone who could raise him like a father, someone who would be around for the rest of his life? What if you denied him that because of fear? Just take it slowly—day by day. You'll know what you feel and you'll know what to do. But don't let fear keep you and Wyatt from the happiness you both deserve."

Olivia got up and wrapped her arms around Callie. "Thank you. You always know the right things to say to me. I'm still not sure, but you've given me something to think about."

"If there's one thing I'm realizing, it's to just let things happen. You don't have to have it all figured out right now." Callie downed the rest of her coffee and stood up. "I need to work!" she said with dramatic flair. "I have spackling to do!"

* * *

There was a knock at the door, and Callie stopped spackling the old picture holes in the drywall upstairs, sharpening her hearing. The furniture had already been delivered and it was still a little early in the day for visitors. The only people here were the crew. They'd started early and cut the power again for the final time.

"Callie!" Olivia called up to her. "Frederick McFarlin's here!"

Frozen, Callie wondered if she could find some reason to stay exactly where she was. She'd lain awake all night, not knowing what to do and scolding herself for prying. It was times like these that she wished she had her mother to talk to. Her grandmother had always known how to listen—why hadn't her mother? Why couldn't she have just picked up the phone and told her how all this was eating her alive? And now Frederick was here. Did it mean he had changed his mind about the mural?

"Callie?"

"Coming!" she said, getting the spackle off her thumb and wiping her hands on her shirt.

When she got to the bottom of the stairs, she found Frederick, holding a large box that she guessed contained paint and other art supplies and a large, flat leather bag. "I thought I'd paint that mural for you," he said, his eyes flickering, his nerves showing.

She nodded and smiled, a pinch forming in her shoulder all of a sudden.

"Wow. You've changed this place. I feel like I'm somewhere completely different." His chest filled with air and he looked relieved.

"Olivia," Callie said, just realizing she'd left her friend standing there in the dark. "Frederick McFarlin is an artist and he's going to paint our mural."

"Oh!" Olivia shook his hand. She flicked a confused look Callie's way while keeping the smile on her face. "Excellent! So nice to meet you."

"I'll show him around."

Callie led Frederick into the formal living room as Olivia mouthed *What is going on?* behind his back and Callie just shook her head. She'd explain later. If she could think of how to explain without giving everything away.

"So, what were you thinking?" asked Frederick.

"I'd like the light blue I've painted to bleed into the sky, but a very subtle beach scene—maybe some sand and seashells or something—along the bottom here."

Frederick set down his paints and scrutinized the wall, while Callie stood beside him, lightheaded with anxiety.

* * *

Callie had let Frederick work while she finished what she had to do upstairs. When she was done, she stopped in the hallway, peering into the formal living room, a thrill running through her like an electric current. "Wow," she said as Frederick sponged on a few shadows in the sand. "That's absolutely amazing."

"Thank you," he said with a grin, his eyes still on the mural. "It's only sand."

"I know, but it looks so real." She walked in and kneeled down beside him.

"I worried I might be rusty," he admitted, mixing more taupe to the yellow on his palette. "But it's like riding a bike: just get back on and go." He examined the color and then added some white. "You know, once, I did a mural for a lady who owned a beach shop. She came in and started sobbing. I nearly had a heart attack. Luckily, her tears were out of happiness. I've never been so relieved in all my life," he said with a chuckle.

"Haha. Have you painted a lot?"

"Ah, not too much. I prefer drawings to murals really. I don't let anyone see them until I'm finished. There's something about the seclusion—just my eyes and my pencil on the page—until I'm ready to show someone.

Sometimes I don't show anyone at all. It feels more personal to me. Sometimes I showed Alice."

"Were you close with Alice?" she asked daringly.

Frederick drew his brush lightly along the wall, making one long streak that, after a few other touches were added, she realized was a piece of sea grass. It was so lifelike she couldn't believe it.

"Very. She and I were always together when we were young."

"Did you drift apart?"

Frederick pursed his lips. "Not really. I just moved away, and distance will take a toll on any relationship."

"Do you still own the house across the street?"

"Yep." He dabbed on some white, his strokes seemingly chaotic until a seashell shape began to emerge.

"Do you ever rent it or anything?" She liked Frederick. He was easy to talk to, like Luke.

"No. I just left it. Like I said, it's too hard. Too many memories." He painted another little seashell and Callie was amazed at how easy he made it look. "Don't feel like you have to entertain me," he said. "I know you have a ton of work to do but you're very kind to sit and make conversation with me."

Callie smiled. "I'm going to run some errands. I'll be right back. Olivia's upstairs if you need anything. Would you like a glass of tea before I go?" Callie asked, standing up.

"That would be nice," he said with that grin that looked like his son's.

* * *

Callie had worked right through her sandpaper. It was nearly as smooth as the wall. She'd spent all morning before Frederick's arrival filling holes in the upstairs bedrooms and hallways, and patching a few odd spots where the movers must have dinged the drywall. She'd had to drive to Rodanthe to the hardware store, and the drive there had been quiet apart from the radio. They were still watching that storm, the clouds lingering, taunting them all.

She couldn't wait to get back and see Frederick's progress on the mural. Now that he'd gotten started, she was so thrilled he was feeling creative again and that he'd decided to do his first piece at The Beachcomber. It made her feel like she'd helped in some way. Perhaps that was why she had been meant to find the lockbox. Maybe things were fine as they were, but Frederick needed to feel like he could come back to this place, that it wasn't so scary after all. Maybe he'd even venture over to his cottage and have a little rummage inside.

When Callie pulled up in the drive, her skin stung with the sensation of a million needles as she came to a stop behind Luke's SUV. She sat at the wheel, clutching the little bag of sandpaper and her purse, not sure what to do. Luke could read her better than anyone ever had, and she knew that if she had to come face to face with him, he'd know something wasn't right.

Then panic set in. What if Frederick had told him? What if Frederick had also said she'd known all about it? Her hands started to tremble. With the car off, the heat was mounting despite the cloud cover, and she'd eventually have to get out or she'd develop heatstroke. Callie opened the door, the sea breeze feeling cool against her skin, and walked up to the house, the bag rustling in the wind at her side.

With a gulp of air, she turned the knob and pushed open the front door. She heard Luke's voice first: unruffled, casual. "So when you put the sunlight on that stem there, did you have to mix colors to blend it, or is that just plain white?"

Frederick answered him. Callie, barely listening through the gale of worry in her head, moved quietly like a cat, coming up on the entrance to the living room. Luke and Frederick were standing side by side facing the painting, their backs to her, and the resemblance in their build was uncanny. She took a step toward them, a board creaking under her feet. Both of them turned around at the same time—even their movements were alike. She forced a nervous smile.

"Hey," Luke said with a wave.

Callie took in the curve of his lips, the playfulness in his expression—there was no hint of worry there. She threw a look over to Frederick. He was smiling too, his face innocent of anything, but a sparkle in his eyes. She knew this moment was huge for him; she just didn't expect to have it go quite like this.

"I thought I'd come over to help," Luke said. "Since you wouldn't go out with me because of all the work you had to do." His voice was droll, to be dramatic.

Always playing.

Well, this wasn't funny, was it? He was standing in front of his biological father. And now Callie was witness to it. She had to watch it unfold, feeling the mortification that she knew he would feel once he found out, and it was only a matter of time because how could they all just exist like this together?

"I was only kidding," he said, and she snapped out of her internal monologue.

Callie looked at Frederick, wondering what to do, but his look of warning made her feel like she should carry on covering everything up. She took in a breath. "Sorry," she said. "I've just been really busy and I don't have time to do anything else."

"You look really tense," Luke said. "Is everything okay?"

Fear blasted through her veins and she just knew her face had turned a ghostly white. She was terrible at keeping secrets. She could hide all her emotions and know people for years without revealing anything about her worries, but when it came to a secret like this, her body language would give her away—and this was the biggest one she'd ever had to keep. It made her so uncomfortable she could hardly stand still. She wanted to tell Luke because, until this moment, she'd been able to tell him anything. He was the first person she'd ever met who made her feel like she could open up and, instead, she had to be closed off.

"Callie, what's wrong?"

She blinked, steadying herself. "Nothing. I'm fine. I've just had a lot on my plate lately with the house." She caught Frederick looking down at the floor and she wondered if he felt guilty for putting her in this position. It wasn't his fault.

"You need a break," Luke said, striding over to her. "Let me get you some lunch. Nothing fancy; just somewhere we can kick back and relax."

She shook her head, but knew she didn't have a good reason to say no.

"Callie…" Luke looked utterly concerned, which only made her panic worse. She felt just awful.

"Okay, fine," she said, raising her eyebrows in an attempt to look light-hearted. She'd caved, faltered, but she couldn't help it. Telling him now would only make things worse. She'd have to be strong. She'd just go out to lunch, have a sandwich, ask him about work, and then go home. That was it.

* * *

"When Olivia let me in, she introduced me to your painter," Luke said right off the bat when Callie got into the SUV. Her heart went a hundred miles an hour and she worried he'd actually see the thudding through her shirt. There was no way this lunch was going to be easy.

"Frederick," she said. "He's really nice."

"Yeah, I like him."

He was probably just making conversation, but she hung on the words: He *liked* him. They filled her with a rush of excitement. Luke was experiencing the one thing she'd always wanted to have with her own father—that chance to talk, with nothing between them—and he didn't even know it.

"I was a little worried about him when I first met him," Luke said.

She snapped her head over in his direction. "Why?"

He glanced over at her and then back to the road. "Olivia mentioned he had a box full of articles about me and my family. She wondered if I knew him. Not sure what that was all about."

Breathe, she told herself. *Smile*. "He just loves the area, I think. He grew up here and actually has a house right across from The Beachcomber. I think he had a bunch of different articles—not just yours." She could barely get the words out, the tiny white lie slithering off her tongue like some sort of foreign serpent. She swallowed hard.

Luke looked at her again; her response clearly had not helped things. Uncertainty swam across his face. She wanted to slide down onto the floor of the car and it just swallow her up. In fact, she was praying for it.

He pulled into the parking lot of a local seafood shop

and put the SUV in park. Then, without getting out, he shifted in his seat to face her. "You're acting weird," he stated. Before she could say anything, he demanded, "Why wouldn't you see me when I called?"

Her mouth opened but nothing would come out, the tiny lie she'd just told stripping her of any possible speech that she might have had.

"Have I done something?"

She shook her head.

"I would've painted that mural for you," he said. "You didn't even ask me."

She felt the crease form between her eyes—the same crease that she got when she was studying for a big test in college or worried about something. She didn't understand his line of conversation, her mind still on Frederick. But then she wondered if he was just hurt that she hadn't asked him to paint. "What?" was all she could manage.

"You hired someone instead."

"I didn't hire him. He's doing it as a favor."

"Why?"

She tried to focus on the fact that he just didn't believe that she'd found a second artist in the Outer Banks who would do her a favor. His questions, instead, felt like he was screaming, *Why didn't you tell me this was my father!* She bit her lip. The heat was rising and she needed air or she might pass out. She opened the car door, trying not to gasp when the breeze blew in.

"Callie, you need to tell me what's going on because I'm thinking that you just don't want to see me anymore." He got out and walked around to her side of the car. When he got to her open door, he said, "And that's fine, but just have the decency to tell me face to face. If it's true, though, know that it'll knock me sideways."

Her head was swimming as she tried to sift through all her thoughts. "What are you talking about?" Callie stood up, worried her legs wouldn't hold her. She shut the door and leaned against it for support.

"I sit at work and think about when I can call you again," he said. "All I think about is when I'll get to see you. I've never met someone who gets me like you do, and I've never shared as much of who I am with anyone." He took a step forward, the gravel beneath his feet crunching and ringing in her ears. "And getting to know you, I think you feel the same. You won't admit it to yourself, but you've opened up to me too—I can tell. Tell me, Callie. Why don't you want to see me?"

"I do..." Her words withered and fell short of the impact she'd wanted to have. Two people walked past them, glancing over with interest. Callie avoided eye contact. The truth was, she did want to see him. And he was right; she felt just as he thought she did, but things were too difficult with this big hurdle between them. It wasn't her place to say anything and she was caught in a terrible situation.

She looked up at Luke; his jaw was set and he looked away, shaking his head just slightly.

"You're so frustrating," he said quietly.

"None of this was meant to happen," she said, the words suddenly tumbling out. "I wasn't trying to meet someone." That was the truth but the way it was coming out, it sounded like some sort of breakup. "That's not what I meant," she scrambled, "I mean, it is, but..."

"What are you afraid of?" he asked, irritation penetrating his words. "Are you afraid of getting close to me?"

"No!" she said loudly, looking around to see if people were staring. The lot was empty.

"Are you afraid because of the press? I could sort of tell, Callie, but I thought we'd gotten over all that."

She didn't know what to say. She didn't know what to do. She just stood there, her mind empty.

Luke's face came into view. "That's what it is, isn't it?" he said. "You actually believe what you've read about me. And now... Now that I know you better, and I see how private you like to be, I'll bet you're worried the press will hound you too." He scratched his face in thought. Then, in a whisper, he said, "I can't believe that you trust the media over me." He let the words hang in the air between them, his pain written all over his face.

She could see how hurt he was by this idea, and it was killing her. He was so wrong but what else was he supposed to think? She shook her head.

"If you believe them, then you do. I'm not going to try to beg you to listen to me, Callie. I fell for you in a big way, and I was willing to give you all my trust, but if you can't do that, then I guess we're at an impasse."

She could feel him pulling away, and it terrified her. That, coupled with the overwhelming sadness she felt about the fact that he thought she couldn't trust him over the papers, made her tear up. "I *do* trust you," she blurted as he headed over to his side of the car. He stopped and turned around. "There's a reason I'm struggling right now and it has nothing to do with you and me specifically."

He walked back over to her. "Then what is it, Callie?"

"I... can't tell you."

He took in a deep, short breath. "You can't tell me," he spat. "You just said you trust me but you can't tell me."

Defeat in her eyes, she said slowly, "I've learned a secret that could literally change everything. It's so big that I was willing to not see you to keep from having to tell you."

"Look. I think you and I are great together. But we can't move forward until you can be honest with me. Whatever it is, you can tell me." His blue eyes bore down on her.

Her hands began to tremble, and her chest felt cold and hollow. "I don't know..."

He tipped his head back in frustration, and it felt like she was losing him. The angry, gray sky above them seemed to echo her feelings. She didn't blame him. How would they ever move forward unless she told him? She had two choices: tell him and hopefully work through it or lose him. But was that being selfish? He was asking her, but did he really want to know?

"You aren't who you think you are." The words floated between them as if they weren't hers.

Luke's eyebrows furrowed. "What?"

"I know where you got your artistic talent from." Her whole body froze, and she had to will herself to keep going. There was no going back now.

His face crumpled. "What do you mean?"

She took a steadying breath. "Remember Frederick McFarlin?"

"Yes?" A group of people who had just parked walked past him but his eyes never left hers.

"He's Alice McFarlin's brother. The woman who used to own our place." Her stomach ached but she pressed on. She'd want someone to tell her if she were in his position. "I found a journal of Alice McFarlin's; it had entries about a boy who didn't know his father."

Luke was still, his face neutral.

"That boy turned out to be someone I know. And Frederick McFarlin—the *artist*—is his father."

Skepticism slid across Luke's face. "What are you trying to say, Callie?"

Callie swallowed.

"You think that some artist guy who gave up his kid is my actual father and you know this because I have a talent for art?"

"That's not *exactly* what I'm saying. But what if I told you that he drew a pencil sketch of a woman and her little boy on the beach in Corolla. A woman who liked to take her little boy there."

"You're crazy."

"I'm not crazy, Luke. Frederick knows you're his son. You said yourself that your mom took you to that beach. Do you remember a man talking to your mother on one of those visits? Or how about the day you dropped a baseball in the street and Alice McFarlin picked it up for you? She mentioned that your birthday was October twentieth... Why do you think you kept seeing her at all your events as a child? She was your aunt."

His eyes had a slight panic in them. "Callie, I need you to stop and think about what you're implying. You're implying that my mother was unfaithful to my father and that I am not a blood relative of the man who raised me my entire life. Get a good handle on this before you go any further."

The fear in his eyes rattled her—he'd always been so sure of himself. She wanted to put her arms around him and make everything okay but she knew she couldn't do anything to fix this or to change it. All they could do was face it.

"I have a handle on it. I talked with Frederick. He cried like a baby over you. He has been without his son your whole life."

Luke didn't speak, and she tried to read his face but he wasn't allowing his thoughts to show. He stared at her and she waited, her hands shaking terribly. His thumbs started to bounce against his legs in agitation and he went around and got back into the car, their lunch date evidently over before it had begun. Callie climbed in beside him and shut her door. The radio buzzed with a quiet hum just low enough that she couldn't make out the words, the hurricane warnings still coming in. She ignored it and focused on Luke, waiting for his response. There was nothing more she could say.

He started the car and drove away in silence. After what seemed like an eternity, they arrived at The Beachcomber. She got out of the car when he did. He spun around and walked toward her but his face took her aback. "I can't believe I let this happen," he said.

"What?"

He brushed past her and headed for the beach. She clambered after him.

When they got to the backyard, he spun around. "This is all a way to get Aiden the company, isn't it?" He shook his head, anger in his eyes. "If that got out, God knows what the papers would say. They'd have a field day. But that's what you all planned, isn't it? So that Aiden would get what he's wanted all these years?" He stormed off again.

"Where are you going?" was all she could manage, the shock of his interpretation of her message causing her so much confusion that she was having trouble finding her words.

He continued walking and she couldn't catch him, his angry stride so much longer and quicker than hers.

Callie jumped onto the new walkway, stopping only briefly to steady herself, her heart pounding like a snare drum. She got to the bottom and ran onto the sand.

"Luke!" she called, but he didn't turn around. "Luke!" she called again.

He was down by the surf and she ran after him, stumbling on the hot sand, her mind racing. Luke refused to turn around, his pace swift as he walked at a clip. She was nearly sprinting, the clouds overhead dark as if they'd explode with rain any minute. The wild wind tore through her hair.

"Olivia and Aiden don't even know!" she yelled, stopping to catch her breath, feeling hopeless. She watched Luke slow down, her breathing heavy, and saw him stop, his back to her. Callie willed him to turn around. The very last thing she wanted was for him to think she'd betrayed him in some way, because she'd never do that.

Slowly, he turned to face her. They stood, a ways apart, as a couple crossed in between them, headed down the beach. Callie ignored their uncomfortable smiles. Luke didn't move. She started to walk toward him carefully, trying to let him know with her stride that she didn't mean any harm. She didn't run to him, she just walked, and the closer she got the clearer his face became until she could see the tears in his eyes. And she knew that he believed her. The more he'd run, the more he'd processed it. When she reached him, she could feel the pain that he felt because she knew that kind of pain. She put her hands on his face for a moment, telling him with her silence that she'd be there for him. He pulled away from her and started toward the house.

"Luke," she called.

"I can't," he said, shaking his head as if he were trying to shake out the information he'd just learned. "I want to shout at my mother for being unfaithful. And then I wonder, does my father—the one who raised me—know? Is that why he's been so hard on me my whole life? Is that why he doesn't want me running the business? But I'd never ask him that, so I'm left to wonder. I feel like an outsider in my own family." He looked down at her.

"Luke," she said gently.

He turned away. "My life is a farce. I don't deserve to have my father's business. I'm not his son! I might as well be a stranger. Aiden's bloodlines are real. No wonder my father would rather give it to him."

"He's never said that, I'm sure. And your life is the same as it has always been," she said to his back. "You haven't changed at all. Edward was the one who raised you. He instilled his work ethic in you. He taught you how to be a man. He is no less of a father to you now than he has always been. But you're right; your bloodlines belong to someone else. And he wasn't a part of your life. But he, too, is a good man. He mourns your absence in his life, still to this day. Wouldn't you rather know him than not know him?"

Luke still hadn't turned around. He ran his fingers through his hair in exasperation.

"Luke, we don't have to solve it all right now."

He started walking away. "I can't stay. I don't want to talk anymore. It's just too complicated."

She let him go.

Chapter Twenty

Callie woke to dreary skies through her window. She turned over to check her clock, but the screen was black. With a yawn, she got up and examined the plug. It was plugged in. Frederick had asked if he could stay over since he was still working on the mural, and he couldn't face going over to his cottage yet. Callie had agreed to let him stay and, not wanting to bring the subject of Luke up anymore, she'd turned in early so she wouldn't have to talk to anyone. She didn't want to tell him what she'd told Luke, or Luke's reaction. She didn't want to meddle anymore.

She'd been up all night thinking about yesterday, replaying every word she'd said, wondering if she could've handled it any differently. She needed her grandmother. She'd know what to do. Feeling completely lost, she rubbed her sore shoulder, a pinch having formed in the night, threw on some clothes, ran her fingers through her hair and headed downstairs, dread building with every step. She'd have to face Frederick and she had no idea what to say to him. On her way to the kitchen, she passed him, asleep on the sofa, and let out a sigh of relief that she'd at least have time to wake up before she faced him.

Through the large window black clouds swirled; they wouldn't get much work done outside today. The building crew had today off anyway, so it was just Olivia, Wyatt, Callie, and Frederick.

Her eyes aching, she loaded the coffee maker and hit start. But her shoulders slumped when she realized that the coffee maker didn't have power either. She tried the lights—nothing. Then she vaguely remembered the crew saying they were cutting the power to do the electrical work on the back deck. Had they not turned it back on before they left? She sat down and looked out at the ocean.

"I texted Aiden," Olivia whispered, startling her.

Callie threw her hand to her chest to steady herself, whipping around from the window, rain beginning to lash at the glass.

"Sorry." Olivia sat down next to Callie at the table. "The crew was in a hurry to get things wrapped up—having spent a very long day—and I think they forgot to turn the power back on. I'd been outside with Wyatt until late, and we both just came in quietly so as not to wake up Frederick and went to bed. I checked my phone a few minutes ago to see if Aiden had texted back, and it's dead. I forgot to charge it. Maybe we can use your phone."

Callie rubbed her eyes and nodded, her head starting to throb.

There was a loud, pounding knock on the door, and both Callie and Olivia jumped. Callie dashed to it before it woke Frederick and Wyatt. The pounding started again, stopping only as she unlocked the door, her fingers fumbling with the lock. She opened it. Luke and Aiden were on the front porch.

"They say we should evacuate," Luke said, without even a hello. That soft, sweet voice she knew so well, the affection in his eyes when he looked at her—gone. "The hurricane is headed this way. We couldn't get you on the phone. Aiden's been texting all morning."

"We have no power and Olivia's phone is dead. Mine's upstairs." She moved aside to let them in, struggling to make sense of all the commotion after having just woken up, her thoughts so preoccupied with everything else that she almost couldn't compute what he was saying.

They stayed where they were, the wind whipping around them. "Callie. If they say evacuate, we need to do it, and quick," Luke said, breaking eye contact to shoot off a text on his own phone. "We're getting everyone together and I'll find somewhere to stay. We need to hurry, though, before everything is booked up. Start packing, keep your phone with you, and if the power comes back on, plug it in. I'll be back to get you."

"Okay," she said, alarm zinging through her. She locked eyes with Luke. "Frederick's here," she said, her head feeling like it was full of water from the stress. "Should he come with us?"

In the infinitesimal pause that followed, she could see a million thoughts run across Luke's face. Finally, he nodded. "What about Gladys?"

"She's already gone. She went to her daughter's house."

"Okay. You have about thirty minutes," he said, all business.

As Luke left, Callie yanked Gladys's plant inside and then paced in circles for a minute, trying to figure out what to do first. She ran in to tell Olivia but she was already heading upstairs.

"I heard," she said.

They entered their rooms and pulled out the suitcases, Callie filling one for herself and Olivia throwing items for her and Wyatt into the other one. They packed clothes, socks, underwear, toiletries, toys for Wyatt, and anything else in their paths that would fit.

Callie grabbed the stack of laundry that was still in the hallway, where she'd folded it, and divided it among the suitcases. She got all her jewelry and her family photo album with old photos of her parents and her grandmother and stuffed them into the smaller bag, then zipped it up and headed downstairs. With a quick swipe, she took Luke's painting off the wall and leaned it against the suitcase.

Callie was packing food into the cooler when Frederick walked in.

"What's all the commotion?" he asked.

"I was going to wake you in just a minute. The hurricane is coming our way. Luke's getting his family. We're all evacuating together. I'm packing enough food for you too. Wyatt, I packed your Legos and your gears buildings set. I've also got your iPad," she said as Wyatt shuffled in.

Olivia told Wyatt to come with her and check to make sure he had everything he thought he'd need, leaving Frederick in the kitchen. He started helping put food in bags. "Luke's coming back?" he asked as he filled a paper grocery bag with bread and chips.

"Yes," she said, asking him with her eyes to be okay with it. She checked her phone—no messages.

He nodded and went back to packing, dropping a box of popcorn into a paper sack.

Callie turned the battery-operated radio on. "If you live

in coastal areas—I'm speaking to those in Kitty Hawk, Kill Devil Hills, Nags Head, Rodanthe, Waves, all the way down to Hatteras—it's advised, if you can, to pack up valuables and family memorabilia. The swells are going to get quite high and the amount of damage we're looking at could be serious."

She looked at Frederick as if he could provide some relief for her worry, but even though he'd probably experienced something like this before, he couldn't offer much more than to say, "This house has weathered many hurricanes. It's just another storm, Callie. Tell yourself that."

By the time they had their bags packed, Callie was wondering how she'd get it all, along with the cooler, in the trunk of her car. Luke came driving in with another SUV behind him. "Don't take your car," he said, getting out. "We can go in mine. It's bigger, so we can get more into it. Mom and Juliette are in the car behind me with Mitchell. She's got two rows of seats. Wyatt and Mitchell can sit in the very back."

Aiden, who had started packing the cars, came out with more bags.

"Aiden and Olivia can ride with Mom, and you and Frederick ride with me," Luke told them as he began to transfer Callie's things from her trunk to his vehicle. He popped the back open—it was already full. He moved his bags to one side to make room for the cooler. "I got three rooms at The Berkeley in Richmond," Luke said, shifting one of his suitcases. "I reserved all they had left." With a pause, he looked down at his painting, blinking for a moment, his face neutral. He put it in the back.

"We can make it work," Aiden said over his shoulder as he headed inside one more time.

Frederick came out and climbed right in with his things

as Olivia and Wyatt walked briskly over toward Lillian, each lugging a suitcase. Luke jogged toward them and took both bags, lifting them easily. He slid them into the back while Olivia helped Wyatt into Lillian's SUV.

"Hop in," Luke told Callie, opening the back door. "Let's try to get ahead of the crowd. Anything else inside that you need?"

Luke looked around, as the group offered a collective "no" from their various locations with head-shaking and worried glances. Callie couldn't help but feel safe watching Luke take charge. He was calm, direct, and focused, and it set her racing heart and flooded mind at ease. She was so worried about their safety that she didn't allow herself to think about the fact that they wouldn't have the funds or time to repair any major damage from this storm or that Frederick was coming along and she had no idea how that would work. She got in the SUV and shut the door, the others doing the same. Luke jogged around and climbed in the driver's side.

Callie turned back to take one last look at The Beachcomber before they drove away.

Chapter Twenty-One

By the time they'd made the almost four-hour trek into Richmond, it was nearly dinnertime, and they were all hungry and tired from driving. The journey had been mostly silent, the only sound being the radio spewing updates—the same information over and over until the station received new weather data, which was about once an hour.

Callie felt like she was going to burst with uncertainty. Every time she looked over at Luke, he wouldn't respond, keeping his eyes on the road. She didn't know what to say anyway because Frederick was in the car, and she hadn't told him that Luke knew everything. Her mouth was bone dry, her hands icy with worry.

They'd stopped for a snack and a bathroom break when they'd crossed the North Carolina state line and entered Virginia. Callie noticed that Lillian had stayed in the car, and she wondered if Luke's mother had realized that Frederick was with them. They'd climbed into the cars so quickly. How would she feel seeing him again?

Were they on good terms? After all, she'd hidden all of this from Luke.

Had Luke even confronted his mother yet? She'd wanted to ask him all these questions, but stayed quiet. The blank look on Luke's face was unnerving. She wanted to read him like she'd gotten good at doing but it was clear that he wasn't going to allow her. He hadn't even offered a glance in the rearview mirror at Frederick.

They didn't stop again until they pulled in front of The Berkeley Hotel. Luke lined up their bags on the curb of the cobblestone street as the valet parked the SUVs. The weather wasn't great in Richmond either, the outer band of rain from the hurricane stretching as far as Virginia, leaving a light drizzle on everything. Callie moved under the large green awning stretching out from the front door of the hotel.

It was an odd sensation to be back in Richmond with Luke. Callie had lived here nearly her entire adult life. Her mother was here in the city. Callie had worked down the street, and she had lived along the James River in an apartment on Tobacco Row. She'd walked past the Berkeley more times than she could count, but this would be the first time she'd stayed here, the first time she'd be considered an out-of-towner.

The hotel was a gorgeous, historical landmark, its elegance incomparable to anything else on the street. It sat along the cobbled road, a grand awning stretched out, a smiling, suited doorman ready to help them. It was a stark contrast to the beachy vibe she'd just left.

The two vehicles were parallel parked, one behind the other, and Lillian, who'd jumped in to help unload the bags from the car before the rain, was struggling to pull her suitcase out. Both Luke and Aiden were already occupied inside and the valets, with their black vests and white gloves, were loading the luggage onto brass caddies. Callie could see Frederick hanging back—only for an instant—as if he were trying to figure out when best to approach Lillian. Callie could hardly breathe. They hadn't seen each other in decades, she was sure.

"Let me help you," Frederick finally said, stepping forward, his words heavy with unsaid thoughts, his eyes on her.

Lillian stopped cold, and it was clear that she just now realized who had been on the drive with Luke for four hours. She looked like she'd seen a ghost. And, Callie thought, in a way she had. Tears filled Lillian's eyes, but she blinked them away, coughing into her fist once as if to take the focus away from her reaction. She squared her shoulders, but emotions kept flooding her face. Callie looked away a moment, feeling as though she were intruding, her head swimming with anxiety.

Quietly, Frederick took Lillian's bag and, with an uneasy smile, passed it to the valet and went inside, leaving Lillian on the curb as Aiden and Luke returned.

Once the others had gathered around on the sidewalk, Luke ushered them inside to check in and get their rooms. The lobby was all dark wood and formal furnishings. Tan valances were drawn in perfect pleats at the top of the windows, the furniture upholstered in burnt orange and dark butter creams. Luke popped over to the front desk and spoke to the clerk. Things had been so crazy and haphazard getting out of town that it hadn't occurred to Callie until now how they were going to split the rooms, so she asked Luke, who'd offered to get their keys. She felt jittery and edgy, wondering how this would all play out.

"I kept our family together," he said. "I've put Mom, Juliette, and Mitchell in one room; you, Olivia, and Wyatt in a second; and then I figured I could share with Frederick and Aiden." His gaze moved over to Frederick and it seemed as if just looking at him was difficult for Luke. He was uneasy and tense.

It was really the only way to divvy it up, but she worried about Luke and Frederick.

"I won't say anything to upset him," he said flatly, still clearly distressed by the situation, but deciphering her thoughts easily.

She let out an anxious breath. "I know."

The front desk clerk gave Luke the keys and told him the rooms were ready. Luke thanked her and handed them out. "Why don't we all settle in and then we can get a bite downstairs?" he told the group as they all moved toward the elevator.

When the doors pinged open, they piled in, their luggage filling half the space. Not everyone could fit.

"I'll wait for the next one," Luke said.

Callie stepped back beside him. "Me too." Maybe if she was alone for a moment with him, she could get him to talk.

She stared at the doors as they closed, not knowing how to begin, her heart thudding in her ears. Time was limited before the next elevator opened, and she had to know what was going on in that head of his. "What a mess," she said, finally looking up at him and bringing the subject out into the open.

He sucked in a breath and it looked as though he didn't want to talk. Then, out of nowhere, he spoke, making her jump. "You know, everything was going along just fine before all this." He rubbed his eyes and then dragged his fingertips over his temples for a split second before dropping his hands.

"I couldn't keep it from you once I knew," she said. She'd have wanted to know.

"Says who?" he nearly stormed. "You? You get to make decisions about my family? If you hadn't meddled in our lives, we wouldn't be facing any of this right now."

The doors swished open, taking her off guard. Luke stepped into the elevator and hit the button. Callie scrambled in, her mind going a hundred miles an hour.

"So you'd rather have had me hold on to this information—sensitive information that wasn't mine to keep?"

"I'd rather have had you not snoop."

As they stood there in silence, she worried that he might have a point. If she hadn't read Alice's journal or tried to open the lockbox, she wouldn't be in this situation right now. It was her nosiness that had brought all this on. Guilt swelled in her stomach. If she had just managed to keep her mouth shut to Frederick, it would have been in his hands. When the doors opened again, Luke got out and walked toward his room. Callie stepped into the hallway and leaned against the wall, trying to get herself together.

* * *

Callie had been in the bathroom trying not to listen to the hurricane updates. They made her so nervous she could hardly stand it. She'd showered, dried her hair and reapplied her makeup, pushing away tears over Luke. As she came out of the bathroom, she couldn't deny how good it felt to be clean and in fresh clothes.

"My turn," Olivia said, standing and stretching her back.

Callie nodded, relenting and turning the television up. The images were too distressing without the sound and she had to know what was going on. The wind had increased and the swells were growing out at sea. The announcer stood in front of an enormous red circular model of the storm, the pathway drawn directly toward the Outer Banks. "This hurricane is not hype," he said. "It's moving dangerously close to the Outer Banks and coming in fast. The National Weather Service warns of catastrophic waves to the barrier islands of North Carolina if our projection is correct. Residents are urged to evacuate immediately. Please take this storm seriously and get out before it makes landfall. Leave storm surge areas as quickly as possible."

Olivia texted Gladys that she was all right and then jumped in the shower while Callie and Wyatt kept their eyes on the screen, but Callie was preoccupied with thoughts about whether or not to tell Frederick that Luke knew that he was his father before they were all caught in a very awkward situation. But that would mean meddling further and she'd already messed things up. And now she had Lillian to think about too. Would Lillian say anything? Callie didn't want to get in the middle of things, especially after what Luke had said, but she felt terrible keeping it from Frederick. Should she just wait for Frederick to say something? Or Lillian? She took in a deep breath and let it out, her head starting to pound.

"Are you okay, Callie?" Wyatt asked, his little face crumpling as he looked at her.

"Yep!" she lied, inwardly cringing that she had to tell yet another fib. "I'm just worried about the storm." She fixed her eyes on the TV. The newscaster suggested that residents call their family members to tell them they were okay. Callie didn't want to consider the fact that her mother hadn't tried to call her or text. But that was just how things were. Seeing Frederick and Luke, however, had made her think about all the time she'd lost with her mother, times they could've been together but hadn't. "I'm just going to step out into the hallway a minute and make a phone call." She held up her phone.

With a nod from Wyatt, Callie let herself out of the room, propping the door open with the lock bar. She wasn't entirely sure what she wanted to say to her mother as she dialed her number, but she just wanted to talk to her. The phone rang three times before she heard that familiar voice. Callie could still recall those golden years before her father had left when her mother used to sing to her before bed to comfort her.

"Mom? It's Callie." She leaned against the wall, running the back of her hand along the patterned wallpaper.

"Oh, hello. How are you?"

Callie chewed on the inside of her lip. "I'm fine. I wanted to call to tell you that. Have you seen the hurricane headed for the Outer Banks? I've evacuated, so I'm not in harm's way." She didn't want to tell her she was in Richmond. She wasn't ready to see her mother yet, and they didn't have the kind of time she'd need for that visit. She just needed to be comforted at this point.

"That's good to hear," her mother said. Surprisingly, her tone didn't sound hollow like she remembered it being.

"How are *you?*" Callie asked.

"I'm okay." One thing that hadn't changed, however, was her mother's unwillingness to elaborate. What made her okay or not okay? Did she miss Callie? Did she ever feel lonely? She'd never say.

"I'm glad you're okay," she said, not knowing how to proceed. But then, all of a sudden, it hit her, and she knew just what she wanted to say. She knew because it was the one thing she'd learned from Luke. Sharing things about herself and opening up made it easier for others to do the same. "I met someone," she told her mom and immediately tears pricked her eyes.

"Oh?"

"Yeah. His name is Luke Sullivan. He's probably one of the best people I've ever met." Her heart ached for better circumstances to share this news, but the words were flowing, coming out so easily that she couldn't believe it. Because they were true. "One day, I'd like you to meet him." As she said it, the fear washed over her again, fear that she wouldn't get a chance to let her mother meet him because he wouldn't have forgiven her for putting him in the position he was in.

"Maybe one day." She didn't have a lot to say, but Callie swore she could hear her mother smiling on the other end. It had been a long time since she'd seen her smile.

"Promise you're doing okay?" she asked.

"Yeah, I promise."

Callie pushed herself off the wall and walked over to the door. "Well, I should probably go. I just wanted to let you know I wasn't in harm's way. Let's talk again soon, okay?"

"Okay, dear."

Callie got off the phone and went back inside. When Olivia came out of the bathroom, she was dressed casually, wearing a sundress and a pair of sandals. "What's the latest?" she asked, shaking out her curls with her fingers.

"They're still evacuating," Callie said.

"I saw a TV downstairs in the lounge. We can probably pop out to check the updates throughout the meal," Olivia said, but she was looking curiously at Callie, her head turned to the side just so, and Callie knew she could tell something was on her mind. "What is it?"

"Well, a lot," she said after Wyatt went into the bathroom, her shoulders slumping in surrender, tears spilling over her eyes with no warning.

Olivia rushed over and put her hand on Callie's arm. "Tell me." She urged her to sit, her face full of concern. "Are you worried about the storm?"

"Yes. But there's more. I called my mom," she started, but the rest just flooded her mind and before Olivia could say anything, it all came tumbling out. "I have to tell you something about Luke," she said. While the television spewed storm updates, the rain pattering at the windows, Callie sat, wringing her hands as she told Olivia the whole story.

"Oh my God," Olivia said through her fingers, her hand clapped over her mouth. She grabbed the complimentary tissue box, yanking one out and handing it to Callie.

All Callie could do was nod her thanks. She felt terrible. Trying to slow the tears, she wiped her eyes and cleared her throat. "I can't face them all," she worried.

"Yes you can. I'll be there with you." Olivia's phone lit up on the table—a text from Aiden telling them he was already downstairs and would order her a drink.

Callie grabbed another tissue, blotting her eyes as Wyatt joined them. Then she ran her fingers through her hair and took in a deep breath.

"Ready?" Olivia asked.

She nodded and grabbed her handbag off the bed on the way out the door, Wyatt following. She wondered what it would be like down there with everyone at a table together. How would Luke behave with her in front of everyone?

When they got downstairs and entered the dining room, the mood was serious. Mitchell was playing with action figures, rappelling them quietly down from the table with a cloth napkin. Aiden was checking his phone, and Juliette, on the other side of him, was bouncing between conversations, a worried look on her face. Lillian, sitting opposite Frederick, had the menu in her hands, and looked up warily.

Luke, who must have also just arrived, kissed his mother on the cheek before pulling out a chair and taking a seat. Callie noticed that Luke sat quite a distance from Frederick, and he didn't make eye contact.

"All things considered," Juliette said from the end of the table as the waitress filled their glasses with water, "we got organized pretty quickly today. Has anyone checked to see the latest on the storm?"

Aiden briefed them all from his phone. "It's made landfall in Waves," he said, patting the chair beside him for Olivia to sit. Wyatt moved over by Mitchell, the two falling into giggles and chatter. "But it's fast-moving. They expect it to be out to sea by tonight. They also think it might lose speed."

Luke unwound his napkin slowly, as if he needed something to do with his hands.

"Thank God," Juliette said. "What if it doesn't and it destroys the house? Where will you go, Luke?"

Lillian sipped her water and gingerly set the glass down, shaking her head. "We have plenty of friends inland. I'm sure we can find someone to take us in for a day or so while we get ourselves organized. We'd find somewhere for Luke to stay until things were rebuilt so he can keep the sailing company running." Lillian turned toward Callie. "How about you? Do you have anyone you can call if you have more damage than expected?"

"She can call me," Frederick said. "So can you, if you need me. You know I'm always here for you." His words were bold and direct, commanding attention.

Lillian knocked her water, causing it to slosh in the glass and spill over onto the white tablecloth. Luke stared at the spot, his jaw clenched. Juliette and Aiden zeroed in on Frederick at once, confusion and curiosity on their faces.

"Sorry," Lillian said, the word coming out breathily as she blotted the water.

Callie's hands started to rattle under the table and she put them on her knees. She glanced over at Luke but his eyes were still on the spilled water.

"Should we tell him now, Lillian?" Frederick said, to Callie's complete shock. Acid burned in her stomach.

Lillian's eyes were as big as saucers. There was an eerie silence among them; the only movement at the table was Lillian's frantic gaze as it darted to Frederick and away again in panic. One could hear a pin drop. Olivia grabbed Callie's hand under the table.

"You don't have to," Luke said, his gaze not leaving the table at first. Then he lifted his head up. "I already know." His words were broken, too quiet for his personality, as if the knowledge had damaged him.

Juliette had her head cocked to the side, complete confusion on her face. Aiden looked on curiously. Frederick was staring at him as if he could see right through to his soul—the soul that he'd created, that was a part of him.

Lillian was getting teary again, and she clamped her eyes on her son as if she could erase whatever she thought he knew with her stare. "What...do you know?" she asked in almost a whisper.

Luke leaned his forearm on the table, his face close to his mother's. "Is it true?" he asked, ignoring her question. "You might as well discuss it here. We're all family." He wasn't accusing her, he was supporting her, letting her know that he was there for her just like she had been there for him all those years, but at the same time, the hurt was evident.

Callie couldn't take her eyes off him because she was transfixed by his expression. She felt out of place by his comment about everyone being family, but she let the thought go.

Olivia stood up and went over to Wyatt and Mitchell. "You two have been so good this whole time. Why don't we go across the street and get a lollipop from that market while we wait for our meal?"

"We get sugar before we eat?" Wyatt said, clearly thrilled with the suggestion.

"Yep. You deserve it."

Juliette offered a silent "thank you" with her eyes.

Once Olivia and the kids had gone, Lillian took a steadying breath. "Juliette. Aiden. I have something to tell you," she said quietly so only their table could hear. "This will come as a shock to you both." Lillian began to tell them about Frederick.

"I couldn't believe it when I heard that Callie—Luke's new friend—had bought Alice McFarlin's beach house," Lillian said, offering a conciliatory smile to Callie. "It's a nice house." She nodded toward Frederick, but she didn't quite meet his eyes. He sat still as a stone, but that sadness Callie had seen on his face when she'd met him had returned. He was worried.

"See, Frederick and I know each other very well. He was Alice's brother."

Aiden turned toward Frederick and then back to Lillian.

"He moved away a long time ago and I haven't seen him since. Not until now." The waitress came to get their orders.

"Could we have a few minutes?" Luke asked the waitress.

When the waitress left, Lillian's eyes grew red and full of tears that fell down her cheeks. She blotted her face with a napkin. "I did everything wrong," she said, her voice quavering. "Everything." She stopped, another tear sliding down her face. Frederick seemed as though he wanted to hop across the table and hold her but he didn't move.

"Edward was away all the time on business, starting up his company in Florida. We didn't have a house there yet, and so I stayed back, but the winters in the Outer Banks were so long and lonesome for me, and he was always focused on his work. Our marriage was crumbling. I was alone. I tried to tell him. I used to take walks on the beach to clear my head, but it didn't help. I didn't know what to do, and I thought that soon, I would have to initiate the conversation about divorce," she said quietly.

"One day, I was walking down the beach and I met this surfer." She set her hands on her cutlery as if she were straightening it before she looked up at Frederick and smiled nervously. "I watched him for quite a while, dipping under the waves and then paddling out, riding them in, over and over. It was so graceful and beautiful—calming. After a while he jogged up, the board under his arm, his hair soaking wet, and the most gorgeous smile on his face. I hadn't ever had a smile like that directed at me."

She finally met Frederick's eyes and there it was: the smile. With acknowledgment of his encouragement, she continued. "He nodded hello and got a sandwich from a little cooler he had on the beach by a blanket. He told me that I was welcome to sit down on the blanket rather than standing. Then he opened a glass bottle of soda and handed it to me. With a wave of his hand, he went back out."

She put her napkin in her lap, her hands unstill, clearly to release nervous energy. "Do you remember that day, Frederick?"

"Of course." His voice cracked and he cleared his throat.

Juliette was on the edge of her seat, her mouth slack, eyebrows slightly raised, her concentration deep as she listened. She looked uncertainly at Luke, but his downward-turned eyes gave her all the confirmation she needed. Frederick folded his hands on the table, his discomfort clear: He didn't like what the news was doing to Juliette. Aiden wasn't much better. His lips were pressed together, his brows furrowed, and he'd put an arm around Juliette.

"When he came up again, we made some small talk, and he told me that he came out there every day to surf when he wasn't working at the little beach shop in town. He told me if I was ever bored, I could look for that blanket and watch the waves. That was what he liked to do sometimes, he'd said.

"I should've known what was happening." Lillian shook her head. "The next day, I went looking for that blanket. I knew I shouldn't have, but I'd called Edward that morning, telling him how much I hated the way we were living apart and, I...It had been months since I'd seen him. I even asked if I could go to Florida. He said..." A flash of anger crossed her face, then went away. "Well, it doesn't matter what he said. He wouldn't come back. He believed that if I could just hold out, we'd reap the benefits. But I knew the benefits he was talking about just meant money. I got off the phone feeling lower than I had in a long time, and that was when I decided to take that walk just to see a friendly face."

"You never told me that," Frederick said, a protective square to his shoulders. It was clear that he didn't like Edward's response to her, even this many years later.

"Why would I have?" she said. "But when I saw you—that surfer who'd introduced himself to me as 'Freddy'..." She smiled as more tears surfaced and turned to the group. "I noticed he'd brought a stack of books. They were sitting on the blanket. He called hello from his board and came up to see me. 'Those are for you,' he said. 'I hoped you'd come back.' A long time later, I asked him why."

There was a moment between them as they stared at each other and there was so much there, just under the surface. Even now.

Frederick said, "I told you it was because I'd never seen such a beautiful woman who looked so sad and I knew right then that all I wanted was to see you smile."

She put her face in her hands and rubbed her eyes before looking up again. "You were so easy to talk to. So kind, gentle, you took me out—we met for ice cream, remember?"

Callie knew what kind and gentle felt like too, being with Luke. It was clear, the more Lillian talked about Frederick, how similar Luke was to his biological father, and she was floored by the similarities. Luke had spent his whole life trying to live up to something he wasn't. If he'd just been told about Frederick, would he have realized that his differences weren't downfalls? He was perfect just the way he was.

"You know why I'm telling you all this, don't you?" she asked Luke.

The whole table waited for the answer.

"Because I can see in your eyes right now, the exact same look I saw in Freddy's eyes when I told him we couldn't see each other anymore: disappointment, anger, sadness. That unique cocktail of emotions that only come about a few times in one's life. Luke, you look so much like Freddy it kills me sometimes."

Luke had a pensive look on his face and Callie had never seen him this quiet before.

"The night I was with Freddy was like magic." She reached out and held Frederick's hand across the table. "We'd seen each other so many times and he was so familiar to me then, like the piece of me that had been missing for all those years. He was such a gentleman that I couldn't believe I'd put myself in that position—that I allowed myself to follow my heart without thinking—because I was falling in love with him."

She offered a shy smile toward him.

"The next morning, in the light of day, I realized what I'd done and I told him we had to end it. Even though I loved him, I told him I'd made the worst mistake of my life out of loneliness, and I regretted how it happened immensely. I left, planning never to speak of it again. Two days later, Edward told me he was coming home. He said he was sorry for not being more sympathetic, that he was just overwhelmed with work, and he promised not to leave me again." She let go of Frederick's hand and crossed her arms. "I have held that guilt for so many years and it weighs on me like a cinderblock tied to my heart."

The rain started sheeting down outside, streaking the windows, the sound on the roof like a crowd at a sporting event. It came down hard and fast like the emotions surrounding them all. The table was silent, but on their faces Callie could see a hundred thoughts at once.

Lillian spoke quietly. "When I found out I was pregnant," she said in a whisper as a family walked in and sat down in the dining room, "I knew right then I should tell Freddy. It was close enough that Edward wouldn't question it, and I was terrified to tell him. When I counted the days, I knew exactly when it was, and I couldn't keep that from Freddy. I arranged to meet him for coffee to figure out what to do."

Frederick smiled a sad smile. "I remember that day like it was yesterday. You looked so beautiful and I hadn't thought I would see you again, so I was over the moon when you called."

Lillian looked at him with a comforting expression, her pain at having hurt him obviously still there. She addressed the others: "I told him quietly and then said..." She cringed, the pain slowing down her words. "...that I'd been thinking all the way there, and the best thing for our child would be to have all the opportunities money could buy. Money that Edward could give him, money that Freddy didn't have. I told him that if I went back to Edward and we raised Luke as our son, however, he could never speak of it again."

Frederick spoke up. "I said okay. And I left." The words came out as if they still surprised him today. He rubbed the scruff on his face like he was trying to wipe the anguish off. "I didn't want to agree to it, but I didn't feel like I could force what I wanted on Lillian. If she wanted to be with Edward more than me, I just wanted her to be happy. I was young. I didn't realize at that moment what having a son would mean to me. But it started to sink in pretty quickly. The moment she walked out, I was a mess."

"I thought I could give him all the love he needed *and* the money to move him forward in life. But money isn't always better," Lillian said. "I should've known that right then, but it took me time to realize what I'd done, and when I did, it was too late." Her voice was breaking and she took a sip of coffee, her hands trembling as she lifted the cup.

Two women came in the door and walked over to the table in the corner, happily hugging the group of people sitting there. It felt like a world away from the table where Callie sat, hurting for this family and for Luke, wishing he'd look at her so she could comfort him, but his eyes were on Lillian, his shoulders high and anxious.

"Freddy wanted to see Luke." Lillian smiled through her tears at Frederick, now speaking to him. "I said that it wasn't a good idea, but you'd taken me to Corolla before and I knew how remote it was. There wasn't a chance, back then, of anyone finding us. I played with Luke that day and you sat on the dune, sketching, on that blanket I remembered so well." She addressed the others. "But he was really watching Luke—watching him laugh, run around chasing the seagulls, build in the sand. I still remember stealing little glances and seeing the smile on his face as he watched Luke play.

"It was a gorgeous day, and Luke had such a ball that he fell asleep on the way home. Before we left, Freddy asked if we'd come again, but seeing him was so hard that I had to tell him no." Her voice cracked again as she finished her sentence. "I'd made a choice to love Edward, and I'd already messed that up once. I wasn't going to do it again."

"But you're divorced now, from Edward," Aiden said, his sentence more of a question. Why hadn't Lillian set things straight then? Why hadn't she gone after Frederick?

"Looking back, my infidelity was a symptom of something bigger, and no matter how hard I tried, I just couldn't make it work. I gave it everything I had. But if I had it to do over, I'd change a lot about what I did. Freddy's been without his son, Luke doesn't know his father, and Edward has been misled this whole time. I feared they would all despise me," she said, hanging her head.

"But, Mom," said Juliette, "didn't you wonder if being hated would be better than keeping this huge secret for all these years? Did you ever think that Luke, that *Dad,* had a right to know?"

Lillian squeezed her eyes shut. "I did consider that—of course I did, every day. But I was scared. I didn't know how to make it right after making it so wrong for so many years. I'm so sorry."

"I don't know how to react!" Juliette said, shaking her head as she processed it all. She turned to Luke, her face full of worry, her lips beginning to wobble. Luke pulled her close, stroking her hair.

Then he got up and put his arms around his mother. She shooed him off sweetly, and Callie could tell she was concerned about blubbering and making a scene. He held her anyway and kissed the top of her head. On the way back to his seat, Luke glanced over at Frederick just briefly and Frederick wiped away his tears.

Lillian picked up her fork and toyed with it. "I worry about what comes next. We're going to have to tell Edward."

Chapter Twenty-Two

Luke had paid the tab for their drinks and they'd all gone back to their rooms, having decided to just get room service. It was clear that everyone needed space. The rain had let up, the stifling heat assaulting them still, every time the doors had opened downstairs, but Frederick had said he was going for a walk. He'd been gone for hours.

Aiden had come to Callie and Olivia's room, and they'd been watching the storm coverage, Callie's mind drifting back and forth between the possible damage to the cottage and the Sullivan family, as surely the others' thoughts were as well. There was a knock and when Callie answered it, Lillian was at the door with Mitchell and Juliette.

"We checked on Luke. He wanted to be alone," Juliette said. "May we come in?"

"Of course." Callie stepped aside to let them enter. Juliette went straight over to Aiden and sat down beside him, while Lillian sat on the chair closest to the sofa. Mitchell found Wyatt, who had built a small fort in the corner with Legos. Aiden put his arm around Juliette, almost as if he could protect her emotions with that one gesture.

They all sat quietly, the TV and the sound of the boys playing filling the silence. As she watched them all, the one thing Callie saw was love for each other. As upset as Juliette had been about her mother's decision to keep the truth from Luke and her father, they had still seemed almost unified at the door. Now Aiden, Juliette, and Lillian were all sitting together, watching the storm coverage but seemingly comfortable in each other's space. Callie focused on the television.

It was as if the newscast was on a loop: After about a half hour of watching, Callie realized that the reporters hadn't really said anything new, and were starting to repeat the major points, which were that the storm was hitting the Outer Banks, causing destruction in some areas, and moving out rather quickly.

There was another knock and Olivia got the door this time. It was Luke. Callie felt herself almost stand up—she wanted to check to see if he was okay. But she caught herself, unsure if he'd want to talk to her, and waited for him to come in.

"I called Dad." He dropped down onto the sofa between Aiden and his sister, his movements edgy as he allowed a little extra room to accommodate everyone. He looked tired. The gray skies outside cast a grim light across the room. "I asked if I could see him."

Wyatt and Mitchell stopped building with their Legos for a moment but resumed making the fort for their action figures when Olivia asked them about their creation.

"I want to be the one to tell him," Luke said. "If you tell him, Mom, he'll just be angry with you, but if I tell him, we could get to the heart of what he really thinks. I said I needed to speak with him in person, and that what I had to tell him wasn't easy."

"What did he say, Luke?" Juliette asked.

"He's on his way."

"What?" Lillian asked, worry showing in her pursed lips.

"I told him where we were. He's reserved a room across the street at the Omni, and he'll be on a plane in an hour. Luckily, there was one available."

"What if he feels like we're all ganging up on him?" Juliette fretted. "This is news he may want to hear privately."

"Yes." Luke nodded. "I've already thought of that. I'm going over to meet him. He's gonna text me when he arrives."

Until eleven o'clock, when Luke got the text, barely anyone spoke a word.

* * *

Frederick still hadn't returned. Olivia and Juliette had put the kids to bed in one room, Olivia offering to stay with them until everyone turned in for the night. It was nearing two a.m., and the hurricane coverage still chirped away on the television. The eye of the storm had passed and residents who'd stayed in the Outer Banks were hunkering down for the last half of the storm.

All eyes were on the screen, but Callie knew where their thoughts were: with Luke. He'd been gone for ages, and she was hoping things were going well. She felt like this was all her fault, and with Luke's noticeable distance from her and the outburst by the elevators, she knew he held her responsible as well.

The door opened and every head swiveled toward it.

Luke's face was stark; he looked completely exhausted. Callie had taken his gentle, affectionate looks for granted, but was now yearning to see them again.

"What happened?" Juliette asked, standing up to meet him. She took his hands, tilting her chin up to look at her brother, concern engulfing her face.

"I, uh..." He let go of Juliette and sat down on the sofa, completely broken, the words not coming out, despite the thoughts that were in his eyes.

Lillian put her hand on his back, tears surfacing.

"I feel like I lost my father tonight," he said, nearly breathless, turning to his mother as if she could help him in some way. "He said he had suspected it, that as I grew up, he had always wondered, but he couldn't imagine it..." Luke ran his hands over his face, complete grief in his features.

"Give him time," Juliette said. She was now kneeling beside him. "He just needs to process it. Let him have a few days, get back to work—you know how he is. He needs to continue on. He'll have to call you to begin the progression of you taking over the company, and it'll force him to talk to you. You're great at being understanding; you'll know just how to handle the situation as it comes."

"Well, it won't happen like that because everything's going to Aiden."

Juliette gasped in exasperation.

Callie remembered that proud look Luke made whenever he was around her. His expression was a far cry from that right now. He looked hurt, sad. Her stomach churned like the wild seas back home.

"I admitted to him that I wouldn't be opposed to getting

to know Frederick." He turned back to his mother and the others.

Lillian's eyes bulged.

"The press will eventually get wind of all this," Lillian said. "We need to have an organized response in case we're cornered. But right now, we need to decide how to approach Edward when we speak to him again."

Callie hadn't experienced it in her own life, but she could spot it—that defending instinct of a mother protecting her child. Lillian was intense as she tried to think through how to handle the situation.

Luke spoke to Juliette in a whisper. They seemed so close, and it was clear that hearing that they were half-siblings, while a huge thing, hadn't tainted anything between them. Callie had worried about how Juliette might take the news, but in the end, he was still her brother. Juliette put her head on his shoulder for a moment.

"I want to be there too," Aiden said, shifting forward. "If you're concerned about me taking the company, Luke, you don't have to worry about that." Aiden leaned in. "I've always thought I could run the business but I never believed that it belonged to anyone other than you."

"I feel like I should be there too," Lillian said, shaking her head. "I have to finally tell him what happened all those years ago. I'm not proud of it," she said, "but it's part of my past and I should be present to answer Edward's questions. He's going to have quite a few for me, I'm certain."

"We'll be there to support you," Luke said. His knee bounced up and down. "He won't talk to me right now. Let's let him cool off—let this all settle in—and I'll call him."

* * *

*Law enforcement is asking that you stay away from any
remaining flooded roadways until the rest of the water
can recede. Flash flooding is still a problem. Tree limbs
and branches cover the roadways due to high winds
and they are causing hazards, along with other road
debris. As you can see behind me, stoplights are swinging into the water, and the wind is still blowing hard,
making clean-up and repairs difficult. I urge you to use
caution upon return. The mayor has issued a manda-
tory curfew of nine p.m. I'll update you every hour on
the hour, right here, on Channel Six.*

Luke came in and sat down. He'd just taken the last
of the things to the car and everyone was nearly ready
to leave, all of them completely exhausted from staying
up last night. Luke had tried to see Edward again, but
he'd checked out already, so he let him go, promising his
mother he'd call him after they'd all gotten settled back
home. After everyone had gone to bed, Frederick had returned quietly, and he hadn't said a whole lot this morning,
clearly immersed in his own thoughts.

The storm wasn't as devastating as they had predicted
but there was still quite a bit of damage and everyone was
eager to get home to see things for themselves. Luke had
had room service bring up breakfast and coffee at five
a.m., and he'd insisted all the ladies stay and have their
coffee while he packed, telling them they needed to watch
the news so they could update him if they heard anything
that might inhibit their return.

"What have they said?" he asked his mother, as Frederick left to take a dolly down to the car.

"It's just a mess down there, like it always is after a hurricane."

Callie had seen pictures on the news in other years, but she hadn't experienced the complete worry that the residents faced every time it happened. It had always been a tragedy, but by the time she'd returned for vacation, the entire place was rebuilt, open for business, ready for the tourists who flocked down and settled on those glorious beaches. Once the damage had been reported, the media moved on to the next story, and the rebuilding process every time went unmentioned. But now, seeing the damage, and knowing it could be like that at her new home, where her life was now, it filled her with fear.

The news program had focused mostly on the villages farther north of Callie's, the major tourist locations where the rest of the country would relate, so she hadn't been able to see the fate of Waves.

"Did you secure your surfboards?" she asked suddenly.

Luke nodded. "I tied them up in the rafters of the shed. Unless it was blown away, they should be just fine."

"Okay," she said with an exhalation, apprehension still assaulting her.

"We'd better get a move on," he said.

Chapter Twenty-Three

They were forced to stay on the bypass when they came across the bridge from the mainland, having only gained access by proving they were permanent residents. Portions of Beach Road had crumbled into the ocean. The water had receded mostly back into the sea, leaving puddles and pockets of flooding in the residential areas. They carried on, hoping they would have solid road all the way to Waves. The car was silent as they drove past the damage.

"I'll take you home first," Luke said quietly, both hands gripping the wheel intently. A power line dipped into the road beside them as he pulled to a stop to yield to any traffic, the stoplights out. He looked both ways, but unless it was by boat, no one would be coming from either direction, as the side street was flooded. He carried on. "It's bad up this way," he said. But he didn't say anything more. Callie wondered if it would be this bad in Waves.

All of a sudden, Luke pulled over. "There's a tree blocking the road over there and that car can't get down it."

Callie saw the driver. He'd exited his car and was pulling with all his might on the trunk of the tree, trying to move it. It would budge just a little and he'd lose grip. There were kids in the back of his car.

"Stay put. I'm going to help him," Luke said.

Before she or Frederick could say anything, he jumped out and ran down the street. Frederick went out after him, leaving Callie. She could see them talking to the man as he gestured toward one of the cottages. Then the three men strained and pulled until the tree had shifted. All three of them got on one side of it and, in a unified effort, moved it to the side of the road. The man shook Luke's hand.

"They rode out the storm," he said, slightly winded, when he got back. "His wife is pregnant and on bed rest. He was worried about the tree blocking their way if they needed to get to the hospital. She's due any day. They thought the storm would've brought on labor, but they were lucky."

Callie shook her head, the enormity of the situation overwhelming her to the point of speechlessness. Luke and Frederick got back into the car and there was a hushed anticipation as they made their way home.

The farther down the road they went, the more hopeful Callie became, the storm having spared parts of the Outer Banks. The road was cracked in places, making it difficult for Luke to maneuver the large vehicle without hitting major dips, but he was a skilled driver and he made it through. Every time she saw some damage, Callie's heart sank, but she knew she couldn't expect the storm to have skipped over her part of the barrier islands completely.

They passed a cottage that was missing part of its front porch and a bit of the roof on the left side. An elderly woman was standing alone in the yard, struggling with a load of bags. Callie shot Luke an apprehensive look. He slowed the car.

"Do you think she's okay?" he asked.

Callie shook her head. "No, we should help her."

He glanced over at her. "But you need to check your own house."

"Getting there sooner won't change anything." It was quite obvious that people around them were struggling and she felt compelled to help after hearing about the man and his wife that Luke had helped.

He pulled the car over and got out, taking his phone from his back pocket. "Let me just text Juliette, and let her know."

The woman, who was carrying bags of debris in her tiny arms, stopped and watched them advance toward her. By the look on her face, and the growing roundness of her eyes, she recognized Luke.

"Hello," he said as he approached her. "Luke Sullivan."

She looked around and set the bags down beside her. Probably trying to decide if she was on some sort of hidden camera show.

"Do you need help with anything?"

The woman's eyebrows shot up in surprise, relief on her face. "Yes!" she said, throwing her hand to her chest, her voice almost giddy. "I live alone and I'm trying to move all that." She pointed to a pile of debris by the porch.

"Well, we've got it from here. What's your name?"

"Paula."

"Hi, Paula. This is Callie and Frederick. Put us to

work." Luke picked up the bags for her. "Where do these go?"

"Just to the street," she said, meeting their eyes with a grateful smile. "I was making a pile until I can find my trashcan or get a new one. It was blown away in the storm."

Luke placed the bags at the street and joined Callie and Frederick as they walked toward the house, Paula leading them to the other pile of boards and wreckage. "Does all this need to be bagged up?" he asked.

"Yes. I'm just piling what will fit into the bags. Be careful, because the wood is full of nails." Then she stopped and looked directly at Luke. "Thank you," she said with sincerity in her voice. "I'll be inside working on the damaged roof. Just let yourselves in if you need anything." She hovered briefly, still clearly in shock at their gesture, but then, once they'd gotten to work, she headed inside.

Carefully, they put what they could into the bags and piled the rest in a more orderly mound. As Paula had warned, every piece was jagged, torn, full of nails and sharp splintering wood, so they labored slowly. Luke was all business, not stopping once to make eye contact, and Callie wished, despite the task at hand, that he'd give her even one small gesture to let her know that he didn't hate her, but it never came.

As they worked, Callie kept hearing a distant sound above the crashing of the ocean, but she couldn't make it out until, all of a sudden, she stopped. "Do you hear that?" she said.

Luke and Frederick slowed to a halt and stood still. The static sound of the ocean filled the air.

"What do you hear?" Frederick said.

Callie tilted her head to the side, sharpening her hearing, waiting for the sound again.

Nothing.

"Maybe it was just my ears playing tricks on me," she said, knowing for sure she'd heard something. Whatever it was, it was gone now. She leaned down to pick up a piece of wood and there it was again. "Did you hear it?"

"I did, " Luke said, looking around and walking away from where they were working. Callie followed.

Their movement seemed to jar whatever it was because the sound got more intense, a high-pitched whimper. They walked across to the next lot, which seemed empty, the owners most likely still out of town. The whimpering came again and Luke looked under one of the cars.

"It's a dog," he said. "It looks scared." He leaned down as Callie peered under the vehicle. "Come here, boy," Luke said gently, patting his thighs. The dog was some sort of Labrador mix—black with a white patch on its chest—and it didn't move. It cried again.

"It's hurt," Callie said. She'd played with enough dogs growing up to tell that it couldn't come to him. Its tail wasn't wagging, and its head didn't rise, but its eyes followed Luke as he walked around the car to try to figure out what to do.

"It's okay," she said to the dog in a soothing voice. "We'll help you."

Luke lay down on his back and shimmied under the car to get a better look at the dog, the whole time talking to it, telling it his next move as if it understood him. Maybe it did because it stopped whining and just lay there. Frederick dumped a couple more bags by the street before joining them.

"It's probably starving," Luke said from under the

car. He ran his hand gently along the dog's side. "I'll bet he got pushed under here in the storm somehow. Or maybe he got hurt and tried to find himself some shelter." He let the dog sniff his hand but it still didn't move, clearly not worried by Luke at all. Luke ran his hand along the dog's head, down each arm, and along its leg. When he got to the bottom of the dog's leg, it yelped. "Yep. He's hurt."

"I'll check with Paula to see if she knows the owners," Frederick said.

Callie reached under the car, gently stroking the dog's head. It tried to lift itself up to greet her but winced and lay back down. "We'll make it all better," she said gently, and the dog took in a short huff of breath that sounded like relief. She fished around its neck for a collar but there wasn't one.

"I think I have a first aid kit in the truck. Callie, could you get the bandages out? I'm going to try to stabilize the dog's leg under the car before I pull him out so he isn't in any pain. See if you can get a few of the depressor sticks out of there too, so we can make a splint."

He wriggled around and pulled his keys out of his pocket, tossing them out from under the car. Callie scooped them up and ran over to get what they needed. On the way to the car, she thought about how much things had changed, how distant Luke was with her now, and she ached to feel his playfulness again. It was painfully clear to her that she missed him. He was right there but he wasn't at the same time, and her heart actually ached being that close to him and not seeing his smile.

She returned in a flash, and stopped alongside Frederick and Paula, who was leaning down to view the dog.

"I have no idea whose dog that is," Paula said. "The

owners next door don't have any pets. I've never seen it before."

Callie handed Luke the items he needed to bandage the dog's leg. As he was wrapping it, the dog whimpered a bit, but allowed him to work. "It's a big dog, but by the size of its paws, it looks like a puppy to me," he said, gently lifting the dog's leg to get the bandage around it. Luke was on his side, his lower half protruding from under the car.

When the dog's leg was properly secured, Luke slid his arms underneath its body and gently drew it near him as he scooted out from under the car. The dog was clearly uncomfortable, its legs moving as if it were paddling, but its injury meant it couldn't make it out without assistance. It tried to stand and its legs buckled under the pain. Luke caught it and sat down on the driveway with it in his lap.

"It's a girl," he said. "She's probably dehydrated and hungry, and her leg's in bad shape. It's definitely broken. We should take her to a veterinarian."

"You two take her," Frederick said. "Callie can help her to remain still while you drive. I'll stay and keep working for Paula."

With a nod, Luke carried the dog to the car and, after Callie had climbed in, he gently set the dog on her lap. She lifted her head and it was then that Callie really got a look at her face. It was black with a white stripe between her eyes that met her white muzzle. Her chest and paws were also white, her floppy ears down as she looked up at Callie trustingly. Callie smiled at her, and her tail smacked Callie's leg just a little.

"We've got you," Callie said. "Let's fix that leg up for you, okay?"

Another few thumps from the dog's tail.

"She's so sweet," she said to Luke. "I can't believe she's probably been there since the storm."

"Well, she might have collapsed there later; we don't know. But from the look of her, she needs some care, and quickly."

Careful not to compromise the dog's leg, Callie cuddled her just a little more.

* * *

The dog had needed IV fluids and a full day at the vet to nurse her back to health. She was also getting a cast on her broken leg—Luke had been correct. No one had called the veterinarian as of yet with a missing dog matching that description, so Callie and Luke promised to return for her, and Luke had stepped forward to take care of the bill. He also left his cell phone number, which the veterinary assistant had stared at as if she'd gotten a famous autograph or something.

As they headed back to Paula's, Callie asked, "What will happen to the dog?"

"I suppose she'll get a name."

"Think we should keep her?"

His eyes stayed on the road. "We?"

It had been an unconscious word choice and she hadn't meant to imply anything. "Well, I was thinking if no one claims her, I'd like to keep the dog at The Beachcomber— I've already fallen in love with her. But I suppose we can share custody if you'd like to have her." She remembered how he'd said he'd like a dog when they'd first met. She wished for those times again but tried not to think about it.

"You can keep her. But then it should be you who gives her a name. What are you going to call her?" He pulled down a side street and stopped at the intersection, checking to see if it was clear to cross.

Callie thought for a while. She'd never expected to have a dog—another being to depend on her. Was she ready? Could she give it the attention it needed? But as she remembered the dog's sweet little face, she just knew that it was meant to be. "I'd like to name her..." She rolled a few names around in her head, thinking about how she had sort of popped up out of nowhere. "Poppy."

"Poppy," he said, pursing his lips in thought. "Poppy the puppy. I like it."

For the rest of the ride, Poppy brought new questions to Callie's mind: Was The Beachcomber a place for a family dog? *Family*...Would it ever be somewhere to raise lots of children? Wyatt would certainly be fine—he acted so much older than his age. But what about more? What if she could've had children with Luke and she'd messed it up? The idea of being happy *and* investing herself in someone hadn't seemed so far off, until she'd told Luke about Frederick.

They pulled up at Paula's, behind Juliette's SUV. They'd all gotten out and were helping with what they could while the kids tossed a ball in the yard. Frederick had piled the last of the wreckage by the street.

"Forgive me," Paula said after she approached Luke and Callie, "but I've been dying to ask...Are you *the* Luke Sullivan? The one from the magazines?"

Luke smiled politely. "Yes."

"Wow," she said, astounded.

"You know, he's more saving-puppies-and-fixing-houses than he is all those things they write in the magazines," Callie said with a smile and a cautious look over at Luke.

He finally met her eyes but only briefly, and then he looked back at Paula, offering a small smile. "I'll stay," he said. "You still have a lot to take care of here. Julie, why don't you take Callie and Olivia home?"

Juliette nodded, rounding everyone up.

"I'll stay too, Luke," Frederick said. Luke walked over and lifted another board, leading the way.

Chapter Twenty-Four

They pulled up outside The Beachcomber and got out of the car. The wind was still strong, whipping against them as they all walked.

Juliette and Lillian stayed with the kids while Olivia, Aiden, and Callie went to see if The Beachcomber had sustained any damage. They got up to the house and went around to the back to check it out. They were on land the whole way, which was a good thing—the waters had receded. The new walkway was damaged, she could already see. Of course the plants were gone too, and the whole yard was a soaking mess, full of debris.

"It can all be repaired," Aiden said encouragingly.

When Callie turned to see the back of the cottage, her confidence faltered. The new porches had been ripped apart, the wood either washed away or dangling precariously from the stilts, and the shingles were missing on part of the house. She blinked, trying desperately not to tear up. The grand opening was only a week away. There was no possible way she could get it all rebuilt and ready in time. It had been risky to open during hurricane season, but they'd hoped for the best, knowing it was their only shot at recovering some of the funds they'd spent on the remodel. She swallowed, trying to alleviate the lump in her throat.

Olivia came over and took her hand, squeezing it tightly, which only made the tears come faster as they spilled down her cheek.

"Let's walk back around front and go inside so we can see if there is any water damage to the interior," Aiden said softly.

They climbed the front steps and Callie pulled her keys out of her pocket, slipping them into the door. She took off her shoes on the porch and Olivia and Aiden did the same. The front of the house was fine, all the new painting and the furniture still in great shape. The air inside was hot, the air conditioning turned off before they'd left, but it all looked okay. With every step she felt relief.

Until they got to the kitchen.

There was water damage to the ceiling at the outside wall, her new paint having buckled under the pressure of the leak. The entire wall would have to be replaced, and the ceiling patched. Callie bit her trembling lip. First impressions meant everything. People were counting on her for a wonderful vacation. Reviews would make or break a business at this stage. They had to have it perfect for the opening if she wanted to make a success of this. Another tear laced with worry slid down her cheek.

"We can fix this," Aiden said.

She shook her head, clearing her throat and trying to push away her tears. "That's very sweet of you," she said, looking over at Olivia. "I'm just worried about the time…"

"I know it'll be a rush, but it's not as bad as you think," he said. "We'll just need everyone to pitch in." Aiden took Olivia's hand. "I promise. You'll open on time," he said.

* * *

Even though Luke had sent a text telling his cousin he was fine, Aiden had insisted they all go to Luke's to make sure that he didn't need any help. Although it pained her to leave The Beachcomber, she knew there wasn't much she could do on her own until Aiden's crew arrived.

Luke's house had some damage: The garage had flooded, so they used large brooms to push the water out; there was some destruction on the deck, which Aiden helped to assess, and a bit of the landscaping would have to be redone. Lillian had been able to save a few of the smaller plants but the stretch to the beach was so large, their acreage so big, that there'd been room for the tide to come up.

It had been a very long day. They all gathered in Luke's living room, exhausted, when Lillian finally spoke.

"I called your father," she said quietly to Luke, but everyone could hear. "I just couldn't sit by and watch him pull everything away from you like that. I told him point blank that he was going to lose you." She leaned against the wall and looked up at the ceiling. "He hired a car to take us home from the hospital when you were born, and he sat next to your seat, cooing to you all the way home." She looked into Luke's eyes. "He helped you take your first steps when you started walking, holding out his hands everywhere you went so you could try to reach them…He spent hours outside, teaching you how to ride a bike, steadying the back of it as it wobbled. You didn't want to go inside that day, and he stayed with you, delighting in your perseverance—do you remember?"

Luke nodded and there was a long silence as they both contemplated the enormity of the situation. "What did he say when you spoke to him?" he asked.

"He's just scared and hurt. I know him well enough to know that. But I could feel his sadness in his silence."

Luke took in a breath. "We've all had a lot going on. Let's try to relax and be thankful that our homes were mostly spared by this storm. Why don't we all just unwind?" He pinched the bridge of his nose and squinted his eyes as if relieving the pain there, then went into the kitchen. "Who needs a glass of wine?" he said over the large island separating the rooms.

They all nodded wearily. While Juliette and Luke handed out glasses, Lillian made an impromptu cheese platter with a few crackers and several cheeses. They had broken into small groups of chatter as they sprawled out on the sofas in the large living area. Luke's face had fallen back into a neutral expression, as if he wanted to block everything out for the time being.

Callie sipped her wine quietly on the sofa, smiling subtly at Aiden as he told Olivia that he'd like to take Wyatt to play mini-golf once this ordeal was over. She also noticed how Frederick had started chatting quite easily with Luke about the dog. She could tell they'd been getting to know one another during their time together at Paula's by the way they were talking.

After quite a while, once the wine had done its job, and everyone had relaxed a little, Frederick sat up and ran his hands through his hair. In that moment, Callie could almost see what he might have looked like as a young man, and Luke's strong resemblance to him was clearer than it had ever been. "I brought something," he said, the other conversations subsiding. He smiled nervously, pulling out the same bag he'd brought when he'd arrived to do the mural. Callie had noticed that he'd taken it with him when they'd evacuated, but he hadn't opened it until now.

They were all gathered around, scooting together on the sofas in the living room. The bag was too flat to have clothes inside, and she'd never seen anything quite like it. He reached over and set it on his lap, unzipping it, and drew out large sheets of paper, laying them down on the coffee table. Callie had to catch her breath.

Lillian clapped a hand over her heart, getting up to view them: pencil sketches of Lillian, the wind blowing her hair, large sunglasses on her face, smiling; Luke pitching a baseball—he must have been about seven; the back of a woman as she sat reading on a blanket on the beach and another of her, leaning against a surfboard.

"Oh my God," Callie said, unable to look away from the pictures scattered along the table.

"Alice was there while Luke was growing up, but I was too." Frederick regarded Luke, his face vulnerable with his admission. "I didn't go to see him as much as she did because every time I did, it ripped my heart out. But I was there. I kept going to Corolla, I was at his baseball games, I saw him riding horses and learning to surf like I did. Whenever I could muster the energy, I went, but after I saw him, I just felt drained, empty."

For the first time, Callie saw fondness in Luke's eyes when he looked at Frederick.

With trembling arms, Lillian hugged them both, and what looked like years of burden fell away from her face, relief flooding it. Frederick had his hand on Lillian's shoulders now, his fingers moving up to her neck as he pulled her into the embrace, Luke by his side. It was as if time stood still. Maybe it hurt, maybe things would be changed forever, but this was right. It should've happened years ago. Once the moment had passed, Lillian pulled back. "What will we say to the press?" she worried.

"I don't care," Luke said. There was a commanding presence to him just then, and it revealed that he'd made up his mind. He wasn't shying away from the press anymore.

* * *

The phone pulsed against Callie's ear as it rang. Sprawled across her air mattress, she looked up at the fresh paint on the ceiling and the recessed lighting that had been installed where Olivia's pencil marks had been. She could barely keep her eyes open after the day she'd had, but she had one more thing that she wanted to do. She couldn't make things right with Luke, but she could start to make them right with someone else.

Callie had seen tonight how right Gladys was when she'd said, "The truth will set you free." She'd learned by letting Luke into her world and her thoughts how being honest with someone made life richer and not so scary when she'd always thought it was the other way around. So, if she were being honest with herself, she'd have admitted that she missed her mother. She missed those days before everything had become so complicated, and she was going to try to mend things.

"Hello?" her mother answered.

"Hi. It's Callie."

"Oh, hi, Callie. How's the cottage? Is everything okay?"

Callie had felt a twinge of guilt for having been in the same city as her mother and not trying to see her, but things had gone so fast, and she hadn't been ready then. Now she was. Her mother hadn't been very supportive after she and Kyle had split up, and they hadn't ever really talked about it, which had hurt Callie. But now, she could step back and see that being supportive might be easier for her mother if Callie would forgive her.

"The cottage had some damage," she said. "But we're getting it all fixed. Thank you for asking."

"That's great. I'm glad you called to update me."

Callie sat up. "That's not why I called."

"Oh?"

"No, Mom. I called because I just wanted to see what you were up to." She balled the sheet into her fist and then smoothed it out, her fingertips light with anticipation. She'd never taken a step like this before.

There was a kind of silence, during which Callie felt that her mother was assessing her, trying to decide her motives, but the truth was, she only had one motive: Luke had lost a lot of time with Frederick—time he'd never get back. Callie didn't want the same thing to happen with her mother.

"I know we haven't been really close..."

"No," her mother said, her voice shaky. "I'll tell you. I'm alone a lot. I used to think that being alone would help me get better, figure out what I needed. I craved the silence, trying to make everything calm down in my head, but now that I have it, it just feels empty. I think about you...Wonder what you're doing."

"You don't have to be alone," Callie said. "Come stay with us sometime. We have plenty of room."

When she didn't respond, Callie said, "The sea air will

clear your head better than anything else. I speak from experience." She heard the small breath before her mother's smile.

"Maybe I will."

"You have my number. Just text or call whenever you want to come."

Chapter Twenty-Five

The next day, they all sat around a table at The Beach-comber discussing their parts in the repairs to the bed and breakfast. Everyone except for Luke. Aiden had said that they could do with Luke's help, but Callie wouldn't let him ask. He'd had too much to deal with already without putting her own burdens on him, and she still wasn't sure if he'd ever forgive her for telling him about Frederick. Gladys had returned home and come over to see the damage, and she was beside herself, but Aiden assured her that it would be just fine.

"How long would you estimate repairs to take, Aiden?" Gladys asked. "I know Callie and Olivia are on a time crunch to get it done by next week."

"It would take two weeks or more usually, but we could do it in less time if we get a whole crew on it. The problem is that I'm not sure I can get a whole crew because builders are in short supply at the moment, as you can imagine, so I'm hoping we can all plan to pitch in."

"Of course," Juliette said.

"I'll be here too," Frederick said.

* * *

They worked all day and all night, then the whole week, on The Beachcomber. Aiden, Frederick, and Juliette helped every minute they could and Olivia and Callie worked around the clock. Even Lillian and Gladys pitched in for small things.

"We've been going full speed," Olivia said over her plate of oysters.

Once everyone had gone home for an early evening to have a much-needed rest, Callie and Olivia took their showers and finally decided they deserved a night out so neither of them would have to cook. They were both exhausted, and they needed to discuss what they were going to do about the guests arriving before all the work would be finished. So they'd had Gladys watch Wyatt and put some food out for Poppy and gone to a little beachside restaurant. They sat outside on the deck, and tried to come up with a plan.

"We still have to paint the kitchen, we have to finish the porches—they've eaten up all our time—and get furniture, and the walkway hasn't been landscaped. Even if we go back home and keep working all night, we just won't be finished in time."

"You're right, the porches are taking forever," Callie said, rubbing her forehead. "With Frederick and the rest of us redoing the entire walkway, Aiden has been basically doing the porches by himself. I know he's going as fast as he can, but we just need more people." She sucked down the rest of her cocktail—some kind of pineapple rum concoction that she'd asked for at the last minute when she'd ordered her dinner. She'd needed a drink. Everything they'd worked for, every moment they'd spent this summer, came down to this, and it was slipping away from them.

Olivia flagged the waitress and ordered them both another drink. "I'm really worried. I have no clue what we're going to do."

Callie looked out at the beach; someone was flying a kite—a rainbow triangle with tails so long they almost touched the sand. The sparkly surface of its fabric shimmered in the sunlight. "I don't know either," she said, turning back to Olivia.

A band was setting up in the corner. They both sat quietly, watching them as the sea breeze blew in off the ocean. The waitress set down the next round of drinks.

"Why don't we invite Aiden and Frederick to come out? Aiden always has such a level head. We could see if he and Frederick have any ideas. If not, they might enjoy the band and it would take our minds off of it."

"You're right," Callie said. "Text Aiden. I'll text Frederick."

Callie hadn't seen Frederick all afternoon. He'd worked in the morning and then spent the rest of the day with Luke. He and Luke had met up just a couple of times, but whenever they had, Frederick had come back beaming. They seemed to be really hitting it off. They'd both gotten involved with a nonprofit Luke had found called Bring Us Home that was rebuilding residences with major damage. The charity was operating on a very strict budget, the destruction in other villages using nearly all their funds for disaster relief. Luke had made a donation, but had also promised he would bring light to their efforts.

"This is the kind of stuff that the media should be covering," he'd told Frederick. "And if my family name will bring it to the forefront, then so be it."

Frederick had joined him on a few building sites. The more they worked, the easier it became for Frederick to be near him. Today, he had been planning to go surfing and Callie had told him not to worry about them. He'd already helped so much with the walkway.

Their newfound closeness made Callie think about Edward. He'd remained in New York without a solid answer about his feelings for Luke or the business; he hadn't been able to see the way the family rallied to help each other, how they'd spent lots of nights around the dinner table laughing over funny things that had happened. Luke had asked him to come home, Frederick had told them one night, but he'd said he had work to get done. Callie wished things could be different with him.

She tried not to think about Luke, but it was proving difficult. She missed him so much, and she felt terrible about how things had turned out. She yearned to have those lighter times, those wonderful moments with him again, and feared with a heart-splitting sadness that she wouldn't experience them again. This was the person she was meant to be with, and yet he would barely speak to her. She knew she needed to get her head straight and just move on, but for the first time in her life, she was struggling to do it.

"I told Aiden we need his help to make a plan," Olivia said. "He said he'll be at the house when we get home. I'll tell him when we'll get there." Olivia tapped on her phone with a silly grin on her face.

Over the week, Olivia and Aiden had been flirty, and whenever Callie had needed Olivia, she'd always been able to find her outside on the porches, getting something for Aiden, holding something for Aiden, checking on him. They both got all their work done, but they could always be found together.

"You really like him; I can tell," Callie said with a smile. She was glad to see Olivia happy.

"I do," she admitted, looking up from her phone and dropping it into her handbag. "I like him so much that I think I'm willing to take that chance and see what happens." She blushed and broke out into a huge smile. She took a drink and the band started to play. "What did Frederick say?"

"He's already talked to Aiden—they were worried about it themselves. He'll be at the house too."

Callie squinted from the sunlight as she looked up at the bright blue sky, still light in the endless days of summer, trying not to feel the heaviness of the situation with The Beachcomber. She wished she could have her grandmother here to talk to. She needed someone to give her the answers that she just didn't have on her own. But Gladys had been with them, which was good, yet she didn't have any way to fix this either.

As she looked around at the vacationers, all sunburned, laughing, eating their yearly dose of local seafood, and enjoying drinks in their souvenir cups, she felt the exhaustion finally wash over her. She was spent—emotionally and physically—unable to enjoy the paradise around her.

* * *

"What's going on?" Callie said as they pulled up behind a team of cars in the drive.

"I don't know." Olivia frowned and got out.

There was a racket going on around the back of the house and they looked at each other in confusion. They walked around to see where all the pounding was coming from and Callie gasped in surprise. Enormous floodlights had been set up to combat the darkness that would be arriving soon. There was an entire crew pounding away on the porches, lifting timber, holding levels, hammers, and saws... She gazed from face to face until she found Frederick, smiling hugely as he looked at her.

"You ladies get your painting done," he called down to them. "We've got this!"

Callie wanted to run and hug him, but he'd gone back to hammering.

"Let's get changed!" Olivia said with excitement as she bounced on her toes. "We've got an opening to get ready for!"

After a quick text to Gladys asking her to keep Wyatt over there for the night, Olivia and Callie threw on some old clothes and got to work. They barely spoke as they painted the new drywall, both of them focused wholeheartedly on the task at hand. This was a blessing that had come out of nowhere and Callie couldn't wait to thank Frederick and Aiden for it, but right now, they had to get the rest finished. Her guess was that with a crew that large, the porches and the rest of the walkway could be done in no time at all. If Callie and Olivia could paint that one wall in the kitchen and get the landscaping laid out and planted, this opening was going to happen!

They painted almost breathlessly, excitement buzzing around them. When they'd finished, both of them went straight outside to start on the walkway. Once they got outside, they decided to find Frederick and Aiden first to thank them. Olivia looked for Aiden and Callie found Frederick.

Callie grabbed him and pulled him aside as she looked up at the porches that were now coming along so nicely, tears of happiness surfacing. She wiped them away. This gesture was more than she could have imagined, and she had many questions about who would foot the bill, and how they'd rounded up a crew of this size. "I just wanted to say thank you," she said, her gratitude showing in the form of more tears.

Frederick smiled.

"We couldn't have opened if this hadn't happened. You and Aiden literally saved us. I don't know what I'll ever do to repay you. Where did you find all these people?"

"They're from the nonprofit I've been working with. But Callie," he said, pulling her attention back to his face, his eyes now serious. "I didn't do this." He turned and pointed to a far area of the porch.

Callie searched the large group of workers, trying to figure out what he was showing her when suddenly a couple of people moved and her heart began racing. There, in the far corner, hidden before by the large crowd, was Luke. He wiped his brow and set a piece of wood in place, hammering it down.

"Luke did this," he said. "He offered to donate double the normal rate for a job of this size to their organization if they'd help him."

She felt her jaw slacken in surprise and had to consciously close her mouth. "Why?" she asked Frederick.

"Perhaps you should ask *him*."

With a dazed nod, she left Frederick and started to make her way down the new porch, forcing herself to acknowledge people along her path as they smiled and greeted her. Her hands tingled with anticipation, her heart feeling like it would burst as she watched him, just waiting for his eyes to fall on her. Then, there it was: He looked up and smiled that smile. She had to will herself to breathe. He set down his hammer and stood up.

"Hi," he said, a slight apprehension in his face.

"Hello." She wanted to throw her arms around him and bury her head in his chest but she stood still. "Frederick told me that you're responsible for all this," she said over the hammering.

"Take a walk with me?"

She caught her breath as he placed his hand lightly on her back, leading her through the workers as they headed for the stairs down to the beach. The breeze blew around them, the pounding fading into quiet as the sound of the waves took over. Tonight they were lapping softly, slapping the shore in a rhythmic motion. Callie tried to tune in to the rhythm of the sound to slow her beating heart.

When they reached the sand, Luke faced her. "I tried to help sooner, but Aiden said you didn't want me here," he said.

Callie frantically shook her head, ready to explain, but Luke kept going.

"I didn't want to push you. I felt terrible for what I said to you at the Berkeley. I was angry and confused, and I didn't know whom to blame. It took me a while to realize that there wasn't anyone to blame really. Not now. And things with my father might never be the same—I'll have to live with that. But what didn't take me long to realize was that I missed you. I missed you so much that it hurt. I couldn't spend another minute without you. I kept asking Frederick how you were, what you were up to, if you were okay."

He reached up and brushed a tear off her cheek and she noticed that she was shaking. He took her hands in his.

"Today, while we were surfing, he told me about how you were shorthanded. I thought, even if you didn't want me there, I wanted to show you that I care about you. I told him I was going to get the porches built whether you liked it or not," he said, that grin finally emerging. Then he looked into her eyes, the most sincere expression on his face, and said, "Will you forgive me?"

"There's nothing to forgive, Luke. I learned something from you," she said, dropping his hands and wrapping her arms around his neck. "That we have to be open and honest with each other, tell each other how we feel. That's what you do when you care about someone. So I have something to say." She pushed herself up on her tiptoes, putting her face right across from his. "I missed you so much when we were apart, and I don't want to spend another minute without you either. I've never met anyone like you and I can't see my future without you in it."

Luke put his hands on her back, pulling her into him, his spicy smell overwhelming her. He touched his lips to hers, his breath tickling her, causing an electric current down her spine, as he said, "Glad to hear it." He broke out into that smile of his, but this time, she didn't want to see it. She wanted his lips on hers, his arms holding her tightly. She reached up and tried to kiss him.

He pulled back before she could. With a crooked grin, he said, "How do you know I'll kiss you on demand?"

She threw her head back with a laugh and replied, "I suppose I don't. I just went for what I wanted." Right then, she knew exactly what she wanted and it was right in front of her. "But I can always buy you a caramel macchiato to prove it."

Without warning, he scooped her up, throwing her over

his shoulder. "Oh, you think you're funny, eh?" he said, running toward the surf.

"Put me down!" She giggled uncontrollably, banging on his back with her fists.

"Nevah!" he called, splashing into the water.

Then all of a sudden, *whoosh!* They were underwater, the waves bubbling over her skin, Luke's strong arms around her, lifting her up to the surface. The air shocked her wet skin as they bobbed behind a wave that crawled to shore. Her thin shirt was soaking and she could feel every muscle in his body against her. His lips found her neck and then moved up under her ear. She grabbed his shirt in her fists to keep herself from going under, nearly gasping for breath. Then, before she could even open her eyes, his mouth was on hers, his salty lips moving all over her, his fingers tangling in her hair. She put her hands under his shirt, against his wet skin and kissed him back, wondering how she'd ever lived without this.

As they slowed down, Callie was aware of a noise and she looked at Luke but then followed his line of sight to the porch at The Beachcomber, full of people cheering and waving.

"Oh my God," she said, laughing.

"Meh," he teased. "I'm used to being under a watchful eye." Then he put his hands on her face and kissed her again in front of everyone.

Chapter Twenty-Six

"I got you a housewarming present," Luke said as he stood beside an enormous furniture truck the next morning, Poppy and Callie coming out to greet him. He'd stayed last night until they could hardly keep their eyes open. It was so late that she'd worried about him getting home safely until he'd texted her that he'd gotten there.

While he'd been affectionate and they'd had a great time together, she still wondered when the topic of Edward would come up again—they'd have to face it sooner or later. And when they did, would Luke come to the realization that his relationship with Edward was ruined because of her? Had Callie not intervened, Luke and Mr. Sullivan wouldn't have had to face this reality right now. Perhaps telling Luke and Edward should've happened at another time, when they could both process it better, when there wasn't so much on the line. Would it always be a sticking point for Luke?

The deliveryman hopped out, went to the end of the

truck, and threw up the door, which rattled as it cranked to the top.

"What did you buy?" She walked around to the back of the truck and peered inside. It was full to the brim with white rocking chairs.

"Enough for all the porches, back and front," he said, putting his arms around her and lifting her up, then setting her back down.

She put her hands on her cheeks in surprise. They'd arranged potted plants on the porches, having run out of time and funds to fully furnish them. Given the circumstances, they'd been very lucky to be able to open The Beachcomber at all, so neither Callie nor Olivia had worried too much about it, but Callie had wished she could have places to sit outside for the guests because it was that million-dollar view that sold this place. "Oh my goodness, Luke! You didn't have to do this!"

"I know. That's why I called it a *present*." He rubbed Poppy's head and she walked away slowly, favoring her good leg, back up toward the house to see Wyatt, who was taking his fishing gear out to the beach.

"Thank you," she said, touched by his enormous gesture. She'd become so close with him that it didn't even occur to her that putting her arms around someone and kissing his lips wasn't typical behavior for her. It came as naturally as breathing and she never wanted to be without that feeling.

He pulled back just enough to focus on her face. "I figured we're going to need somewhere to sit when we drink all those morning caramel macchiatos."

"And what will you be doing over here in the mornings if the renovation is complete?" The workmen had put the finishing touches on the porches out back, and the remaining end tables and side chairs that had been delayed due to the hurricane were coming first thing this morning.

"I thought maybe I could stay over sometimes."

"I'm hoping that business here will be booming and all the rooms will be full."

He stared at her, chewing on a smile, waiting for her to realize what she was suggesting.

With a gasp, she shook her head, sucking in her smile. She'd meant that he couldn't stay because the rooms were full, not that she'd hoped he'd be in *her* room, even though that wouldn't be out of the question. "I meant..."

"Mm hmm," he said, pulling her close to him. He leaned down and pressed his lips to hers. Then he said, "I brought you something else."

"You've done enough," she said, following him over to his SUV as the deliverymen finished taking the rocking chairs up to the porches.

"I took the nearly empty paint can from the kitchen last night. I got it right past you!"

"I was looking for that! I thought someone had thrown it away."

"No. I took it home." He opened the back hatch of the SUV and pulled out the most stunning painting of a gaillardia on a bright white background with yellows and the most perfect pink to match the kitchen. "Try not to touch it; it's still tacky. I painted it this morning. I thought it could go on that big wall by the window."

"It's gorgeous!" She covered her mouth in surprise, unable to verbalize how beautiful it was. "It'll tie in the paint so perfectly!" Her heart couldn't be fuller. "Do you think you could help me hang it?"

"Absolutely." He turned to her, raising his eyebrows. "Today's the day! Everyone's coming! Are you excited?"

She giggled. Her phone went off in her pocket. When she pulled it out, she almost lost her balance. "It's my mom..." She read the text, and then smiled up at Luke, giving him another kiss.

* * *

The atmosphere was as lively as Callie's emotions. "Your bags are in your room," she said, delighted to show her mother all they'd done. She and Olivia had tied a powder-blue ribbon in a perfect bow across the porch that morning and strung silver and blue helium balloons from the railings with more ribbon bobbing in the wind. Once the local crowd had gathered, they had ceremoniously cut the ribbon. It lay now on the table next to the guestbook and pen for visitors to sign and share a few words about their stay.

She showed her mother around the downstairs, passing the small staff she'd hired with trays of drinks for the guests. The French doors were all ajar, and it was as if the entire back of the house was open to the sea. They meandered through the buzzing crowds, the beautiful breeze coming off the ocean, beach music sailing upward from the band playing on the patio below. Her mother was holding a celebratory glass of champagne. She had swept her wispy hair into an up-do, clearly having spent more effort on her appearance than Callie had seen before. She stopped to admire a painting that Lillian had brought for them as a housewarming present. It was Frederick's painting of the horses that he'd done so many years ago. Lillian had said it belonged here.

Yesterday, Callie's mother had texted to say she was coming. Callie had sent her an invitation for the opening, to let her know that Callie was thinking of her, but not expecting anything from it. She'd been delighted to get her mother's text telling her that she was thrilled to be invited and she couldn't wait to come.

"They've really done well, haven't they?" Gladys said with a wide smile as she joined them. She'd been there to greet Callie's mother when she'd arrived.

"Everything's just lovely," her mother said, looking around, wonder on her face. "Callie, I'm so proud of you."

Callie reached out and embraced her mother, her familiar citrusy scent taking Callie back to those nights of laughter and bedtime stories. She breathed it in, realizing how much she'd missed it.

The house was brimming with people. Olivia's whole family was there as well—her parents and her sister. They'd brought a gorgeous sand-colored mirror as a gift, all of them chipping in together to buy it. Olivia had placed it on the mantel, leaning against the wall. The sparkle of candles shimmered off the surface of it—it was perfect.

"Hey," Luke said with a grin as he ducked away from a few of the reporters, throwing a hand up to signal that he'd return. "How's my girl?" He gave Callie a squeeze around the shoulders.

"Fantastic."

Luke took a deep breath and grabbed a glass of champagne from one of the staff. "I'll be back. I have a few more reporters who want to know about my father's plans for the company," he said, with slight apprehension on his face. Callie was keenly aware that he was keeping his worries at bay so as not to spoil the day. She didn't want to think about what would happen after today. Pushing it out of her mind, she offered an encouraging smile. Then he darted off into the crowd.

"He is an absolute delight," Gladys said. "He's been here through everything."

Callie twisted the new bracelet on her arm nervously, hoping to channel her grandmother's calm. To her surprise, her mother had also brought something for them. She had brought a bottle of wine for everyone, and offered her another gift privately. Before everyone had arrived, she'd asked Callie to join her in the formal living room, which was now full of white linen-covered sofas and chairs with denim and burlap throw pillows, gauzy white curtains at the windows, and a soft, driftwood-colored rug in the center of the room, Frederick's mural providing all the color the room needed.

"I haven't been there for you like I should have," she said, concern causing her to frown. She'd told Callie that same thing once when she was in high school, but until now, Callie hadn't been ready to believe her. "Time has passed so quickly," she said, shaking her head, the lines of worry over the years etched into her face. But then, she offered a cheerful expression, her thin lips pressed into a bright smile. "I'm so happy for you. You deserve all of this." She waved a hand in the air, taking in a few breaths as if she were putting in order what she was going to say. "Anyway, I wanted you to have this." She dug around in a small sack she'd brought in with her, pulling out a tiny gift bag and handing it to Callie. Callie reached into the bag and pulled out a gift box, opening it gently.

She gasped quietly as she pulled from the cotton batting a delicate silver bracelet with a single charm. She held it up and inspected it, admiring its beauty. "Is that a diamond?"

"It's the diamond from your grandmother's wedding ring. She wanted you to have it. I made it into a bracelet for you. She told me to wait for the perfect occasion—you know how she was. She liked to make a statement."

Callie smiled. "I do remember. I love it." She slipped it on and hugged her mother, closing her eyes and squeezing her tightly.

"I brought a little something for the house too," she said. "It's up in my suitcase." Callie had taken the gift out to Olivia later that morning and they'd opened a small picture frame with little sand dollars at the corner.

"We should all take a picture today!" Olivia had said.

They'd agreed that once the crowds had gone, they'd take a photo for the frame. But for now, it was time to entertain. Callie and Olivia had hired a band to play outside on the patio, they'd put fresh flowers in tiny pots on every table inside and out, and, while they'd had to cancel their original caterer because they were low on funds, the ladies had worked quite hard to make the spread of food elegant and simple, hiring only a small staff to work the party. Even Gladys had joined in, delighting in having a reason to make her favorite dishes all at once. The paddle fans on the porches whirred, causing the beaded driftwood mobiles to tinkle like wind chimes, the ocean calmly lapping as if it were celebrating this moment of completion and relaxation. It had all come down to this: opening day.

All the Sullivans were there for the opening—all except Edward. Luke had called to tell him about it, but had had to leave a message as Edward had not picked up. Juliette had been helping all morning to prepare, Mitchell arriving with Lillian for the ribbon cutting.

The opening had gone off without a hitch. An area restaurant had offered to partner with her, providing dishes that she could serve at the bed and breakfast, and the local paper was going to run a full-page story on The Beach-comber. Luke had promised interviews to generate a buzz in the media, the press also taking photos of Callie and Olivia as well as the house itself. The reporters wrote notes in their notepads, their companies' photographers busy behind their lenses taking photos. Callie gave one reporter the address of the new website for The Beach-comber. She'd never thought they'd be able to open when they had, especially given the storm, but they'd done it. She couldn't have asked for a better day.

* * *

When Luke had given his last interview, he met Callie on the porch. She'd followed her mother outside. The crowds were dwindling now, and they were settling down, the champagne and good spirits showing on their faces.

"So you are the famous Luke Sullivan," her mother said, finally able to talk to him, as Juliette filled her glass again with what was left of the champagne. It had been so busy that they'd barely had a chance to talk, only meeting briefly.

Luke nodded graciously.

"My daughter speaks very highly of you."

He grinned at Callie. "Does she?" He poured two more glasses of champagne at the small table they'd set up for guests. It was now littered with empty glasses. He handed one to Callie, affection in his eyes. Poppy, who'd been running around the grounds most of the day, plopped down at his feet. As they all settled in, Callie wished the day could stretch on forever. She took in the curve of Luke's jaw as he smiled at her, the lack of tension in his shoulders, the interest in his eyes.

"Yes. And that's saying a lot because she's never told me much about anyone she's dated."

Callie pulled her attention back to the conversation.

"Well, I charmed her with caramel macchiatos and crab cake dinners."

Callie laughed.

People had filtered in and out all day, but Callie was glad that the Sullivans had stayed after the rest of the public had gone and had settled on the porch with them. With the last of the crowd still lingering around the band below, the Sullivans, Olivia, Gladys, Wyatt, Callie, and her mother had all remained there, talking. Luke made a silly face at her as if he were exhausted, and she felt that familiar adoration swim around inside her. She knew he hadn't wanted to talk to the press but he'd done it for her, to help get her name out there. He pulled an empty rocking chair next to her.

"Today was good!" he said, looking out over the ocean. The sun was beating down but it wasn't terribly humid, so the sea breeze cooled them easily. Someone down on the beach was playing with his child, lifting the little girl up onto his shoulders. The band continued to play—they'd paid them until five—and there was a sort of magic in the air. Callie peered over the railing at the new walkway and a smile inched its way across her face: The wood was sparkling in the sun. With excitement, she looked over at Gladys.

"Stardust," she said with a wink.

As they all sat around, the hum of chatter in the air between them, Poppy hopped up and turned toward the door, her ears perked. There was a hush, and Callie felt the serenity of the moment slide away. Slowly, she turned around. Edward was standing in the doorway.

"Hello," he said, walking in, his stare fixed on Luke but his words clearly meant for everyone. He pulled his focus off Luke to offer a polite smile to Callie and the others.

Lillian stared at him, an apprehensive look on her face.

Luke stood up. He walked over to one of the tables and pulled a bottle of beer from a melting bucket of ice, popping the top and handing it to Edward as if it were a peace offering.

"Thank you for coming," he said, feeling in his words. "This is Callie." Luke took her hand and guided her up. "You haven't met; let me introduce you."

Edward smiled warmly at her and then his attention settled back on Luke, the seriousness returning.

"I've never introduced you to any of the girls I've dated before," Luke pointed out. "And that was because they didn't mean anything to me."

Callie wondered where he was going with this when he and Edward certainly had other things to discuss.

Luke continued, "I didn't realize that the other girls didn't mean anything until I met Callie. She showed me who I was, and I learned about the things that I care about. I care about her and I care about my art." He took a step, planting his feet right in front of Edward. "And I care about what you think of me. I always have. I've spent my whole life trying to make you proud of me. I can't change who I am, but I can promise you that I care, because I love you—even when you and I disagree on how to be aggressive in business or what to spend our time doing. If you want to give the company to Aiden, then do it. I won't run it like you did. I'm not you. But I can give you my word that if you pass it on to me, it will continue to thrive." Callie saw the sincerity in his eyes that she loved so much. "You and I will never be alike, but you taught me how to be honest and focused and strong. And I will forever be thankful for that."

Edward's eyebrows rose and he looked down at his beer in contemplation. He was so intimidating that Callie found her own hands shaking. She clasped them behind her back and took in a steadying breath as she noticed how calm and cool Luke was. But that was just the way he was wired.

"What are you going to do, Luke, when this news about our family gets out? It could ruin our reputation." His voice wasn't harsh; it was concerned.

"Or make us more relatable."

"You've got your head in the clouds," he said, taking a drink from his bottle. Luke touched his arm, stopping him.

"Let them talk, Dad. They're doing it already. Aiden and I have an idea for the business. He's great with real estate—we've both always known it. But together, he and I can build up the other pieces of the business. If the press sees us working as a team, what can they say about the rest of it? It's water under the bridge at this point."

Edward took another drink without saying anything. Then he finally said, "They're not always kind, Luke. Shall we invite bad press?"

"Nope. We spin it to sell our products. If people feel like they know us, they will want what we've got to sell."

Callie couldn't believe her ears. Luke was actually confirming exactly what she'd banked on when buying The Beachcomber. And she knew he was right.

Edward walked over to the edge of the porch and put his hands on the railing, looking out, his back to everyone. The band played below.

Then, as if something clicked, he turned around. "I apologize, Callie," he said, offering a smile. "Where are my manners? I've completely ignored you and I'm so sorry about that. Forgive me."

She shook her head, smiling nervously.

"Please sit," Edward said to them both, glancing down the porch and then pulling a chair over to Luke.

"Callie and Olivia, The Beachcomber is just gorgeous. I wish you two so much success," he said as he sat down. His words were very kind, but they all were on the edge of their seats to hear if Luke had been able to change Edward's mind at all.

"Thank you," Callie said.

Olivia smiled uncomfortably and nodded.

Edward took in a deep breath and smiled. He looked out over the ocean again from his chair and then turned to Lillian. "I'm sorry," he said finally, shaking his head. "I'm sorry that I pushed you away for the sake of the business. I was young and overly eager, and I didn't realize what I was doing."

Luke and Juliette looked at each other in surprise, probably in disbelief that Edward would admit this in front of everyone.

Edward continued, "We didn't handle things in the right way—either of us. But I'm truly sorry for all those nights I left you alone."

"It's done now," Lillian said, kindness on her face. "But I've never worried about myself. My concern has always been Luke."

"I've been wrestling with all this," he said as he looked into the faces of everyone there, and Callie could see that expressing himself in this way was very difficult for him. "I've been thinking a lot about you, Luke. I'm sure all of this has been a terrible shock to you too."

"I can deal with it," Luke said. "I just don't think it should affect the company."

"You're right." He pursed his lips, thoughts on his face. "How would you change it?" Callie watched closely, her protective nature kicking in for Luke, but Edward was clearly ready to listen. He'd leaned toward Luke, his head slightly tilted, his demeanor unguarded.

Lillian threw an excited but still slightly uneasy look over to Juliette, who had scooted on the edge of her rocker. No one moved a muscle as they waited.

"I'd like to have Aiden on board," Luke said, his words careful. It was clear that he knew how big this was for Edward. "I want to expand Blue Water Sailing, incorporating more retail—not just my own designs; possibly more. But we could start there. I've started painting surfboards."

"He's talented, Edward," Aiden said, speaking up. "I have the business sense, certainly, but Luke has the vision. He sees things that I don't. We'd make a great team."

Edward nodded, reflecting on this as he looked back out at the ocean. Then his eyes met Luke's and then Aiden's. "I trust you two," he said. "You know, when I started this business, I was told it wasn't lucrative, that the area was just too rural. But I had a vision and when the boom hit, we soared. I believe you two could have success, albeit in a different manner than I achieved mine. I'm willing to put my trust in family. Maybe we could put your business model down on paper and get started."

Lillian burst into a smile. "Oh, Edward," she said, her eyes glassy. "That's fantastic."

"I'm excited to see how it goes."

"We need to celebrate," Juliette said, getting up and wrapping her arms around Edward. "Let's pour ourselves a drink, kick off our shoes, and go downstairs. They've got that wonderful band down there. We should dance,

Daddy." For the first time, Callie saw Edward really smile. He patted his daughter on the arm and nodded.

Luke stood and pulled Callie up, his smile still directed at Edward. "I think that's a great idea," he said.

They all went down to the patio and settled at the tables by the band. With a hoot of laughter from the few who'd lingered from the crowd, Luke grabbed Callie and pulled her onto the patio to dance. Gladys joined them, dragging Frederick onto the dance floor, followed by Aiden and Olivia. Edward and Lillian were on the side, grinning. While Juliette poured the champagne, Edward held out a hand to Lillian with a conciliatory smile, and she let him lead her out to the patio.

As they danced, Gladys winked at Callie. *Stardust,* she mouthed.

Callie took a look back at the magnificent cottage in all its glory, the paddle fans going on the porches, the mass of glass showcasing the beautiful furnishings inside, the tables of food in the window of the new sitting area. There was a thrill that she couldn't deny. This old house had been renewed, made into something different, something better. Just like this unexpected group of people around her. The sky was an unusually brilliant shade of orange and pink, a burst of color over them, and Callie wondered if Alice was looking down on them—all her family together. In her house. Finally.

Epilogue

Callie stared at the enormous rock of a diamond as it swung around on her nervous finger. This was the last time she'd wear it without a band beside it.

She'd never expected Luke to propose when he had—he'd completely surprised her as he often did. They'd gone camping, and she noticed he'd brought along mason jars. He pulled one out and showed her the lid punched with holes, like she'd remembered doing as a kid. "For catching lightning bugs," he'd said over a glass of local wine as they sat next to the campfire. They'd gone deep into the woods, where the last of the moonlight was hidden by the thick brush, and—she could still remember it like it was yesterday—the black expanse before her had lit up with them. The whole forest had seemed as though it were strung with dancing twinkle lights.

She caught one in her hand and Luke helped her put it in the jar. "We'll let it go later," he said, catching another one. When they'd gotten back to the campfire, they had a whole mason jar full. He set it on the small portable table he'd brought. He was pensive and she asked why. He turned to her and said, "This jar represents the present." Then he pulled a second jar out of his bag and handed it to her. It had something in it. "The past," he said.

She unscrewed the lid and pulled out a black and white photo of her grandmother. She had pin curls, her face so young. The image blurred in front of her. She ran her fingers along the diamond bracelet on her wrist, emotion welling up.

When she'd finally blinked away the last of the tears, Luke gingerly placed the photo back into the jar. "So we have past..." He set the jar down on the table. Then he picked up the lightning bugs and unscrewed the top. He released them, the golden lights filling the dark sky all around them. "And present..." Under the glow of the fire and the lightning bugs, he pulled a third jar from his bag. "And hopefully," he said, "we have a future." Suspended from the lid, from a red velvet ribbon inside the jar, was the ring that was now on her finger.

He'd told her that he'd contacted her mother, driven all the way to Richmond, and asked for Callie's hand in marriage. Later, her mother had said he'd charmed the dickens out of her, making her laugh. He'd brought her flowers and he'd taken her out to lunch.

* * *

The Beachcomber was full to the brim, but this time all the rooms held friends and family. The porches Aiden had built were draped in a garland of fresh flowers—daisies and gaillardias—and the patio was a field of white tea light candles in mason jars. The walkway, too, was lined with them and white folding chairs were set out on either side of it leading down to sea.

"Ready?" Olivia asked, as she straightened Wyatt's tie. He was now ten, lanky and tall in his tuxedo, holding a ring bearer's pillow.

Callie's mother blinked rapidly, wiping her tears with a hanky, as she stood with them in a pale pink gown. She'd spent a wonderful week talking and catching up with Callie and Olivia and finalizing the wedding plans. Callie had never seen her smile as much as she had since she'd arrived.

Callie nodded, her nerves melting away at the thought of standing next to Luke and promising to love him forever.

They both had laughed at the headline in the local paper: *Pretty boy Luke Sullivan has been tamed!* The papers had been in a whirl since the public revelation of Frederick McFarlin's connection to the Sullivan family, as well as the merger between Parker Industries and Sullivan Enterprises, when Aiden and Luke had announced their partnership.

And now, they'd surprised them once again with the wedding. But Luke had been right about the press embracing their family turmoil: They were the new darlings of Waves, and the people there couldn't get enough of them. Callie had to insist on paying for coffee at the coffee shop, the owner refusing to take her money for all the wonderful things they'd done for the community, and when they walked past people in town, Luke got stopped but only to receive well-wishes and offers of gratitude.

Luke hadn't just donated to the relief effort that year during the hurricane, he'd initiated an annual auction in which he auctioned off ten of his prized surfboards, donating all the proceeds to the nonprofit Bring Us Home. Other companies had jumped on board, and the whole thing had gotten so huge that it had become a local fair. There were carnival rides, booths of local products, cotton candy and twirling, light-up toys for the kids. Luke and Aiden organized the whole thing every year, and the community loved it.

Callie took a peek out the French doors, warmth spreading over her when she saw Luke. His eyes were on the entry to the walkway, waiting for her. The music had started. Just before she turned around, she caught sight of Edward and Frederick, sitting beside each other. They looked like they were chatting.

"It's time," Olivia said.

Callie grabbed her bouquet, made specially of gaillardias, and held it close to her white silk dress, which fell in one smooth wave to the floor where it puddled at the back into a small train.

After they'd gotten downstairs, just before going out, she picked up the basket they'd filled with petals. "Ready?" she said in a commanding whisper as she bent down—they'd been practicing this all summer. With a giggle, she handed the basket to Poppy, who carried it in her mouth. Wyatt took the white ribbon leash and they walked out together as the crowd shifted in their seats.

"Okay, Mom," she said, turning to her mother. She'd cried when Callie had asked if she could walk her down the aisle. They'd talked for over an hour that night over wine and good music.

The doors swooshed open and all Callie could see was Luke's face, the glisten in his eyes, and the awe that overtook him as she walked toward her future. And she couldn't imagine anything better.

A Letter from Jenny

Thank you so much for reading *The Summer House*. I really hope you found it to be a heartwarming summer escape!

If you'd like me to drop you an email when my next book is out, you can **sign up here**:

www.ItsJennyHale.com/email-signup

I won't share your email with anyone else, and I'll only email you when a new book is released.

If you did enjoy *The Summer House*, I'd love it if you'd write a review. Getting feedback from readers is amazing, and it also helps to persuade other readers to pick up one of my books for the first time.

If you enjoyed this story, and would like a little more summer time on the beach, do check out my other summer novel—*Summer at Firefly Beach*.

Until next time!
Jenny x

Acknowledgments

I'd like to thank my husband, Justin, who has endured many years now of my coffee-drinking sprees and frantic sprints to the computer. He has listened and been there every single minute.

A giant thank you to Oliver Rhodes for his support. I'm so thankful for his great instincts that keep it all going smoothly.

My editor, Natalie Butlin—I am thankful for her fantastic ideas and her willingness to hear my million questions and concerns while I find my way through every new book.

When the summer sun turns to winter snow, snuggle up with Jenny Hale's cozy holiday romance, now a Hallmark Channel Original movie!

Please turn the page for an excerpt from

Christmas Wishes and *Mistletoe Kisses*.

Chapter One

Twenty-six—that was the number of windows across the front of this house. Four—it had *four* chimneys. Abbey had only just counted them all as the enormous, Georgian revival–style mansion came into view at the end of the mile-long driveway. She'd had to be let in via an intercom at a pair of iron gates bigger than her apartment building. As she'd snaked along the property in her car, miles of perfectly manicured grass—green, despite the winter weather—stretching out on either side of the drive, and the James River angrily lapping on the edge of the property under the winter clouds, her hands had begun to sweat. Abbey had always been impulsive, even though she'd tried very hard not to be, but she'd done it again.

She'd dressed up. Abbey wasn't used to dressing up. Normally, she had on scrubs at work, and on her off time she wore hoodies and jeans. But this was a business meeting, and she'd wanted to look prepared; however, nothing had prepared her for what was in front of her now. She shifted her portfolio case on the seat of her car to keep it from slipping onto the floorboards. It was a gift from her gramps and had sat empty until now.

You can do this, she said to herself as she tried to keep the seatbelt from wrinkling her clothes. *You're gonna have to do this. You made your bed. Now you have to lie in it.*

The owner of this home was in a league beyond comprehension. He was the grandson of a woman named Caroline Sinclair for whom Abbey cared. Caroline lived in a small cottage on the edge of the Sinclair property, and Abbey had always reached her cottage using a private side road. The estate was so large and wooded that the cottage seemed to be all by itself; the main house wasn't even visible. Caroline had explained that she wanted it that way.

"If Nick is making me live on the property, I want to at least feel that I can come and go as if it's my own residence. I don't want to live out back of the house, or something demeaning like that. I want my own place, not a guest quarters."

Abbey had gotten the job caring for Caroline while working at an upscale retirement home. Nicholas Sinclair had called to ask if they had a service for in-home nurses. When she'd said that they didn't, he'd offered to pay her more than what she was making there to care for Caroline at home, because he didn't want to put her in a facility. Caroline had mentioned that her grandson, Nick, had a "big house," but this kind of wealth was something out of a storybook.

As Abbey looked at the house, it shed new light on Caroline's quirks—the way she'd held the thick mug that Abbey had gotten her for her birthday as if it were a delicate piece of art, the straightness of her back when she sat on the edge of her chair, the manner in which she nodded and said "thank you," for the smallest of things. It was all clear now. What had seemed like generally polite behavior had actually been the behavior of a privileged upbringing. Abbey had never met Mr. Sinclair face to face. She'd always just provided Caroline's current health status and data from her tests via phone—usually leaving a message—and he'd mailed her paychecks. She wondered if she'd notice the same small indications of wealth when she met him.

Abbey parked her car in the large circular drive and turned off the engine. Snowflakes dotted her windshield as she took a peek in her rearview mirror to be sure she was as presentable as possible. She dabbed on some lipgloss quickly and dropped it into her handbag. With a deep breath, she got out of the car, her heels wobbling slightly with her nerves. Hoping the snow wouldn't begin to pile up when she was inside, she clicked along the brick patio-sized pathway to the front steps. With every stride, she could feel the crescendo of the pounding in her heart.

She stopped between two urns, each one containing a spruce tree the size of her Christmas tree at home, and pressed the doorbell. The double doors in front of her were so ornate and grand that she almost feared what was behind them. What was she thinking, telling Caroline she'd do this? Was she out of her mind?

The door opened, and, standing in front of her, was a short man wearing a charcoal gray suit and a red tie, his hair balding on the top. Abbey had heard about Nick Sinclair from the other nurses at the retirement home. They'd described him as tall, quiet, handsome—gorgeous, one had said—with dark hair and perfect clothes. While there was nothing wrong with the man in front of her, he was a far cry from the description she'd received.

He smiled, his lips pressed together, and took a step back to allow Abbey to come in, the large door closing behind her as she entered the home.

She refocused on the man. "Hello. I'm Abbey Fuller. You must be Mr. Sinclair?"

"No, ma'am. He'll be with you shortly."

Wow, she thought. *He doesn't even open his own doors.* Her eyes moved around the space, taking in everything that surrounded her. The floor was a white-and-slate-colored marble, with matching columns that looked as though they were holding up the entire second floor. The upstairs ran along an oval balcony that completely circled the room. The space in that one room was the size of the house where she'd grown up. It was so grand that it had to have three massive chandeliers to light it, but the windows spanning every surface were large enough that the natural light coming in was plenty.

"Follow me, please," the man said as he led her across the marble floor, between the two wide, curving staircases flanking each side of the room, and through an ornate doorway with more pillars on either side, the woodwork all painted cream to match the walls. Each piece was carved into swirling perfection that rolled to a peak at the top of the doorframe. The more she walked, the more nervous she became.

Her breath caught, and Abbey swallowed to cover it up as she entered the next room. A wall of windows on the east side offered an almost blinding white light from the clouds outside. The grass had been dusted with snow in just the amount of time she'd been in the house. In front of the windows sat a black grand piano, the top propped up, the keys so shiny she could see the reflection of the panes of glass on their surfaces. On the south side of the home another wall of windows stretched to the top of the thirty-or-more-foot ceiling and overlooked the grounds. The walls had intricate woodwork framing their surfaces, the color between the woodwork matching the blue of the rug.

The man had walked over to two facing cream-colored sofas that seemed so comfortable that she wanted to snuggle up on them with a blanket and read. Their billowy cushions were juxtaposed to the formality of the blue and cream patterned rug that extended the entire length of the ballroom-sized space, and the general emptiness and sterile surroundings. He gestured for her to take a seat.

Abbey's eyes could not stay still in this room because she'd never seen anything like it in real life. It was such a stiffly styled room, yet those sofas were sitting at one end, and she wondered if anyone had ever sat on them.

What kinds of things would someone do in a room like this? Did Nick Sinclair play piano? Had he ever played for anyone before, or was it just a prop, a piece of furniture?

She sat down and the man left her alone with her thoughts, having never even introduced himself. Abbey put her hands on her knees as she sat on the edge of that gorgeous sofa. How impressed must Caroline have been with her decorating skills to suggest that Abbey decorate this mansion for her grandson? She couldn't even allow her pride to slip in because the whole situation was so baffling to her. She was shaking—partly from nerves and from the fact that the house was just slightly colder than she found to be comfortable. She shivered outwardly. The snow had really started coming down now in the few minutes she was there, already covering the ground outside. The scene played out before her through the towering windows, like a movie. Her mouth was so dry at this point, she couldn't even lick her lips, and she worried that her lip-gloss wouldn't last.

If Abbey had to sit there much longer, she would explode—she needed to talk, have some kind of interaction—so she stood up to try to burn off her nervous energy. Her heels tapped on the marble floor that ran along the edge of the rug, and made hollow clicks that echoed throughout the room. "Rug" was not the best term for this piece. It was half the size of a football field, it seemed. Her back to the room, Abbey looked out through the windows and, when she realized what was out there, she had to consciously keep her mouth from hanging open.

Covered in snow were tennis courts, a brick gazebo as big as a four-car garage, and, off in the distance, closer to the river, was an Olympic-size swimming pool. As she looked out at the grounds, the cold of winter seeping in through the icy glass in front of her, she wondered what Nick could possibly be doing. Why hadn't he greeted her when she'd arrived? Did it take him that long to walk from wherever he was in the house? She'd left a message, as he'd directed, and told him she'd be there at two o'clock. She'd just expected him to answer the door.

"Hello, Ms. Fuller," she heard the words echo across the room.

Abbey turned around. As she fixed her eyes on him, she had to work to keep her breath from coming out in ragged, nervous jerks. He *was* gorgeous. He was probably the most handsome man she'd ever seen. He had on navy trousers and a buttercream sweater with a thick collar that made the icy blue of his eyes visible even at a distance. His hair was perfectly combed, not a strand out of place, and his face looked soft, as if he'd just shaved a few minutes before their meeting. Perhaps that was what he'd been doing…Abbey shook the thought from her mind.

"Hello," she returned. She wanted to walk toward him,

but she didn't trust herself in heels, and she worried that she might fall. He crossed the room and stopped in front of her, giving the two of them a large amount of personal space. He held out his hand in greeting, the starched cuff of his button-up shirt peeking out from underneath his sweater. She shook his hand.

"It's nice to finally put a face with the voice," he said. "Shall we head into my office?" He moved aside so that she could step up next to him. "We can discuss the details of your employment more easily there." He smiled. It was a pleasant smile, but it didn't seem to sit comfortably on his face.

They walked along the corridor, a lofty area so wide and open that it couldn't possibly be called just a hallway. It, too, was quite empty—no pictures, no accent tables, nothing. Abbey was shocked at the lack of decorations. The house was so cold and unfriendly that it made her wonder about Mr. Sinclair. Was he as cold as this house? They finally stopped outside what looked like Nick's office.

"You can just call me Abbey," she said, gripping her portfolio case to keep her hands steady.

He smiled down at her.

"Did you just move in?" she asked out of curiosity. There was nothing in this home to suggest that it was regularly lived in. There were no photos, no memorabilia anywhere—not a thing to tell her about who he was.

"No," he said, sitting down behind a shiny desk with a mahogany finish. His chair rolled on the slick marble floor beneath it. Then, he made eye contact. "My grandmother tells me that you are a very good decorator," he said, offering that manufactured smile again. This time, Abbey could almost tell that he'd practiced it. Was he used to having to smile when he really didn't want to? She wondered what he looked like when he laughed—really laughed. What would his mouth do then? Would he keep still or throw his head back? Would she be able to see amusement in his eyes?

She sat down in one of the leather chairs facing his desk and crossed her legs at the ankle. With a tiny breath to steady herself, she put her portfolio case on her lap and unzipped it. She'd taken a few photos of her best decorating and had them blown up to a larger size for her presentation. "I've never had a project this size," she warned. What she really wanted to tell him was that the only decorating experience she'd had was when she'd decorated his grandmother's cottage because Caroline didn't have the ability to paint and decorate herself. Abbey had worked hard to make her presentation professional, and there was a lot riding on this. She had Max to think about.

Abbey's son, Max, was in first grade. He needed lunch money, school supplies; he was on neighborhood sports teams. There were things she *had* to pay for if she wanted Max to have a regular childhood. Her poor judgment with his father had been her fault, not Max's. And the fact that her grandfather needed medicine that she had to help her mother pay for—that wasn't Max's fault either. Her son deserved nothing but the best, and she was going to give that to him, even if it meant that she went without. And she had before. Abbey had gone nights with no dinner, skipped parties with her friends, and lived on meager funds so that Max would never know that he was any different than anyone else. Secretly, she worried about him. Would he wonder why he didn't get beach vacations with his family? Would he wish that he could have big birthday parties with all his friends? She fretted about it all the time. And this was her chance to do something great for his future.

"I'm not concerned about any lack of experience. You come highly recommended by my grandmother, and she's hard to please, so I trust you'll do just fine."

She pulled back the flap on her portfolio and retrieved the first photo from it, turning it around for him to view. "I have experience decorating in a small variety of styles..." she said apprehensively. She'd practiced her presentation last night a hundred times but it was quite different with Nick's eyes on her. "As you know, this is a picture from your grandmother's cottage. I thought I'd start with hers first, since you could envision the before and after..."

He cleared his throat. "You don't need to sell me," he said. "I'm already hiring you." He offered a pleasant expression, and it was clear from his face that her presentation was over.

She slid the photo back into the case and closed it.

"Are you planning to charge a flat rate per square foot, or would you prefer a salary with a decorating budget?" he asked.

"Uh-mmm..." Abbey chewed on the inside of her lip, trying to scramble for an answer. She didn't know. She didn't have a clue. She'd only ever been a nurse. The idea of how to charge him hadn't even crossed her mind. That thought alone was unsettling enough to cause her chest to burn with anxiety.

Abbey had gone online during a few of her breaks, ordering things that were more extravagant than she'd ever bought, but she knew just how to place them to give them life in Caroline's cottage. She'd done it as a favor to Caroline, but she hadn't made any money doing it, and it never occurred to her to ask for any. She realized that she hadn't thought this through at all.

"I, uh..." She felt ridiculous that all she could produce

were unintelligible sounds. *Get a grip!* she scolded herself. *Answer him!* This was too big a leap for her. She wasn't a decorator. She'd always dreamed of being one. She had files of magazine clippings just in case she ever won the lottery and was able to buy what she really wanted for her and Max.

Her passion for art ran deeply through her—she painted, she could draw, she saw art in everything—but when it had come down to it, she'd had to choose the career that would be the least amount of risk. She'd had to pick something that would provide for Max. Because of that, she'd gotten a nursing degree as quickly as she could. It gave her steady income. She'd taken as many classes as the local community college allowed, and she'd done nothing but study so that she could get her degree. Abbey still believed there was art in everything; she just didn't always have time to notice it anymore.

As she sat across from Nick Sinclair, she felt very small, heat filling her cheeks. She blinked to keep the tears at bay. Never had she come to tears about anything before now—not even raising Max alone. She'd always been able to handle it. So why was she about to cry now? Abbey tried not to process the answer, but it was bubbling up: She knew her artistic talent was that one piece of her that she could always hold on to when she'd lost everything, hoping that one day she could tap into it. It was the only thing besides Max that she was proud of. Now, finding herself out of her league, she didn't want anyone telling her that it wasn't good enough because that would crush her.

And the last thing she wanted was for Nick to think less of her, but she didn't know a thing about how to charge him for this job or the etiquette in a business relationship like this. She felt guilty charging him at all.

Abbey was silent, still trying to formulate an answer while not giving away how she was feeling. She didn't know what to say, so she just sat there, inwardly screaming at herself to say *something*. "I'll do it for free if you'll let me take photos for my portfolio when I'm finished," she said finally.

Then, his light blue eyes changed as he looked at her. He looked curious, and there was a gentleness in his face that she hadn't seen until right then.

"My grandmother has wanted me to do this for a while. Before she was set on having you do it, she'd even called around and given me quotes. I've had quotes for upward of a hundred fifty thousand dollars, so, with that said, I won't let you do the job for free. My grandmother might disown me if I did. Why don't we settle for seventy-five thousand dollars to decorate the whole house?" He searched her face for a reaction. "And that will be your salary. Then, I'll buy whatever you need in terms of furnishings."

Abbey blinked to keep her eyes from popping out of their sockets. Seventy-five *thousand* dollars? That was three years' salary for her, and she was about to make it in a matter of weeks. All of a sudden, she felt light-headed, her excitement swelling up inside. This could change everything. With money like that, she could pay for extra childcare—private sitters when she needed them. That would take the burden off her mother, who was caring for her grandfather and watching Max. She might even be able to get Gramps that medicine he needed so badly.

"Does that suit you?" he asked. "Are you okay with those terms?"

"Yes." She couldn't say anything more than yes. Her emotions were getting the better of her. She wanted to get up and hug him and tell him what a Christmas miracle that money would be for her and her family. She wanted to thank him for being so generous despite the fact that, clearly, she was inexperienced.

"Great." He stood up and walked around to her side of the desk. She followed his lead and stood, tucking her portfolio under her arm.

He was so close that she caught his scent, and it caused a tickle in her chest. Abbey had never smelled cologne that good before, and she wondered what it was that he was wearing. Had she ever even heard of it? It was probably very expensive.

"Let me show you the rooms that you'll be decorating," he said, distracted, as he pulled out his phone and put it to his ear. She was glad to be up and moving again, and hoping to have a normal conversation, but he was already barking into his phone. "I don't care how much it costs," he said. "It's a car. Just buy it…I'd like it detailed and cleaned before it leaves the lot this time." After a minute's more conversation, he ended the call and responded to her obvious interest. "I collect cars—mostly Ferraris," he said, with an air of pride.

"Cars?" she asked. Max collected cars, but she wondered if he might be talking about a slightly different kind.

"There's a Lamborghini that's up for auction—very limited number of them. I've got someone bidding for me and I'm trying to manage that while I show you around. My apologies."

She stared up at him long enough to realize that it was becoming awkward, so she looked down at her feet. Her grandfather couldn't even buy the medicine he needed and this guy was wasting money on luxury cars.

"You need more than one car?" she asked.

He looked at her, the skin between his eyes wrinkling

as if he were trying to make sense of what she was saying. "I *collect* them. I don't necessarily drive them."

"Where do you keep them?"

"I have a garage on the property. They're displayed there."

She knew that her face was showing her distaste, and she couldn't straighten it out no matter how hard she tried. She had no right to offer any opinion about what he did with his money. "So who comes to see them?"

He eyed her again. "No one," he said, his voice sounding slightly exasperated. "I collect them for my own amusement. No one else's."

She was quiet after that; the idea of all that money sitting somewhere in a garage helping no one had silenced her.

"Basically, you'll be decorating all the rooms except for a couple. I know that's a big job..." He looked down at her as they walked, changing the subject. Had he been able to interpret her opinions? "And you'll have only a short time to do it." He stopped, so Abbey did too. "I have family coming and I'm having a Christmas party. I want you to make the house look *lived in*."

A punch of laughter rose in her gut, but she cleared her throat to remove it. She remembered the ballroom with nothing but a piano and a set of fluffy sofas, and thought to herself, *How can I make a room like that look livable?*

If she'd chosen to be a full-time decorator instead of becoming a nurse, Abbey would take something like a cozy corner nook, paint it a warm color, add a pop of white furniture, and fill it full of bookshelves. She'd arrange the books on the shelves between knickknacks from various locations around the world that her client had gotten on his travels. She'd even drape a snowy-white throw across the arm of the chair and add a floor lamp for ambience. *That* would look lived in. This house was like a museum. It was too big to make it even *seem* like someone would live in it. But then, her thoughts went to Nick. He lived here. And as far as Abbey could tell, he lived here all by himself.

Caroline had never mentioned a family when she spoke of her grandson. She'd only said that he needed help with his home because he was too busy working to do anything with it. How sad to have to walk these giant hallways alone.

They rounded the corner and headed up a curling staircase to the second floor. Everywhere she looked, she saw lofty ceilings and balconies. It made her feel the need to take a deep breath to release the growing tension she was feeling about this job she'd taken.

All the doors to each room were shut, which was odd to Abbey, but then again, perhaps it was hard to heat such a large house. He stopped at the first one and opened it. It was another colossal expanse of space with vaulted ceilings, ornamental woodwork, and more chandeliers.

"This is a bedroom," he said as she walked around the room, snapping photos of walls and architectural features. She looked up at the intricate crystal chandelier above her, with its strands of diamond-like jewels dripping down, and took a photo. "There are eight bedrooms in total. I'd like each room to feel distinct, yet consistent with the style of the home. What you do with them is up to you. I trust you."

Abbey dragged her hand along the ornate woodwork in the recessed doorway, noticing how the patterns in the wood emerged from under the thick coats of shiny white paint. She'd keep that, she decided. She imagined Georgian-style furniture to maintain the integrity of the home, but with a few present-day traditional accents to make the look current. In such a large space, she'd want to focus on breaking the room up into smaller pieces— perhaps put a sitting area at one end of the bedroom. The key was to make this cold house seem warm and more personal. The walls needed neutrals but in inviting colors like light buttery yellows and subtle mint greens, rather than just plain white. She jotted down notes in the notebook that she'd included in the front pocket of her portfolio.

They opened the next two doors, and he explained the purpose of each room. She wrote down where the light came in and areas on which she wanted to focus. When they came to the fourth door on the hallway, he skipped it and walked ahead, his thoughts seemingly preoccupied all of a sudden. It was subtle, but she'd noticed. What was behind that door?

"Did you want me to see this one?" she said, stopping in the hallway and pointing back to the closed door.

"No," he said. "I won't need you to decorate that room. It's fine." He walked ahead and opened the next door. It was just like the others.

"I'm sorry." She stopped him right there in the hallway. She was going to have to really make sure he understood if she ever wanted to feel comfortable in his presence. "I must drive home the fact that I haven't ever had a decorating job of this magnitude. Ever. I've only done the cottage for your grandmother and I've decorated my mom's house. I've never even been in a home on River Road before."

Everyone in the vicinity of Richmond knew where River Road was. It was more than just a road; it was a landmark, a stretch of real estate showcasing Richmond's finest. "I mean, my mother's house is nice. She's on the corner of Maple and Ivy Streets," she kidded, trying to joke about the insignificance of where her mother's house was located. Clearly, he didn't get it. Maple and Ivy obviously didn't have the same impact as River Road. Her joke had fallen flat.

He stared at her, as if waiting for something more.

"What I'm trying to say…" She swallowed. "What I'm wondering is…" She didn't want to *not* take the job. But telling him the truth was the right thing to do. "I'm inexperienced. With all the money that you have, why don't you just hire an experienced decorator?"

He was silent a moment as if he were trying to get his answer just right. "I mean no disrespect," he said. "This was my grandmother's idea. She thinks I need to make this house presentable for my family and friends when they come for Christmas. I agree, to a certain extent. And I think the emptiness bothers her in general. The problem is, I only want to make her happy. I don't care enough about it to spend time searching for a decorator. I just want it done, and if she thinks you're the person to do it, then so be it."

So he didn't care that Abbey wasn't a seasoned professional. He didn't care about any of it. Any feelings of achievement she'd had by securing this job came crashing down. He was telling her loud and clear that it wasn't about him trusting her abilities; it was just something to tick off his list. Nick turned and headed down the hallway again. Trying to look on the bright side, Abbey walked along beside him, thinking of all the possibilities.

About the Author

Jenny Hale is a *USA Today* bestselling author of romantic fiction. Her novels *Coming Home for Christmas* and *Christmas Wishes and Mistletoe Kisses* have been adapted for television on the Hallmark Channel. Her stories are chock-full of feel-good romance and overflowing with warm settings, great friends, and family. Grab a cup of coffee, settle in, and enjoy the fun!

You can learn more at:
 ItsJennyHale.com
 Twitter @JHaleAuthor
 Facebook.com/JennyHaleAuthor
 Instagram @JHaleAuthor

Fall in love with these charming contemporary romances!

SUMMER ON HONEYSUCKLE RIDGE
by Debbie Mason

Abby Everhart has gone from being a top L.A. media influencer to an unemployed divorcée living out of her car. So inheriting her great-aunt's homestead in Highland Falls, North Carolina, couldn't have come at a better time. But instead of a cabin ready to put on the market, she finds a fixer-upper, complete with an overgrown yard and a reclusive—albeit sexy—man living on the property. When sparks between them become undeniable, will she be able to sell the one place that's starting to feel like home?

PRIMROSE LANE
by Debbie Mason

Olivia Davenport has finally gotten her life back together and is now Harmony Harbor's most sought-after event planner. But her past catches up with her when she learns that she's now guardian of her ex's young daughter. Dr. Finn Gallagher knows a person in over her head when he sees one, but Olivia makes it clear she doesn't want his companionship. Only with a little help from some matchmaking widows—and a precocious little girl—might he be able to convince her that life is better with someone you love at your side.

Find more great reads on Instagram with
@ReadForeverPub.

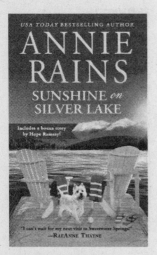

SUNSHINE ON SILVER LAKE
by Annie Rains

Café owner Emma St. James is planning a special event at Sweetwater Springs National Park to honor her mother's memory. Which means she'll need the help of the ruggedly handsome park ranger who broke her heart years ago. As their attraction grows stronger than ever, will Emma find herself at risk of falling for him again? Includes a bonus story by Hope Ramsay!

STARTING OVER AT BLUEBERRY CREEK
by Annie Rains

Firefighter Luke Marini moved to Sweetwater Springs with the highest of hopes—new town, new job, and new neighbors who know nothing of his past. And that's just how he wants to keep it. But it's nearly impossible when the gorgeous brunette next door decides to be the neighborhood's welcome wagon. She's sugar, spice, and everything nice—but getting close to someone again is playing with fire. Includes a bonus story by Melinda Curtis!

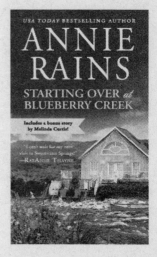

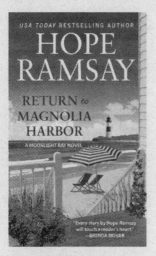

RETURN TO MAGNOLIA HARBOR
by Hope Ramsay

Jessica Blackwell's life needs a refresh. So while she's back home in Magnolia Harbor, she's giving her architecture career a total makeover. The only problem? Jessica's new client happens to be her old high school nemesis. Christopher Martin never meant to hurt Jessica all those years ago, and now he'd give anything to have a second chance with the one woman who always haunted his memories.

CAN'T HURRY LOVE
by Melinda Curtis

Widowed after one year of marriage, city girl Lola Williams finds herself stranded in Sunshine, Colorado, reeling from the revelation that her husband had secrets she never could have imagined, secrets that she's asked the ruggedly hot town sheriff to help her uncover. Lola swears she's done with love forever, but the matchmaking ladies of the Sunshine Valley Widows Club have different plans...Includes a bonus story by Annie Rains!

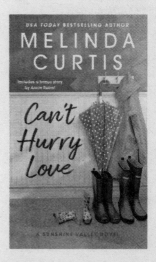

Discover bonus content and more on
read-forever.com

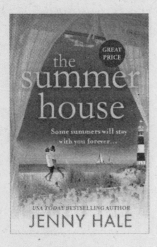

THE SUMMER HOUSE
by Jenny Hale

Callie Weaver's too busy to think about her love life. She's invested her life savings into renovating the beach house she admired every childhood summer into a bed-and-breakfast. But when she catches the attention of local real estate heir and playboy Luke Sullivan, his blue eyes and easy smile are hard to resist. As they laugh in the ocean waves, Callie discovers there's more to Luke than his money and good looks. But just when Callie's dreams seem within reach, she finds a diary full of secrets—with the power to change everything.

PARADISE COVE
by Jenny Holiday

Dr. Nora Walsh hopes that moving to tiny Matchmaker Bay will help her get over a broken heart. When the first man she sees looks like a superhero god, the born-and-bred city girl wonders if maybe there's something to small-town living after all. But will Jake Ramsey's wounded heart ever be able to love again?